LIFE HERE BELOW

GW00778049

Life *here below*

A collection of stories

By *Michael J. Farrell*

NEW ISLAND

LIFE HERE BELOW
First published 2014
by New Island
16 Priory Office Park
Stillorgan
County Dublin
www.newisland.ie

PRINT ISBN: 978-1-84840-355-0
EPUB ISBN: 978-1-84840-356-7
MOBI ISBN: 978-1-84840-357-4

Typeset by JVR Creative India
Cover design by Mariel Deegan & New Island
Printed by Clondalkin Digital Print

New Island receives funding from the Arts Council.

10 9 8 7 6 5 4 3 2 1

Notes

The first segment of *The Ronan Chronicles* is an edited version of *Pascal's Wager*, which was runner-up for the Francis McManus Award in 2006 and was included in *Life in the Universe* (Stinging Fly Press, 2009). The remainder of the story is new.

All That Delirium is an edited version of the first chapter of a novel awaiting a publisher. *À la Descartes* and *Strangers* have already appeared in *The Stinging Fly*, while *Pagans* appeared in *The Moth*.

About The Author

Michael J. Farrell is a native of County Longford. A varied career included many years in journalism in the USA. He reviewed books for the *Los Angeles Times,* and was a long-time editor of the *National Catholic Reporter.* His novel, *Papabile*, won the Thorpe Menn Award in 1998. He retired to the Irish midlands in 2003 to write fiction. His work has been published widely.

Dedication

For Marilyn

Contents

The Local Paper

In the newspaper world, tragedy is king. The media will beat the breast, but deep down they are waiting for the grim reaper or some lesser malefactor to do them a favour. If the journalist feels giddy though, it is not from cruelty or even greed. It is, rather, some primordial urge in the journalistic soul to make sense of good and evil.

None of this entered my mind the day Evie Adams fell down on the side of a country road as I was driving by. Yet for some reason, I stopped. There is, it transpires, only a narrow divide between what is and what might be.

A year or two earlier, I prowled for an hour, hating myself, before venturing past the brass plaque declaring that the *Midland Observer* was founded in 1893. Inside, the buxom girl, a defiant red ribbon in her hair, insisted on ignoring me.

"I'd like to apply for the reporter position."

"Have you an appointment?" She eyed me with that lack of civility I have lately noticed creeping through the culture.

"Sorry." I'd be humble, and when eventually I became editor of this pitiful rag I'd fire her first thing some sunny day. It's not that I'm thin-skinned on the one hand or malicious on the other, it's just that Ireland needs to snap out of this mood it's in.

She led me down a narrow corridor to a door with *Editor* written in gold on frosted glass. She opened the door without knocking. What if he has just farted, I couldn't help thinking. Or worse – we're all human after all. In the light of such misgivings, it was edifying to find Liam O'Lally face to face with a computer amid clouds of smoke just when one thought tobacco had been banished from the land.

"Someone to see you," and the sassy girl disappeared. The office was impressively untidy, an appropriate confusion of paper and bric-a-brac; but gloomy, an ideal refuge for outmoded ideas.

"Can you give me another word for *layabout*?" he said, without looking up.

"I'm here about the reporter job." If he wanted a word he'd have to pay for it. I had hoped to find an outsized character, a throwback, perhaps a white-suited eccentric with a Mark Twain mane. Instead, he had the standard country face on which life had made little impression except for a bulbous nose and, higher up, tufts of parched hair that reminded one of the Burren in July.

"I suppose you're qualified?"

"Why certainly." Job interviews have not kept pace with our general progress as a species. I was grossly overqualified but there was no formula for saying so. "A master's degree from Dublin," I said. "Another from Cork. A spell in Oxford." At that his eyes widened. I decided not to mention my world tour, on camel and bicycle, from Kiev to the Himalayas and back to Ballinasloe. I also failed to tell him my spell in Oxford was on a building site.

"A master's, is it? What's your name?"

"William Wilde." Fortunately this was the truth. There is a lot to be said for names, windows on one's pedigree, though in my own case the mists of time had covered the family tracks. I had, all the same, the best of intentions, which were two-fold: first, to make enough money to support a convivial lifestyle; and second, to improve the human condition because anyone could see it had lost its moral compass. Yes, I know: I, too, saw the Sisyphean dimensions of my ambitions, but that's life: a walking, talking paradox, most of us hovering between pie in the sky and old-fashioned sin.

"I presume you're a regular reader?"

"Why wouldn't I be?"

"I mean, the *Midland Observer*."

"Oh not the *Midland Observer*. I'm afraid it stinks."

I am, as anyone can see, a high-energy individual. I was already twenty-five. My generation was in a hurry. Nearly everyone I knew already owned a BMW and a two-storey house or two. The smart ones had gone into engineering, while I, in the throes of some metaphysical hangover, opted to be a poet – not necessarily writing verse, which demands grammar and that, but I pitched my tent on the Dionysian side of the river, where the sun shines brighter and the maidens dance with longer legs.

"Stinks, does it?" His pipe was now smoking like a volcano.

"Look at it." I grabbed a copy. "A few beatings; a murder or two, because deep down people love murders; or a few drunks getting their comeuppance, because readers hanker to see their neighbours humiliated. And football. I'll grant you, you cover football thoroughly. If I came in from Mars I'd know at once that football was our bread and butter here."

"From Mars, is it?" He seemed so serene, with a ginger cat under the chair.

"Speaking of which, why don't you do an article about the recent shady past and dim future of the race? About what's happening up in the Milky Way? What would Einstein say, or Pseudo-Dionysius?" Sure, I was showing off, and once one heads down that road hubris takes over. "There is a whole new paradigm out there. It's up to you to bring the Irish midlands into Europe, which is the next big thing. Think of Charlemagne and De Gaulle and Maggie Thatcher, or, if you prefer, the Spice Girls. Between ourselves, Mr O'Lally, you're talking down to people. They buy all that guff only because they need to find out who died in the obituaries. It's an insult. They're educated now. They don't need an article on the new traffic lights." I'll be sorry, I was thinking as I ranted. But it would never be a BMW kind of job anyway, more likely a Ford Fiesta kind of job. I should have signed up for engineering when I was young, that's what I was really talking about.

"Thank you," Liam O'Lally said, all placid, tamping the tobacco with his stained thumb. I had dug a hole in his life and thrown him into it. "You may be right," he was saying. The smoke curled beautifully. I resolved to try a pipe as soon as I got a job.

"I suppose I might as well go now."

"What's your hurry?" It's not easy to look sad and sly at once, but he managed it. "You're the only applicant," and he actually winked; it would be our secret.

That very evening, he sent me to cover a football match.

"Are you sure I'm ready?"

"It's not an important match."

My report was on his hard drive when he arrived in the morning. There was, I declared authoritatively, a paid attendance of twenty-seven. I reported on who scored what, and the "altercation" (*fights* were so twentieth-century) in the second half that resulted in a bloody nose and a sending-off. I realized that all this was just an excuse for the two pages of photos taken by our prize-winning photographer Red O'Brien.

"That about covers it," O'Lally said with satisfaction, and in a euphoric moment suggested I try an editorial.

"About what?"

"Whatever needs to be said."

Football was fine, new supermarket launchings were inevitable, but editorials got down to saving the world. I recalled some of the great historical occasions, from world wars to landings on the moon, and the editorials, without which they would never have been embedded in the great scheme of things. Then I thought of the philosopher Kierkegaard, whose ideas had finally caught up with my own. On a Sunday afternoon, a century and a half earlier, smoking a cigar in a Copenhagen park, Sören Kierkegaard realized his peers were getting rich and famous from new inventions and discoveries, while he languished in obscurity. Their success, he saw, came from making life easier for people. But K wasn't a curmudgeon for nothing. A day would come, he speculated, when people would get tired of the easy life. After a million years of assorted hardships, human nature and misery were a better fit than human nature and happiness. So K figured he would eventually grow rich and famous by making life hard again. I waxed for a page or two about the sagging standards of our day. Making life harder, I wrote, may sound unsavoury to a narcissistic generation, but survival is a commendable prospect when one considers the alternative.

"Tell me the truth. Did you make that up?"

"Certainly not," I pretended to be insulted. "You'll find it in Kierkegaard's *Concluding Unscientific Postscript*."

There was, it transpired, a staff of thirteen at the paper, but most of them were in accounting and advertising, unsung heroes keeping reality's wheels turning. A Lithuanian blonde named Lillie tended the website and filled pages of the paper with flighty gossip about Hollywood borrowed from the Internet.

O'Lally sent me to report on a controversial new car park. Such progress often splits people into vested interests or even enemies. The trouble was people. Behind a façade of amiability the island was having an identity crisis. Once wild, then tamed, first by the saints and scholars, then by the British, and latterly by ourselves, we Irish were returning now to a savagery that left no room for loving your neighbour as yourself.

The pipe would stick straight out from O'Lally's yellow teeth as he let the smoke have its way. The delete button kept him from going berserk.

I was not, in short, galloping up the ladder to success.

Then Evie Adams fell down and my rusty Ford Fiesta insisted on stopping.

"Are you all right?" She was spreadeagled in the tangled grass amid dandelions. She had bronze-black hair, short and choppy. From the corner of my eye I had seen her turn to rubber, the knees buckling this way and that, throwing her arms out as she folded.

Since going to work for O'Lally, I had occasionally longed for a tragedy to challenge my youthful ambition. I never thought of longing for a rubber woman with one eye closed and the other looking beyond me at the sky. "Hello?" It's plain to see why people don't stop in cases like this. Stopping is the easy part, but then what?

I got down on my knees and folded her into a dignified posture. She had a flat chest under a summery dress sprinkled with flowers; probably daisies, and she looked like a scarecrow. "Can you hear me?"

When she failed to answer I tried her pulse, took note of her steady breathing. "I'm stuck with you now," I said out loud. "We'll have to wait until help arrives." I had to be cool. I had noticed that in the new, heartless Ireland, people would sue you for doing them a favour. "Took a jar too many, did you?" Silence. "If you could tell me where you live, we could both get this episode behind us."

"Over there," she then pointed her rubbery arm vaguely down the road.

"Can you stand up?"

"You'll need to carry me."

And I did: to a neat cottage a mile away with roses round the door and a lazy sheep dog by the sheltery side of a wall.

"Give it a push," she said as we approached the door. I placed her on a sofa. "I'll be all right now."

I gave her every chance to thank me but she just watched with that vacant gaze. I nodded repeatedly as I backed out. I even nodded to the dog. I planned to think no more about her. That's how innocent I was.

"This is Evie," she said on the phone.

"I don't know any Evie."

"You carried me home when I had my spell."

"Is that what it was?"

"Aye, a spell."

"What can I do for you?"

"It's not as simple as that," Evie said.

An hour later we were eyeing each other across cups of tea in Fred's. The orange-black hair had a sheen like certain birds in spring. She was neatly dressed and looked more trendy than on the grass; and younger, maybe thirty-odd.

"I heard what you were saying."

"What was I saying?"

"When I was on the side of the road. I heard you."

"Sorry." The world was on edge because we had kept the Furies locked up so long. I used to make apologies, therefore, for all manner of things rather than go to war over them. "If I offended you, I'm sorry."

"You work for the newspaper?" She had to look sideways for her one good eye to focus on me.

"Aye, the *Midland Observer*."

"Are you going to write about me?"

"Alas, you're not news."

"I'm as much news as that car park." Her shoulders rose and fell and her body wriggled like an eel. "I wasn't a bit drunk."

"Is that right?"

"I'm mad." She stared steadily at me, defying me to deny it. "I admit I take a sup. But I fall down on account of the other."

"What other?"

"Insanity."

"Is that what you want me to write?"

"Whatever you think yourself." At one moment she looked abject and ugly, then a light would pass over her face like the sun over countryside and make her beautiful. The tortured body would lean forward or back, and her mind, too, squirmed like an eel.

I made enquiries. She had been in and out of institutions, I was told. She lived alone. No one knew about relatives except for an uncle who, years ago, had drowned himself after allowing an easy goal during the dying moments of a football match.

"Wise up or I'll sack you," O'Lally warned, and put me on a regime of county council meetings. I smuggled Plato, Erasmus and other luminaries into my reports. He never said a word, just yanked the interfering luminaries.

"Are you hungry?" I would drive out to Evie's fairy-tale cottage on my day off.

"I love you," Evie would say, over and over.

"Not so loud, Evie." I had quickly gained my own small reputation as an eccentric. I didn't mind: it was part of the package I aspired to be. Kierkegaard the quasi-hunchback had in his day been dogged through the streets of Copenhagen by snotty urchins taunting him, "Either or, either or," which is a whole other story.

The secret is to avoid seeing their faces, whether Evie's, or the Third World faces expiring from hunger, or the Bosnian faces bound by the wrists going down a briary lane to get their bullet. I was beginning to feel sympathy for the smoking O'Lally. He wasn't so much editing a newspaper; he was editing life. He got up every day to face life-and-death decisions as to whom the people of the midlands would care about and whom they could with good consciences ignore. His decisions, in a roundabout way, were crucial to the great scheme of things.

"Who have you belonging to you, Evie?"

"Kith and kin, do you mean? Neither kith nor kin."

"So who looks after you when you, you know, take a turn and fall upside down on the road?"

"I snap out of it." She was cheery and even frolicsome. Her nerves gave her body no rest, there was surely a medical name for what ailed her. "Are you going to write about me?"

Too few appreciate the awesome power of the local paper. The *Midland Observer* came out on Wednesdays. By nine o'clock, irrespective of world events, the paper had insinuated itself into every household. On outlying farms, animals were often neglected. A similar spell gripped towns and villages. All this concentration had an extraordinary effect on the community. Tens of thousands of people reading the same thing at the same time, guided by the slick words of journalists and the wise choices of editors, became a force for good or evil that not even money could buy. The result was akin to mass hypnosis. When, therefore, a villain came into view, and the paper shone its spotlight on him, the public vilification soon had him, or even her, paying the piper. In like manner, when sympathy was brought to bear, compassion flowed like a mighty river, with an energy not unlike the prayers of yesterday's mystics. That is why, even in this cynical age, there are still miracles in the world.

I took this hypothesis to O'Lally.

"Forget that nonsense," he said kindly, like a childless old uncle.

All that spring I would go out to the cottage to see her. Last year's roses had scarcely died when the new buds appeared, yellows and reds. I preferred them young like that, all promise, for I had never seen a grown rose that lived up to its potential.

One day, curled up in a bloated armchair donated by the Vincent de Paul, she handed me a letter. "Read it," she said. She hadn't opened it. "I can't read with one eye," she explained. "The eye that went blind was my reading eye."

The letter advised her that she was expected at the hospital for treatment.

"It's for my multiple sclerosis," she sprang out of the chair and plugged in the kettle, all business. "Evie is off to the hospital." She always talked as if she had a handful of pebbles in her mouth. "Evie is going to die." And then she fell down in a heap. I put her on the sofa. She covered her swollen eyes with two little knuckles. I made her tea and for an hour told her how the world worked and how the infamous O'Lally was dragging his feet, refusing to tell readers about the criminal profits of oil companies and especially about her own poignant story.

She would laugh on inappropriate occasions. This made sense in light of my theory that even sticks and stones know well what's going on. Such as whether it's raining or not. And when I look sheep or goats in the eye I fear they know what I'm thinking. I can't prove any of this but neither can the enemy prove the opposite. We're all waiting for someone to come along and reveal the whys and wherefores. But forget sticks and stones: Evie Adams was a puzzle entirely. She would talk smartly at times, stupidly at other times. But who's to say what's stupid and what's not? I who usually gave hens and geese the benefit of the doubt could not but do the same when Evie acted oddly.

She vomited the spring away. She refused the hospital treatment. Bravo, I told her, I don't know why, and in return she vomited all over my only suit. Social workers and neighbours descended on her with offhand love. They eyed me with suspicion, which seemed all the more justified when Evie would tell them she loved me.

It was not as if I had no other life. I hobnobbed with engineers and bankers and rugby footballers. I attended poetry slams and art openings. I drank lager and vodka while putting off the day when I'd be ready to smoke a pipe. On slow Saturday nights I squired that overweight receptionist whose career I had long ago vowed to torpedo. I had postponed the hunt for wealth, but a young man never abandons the hunt for love.

"Just once, if you could put her in the paper," I said again to O'Lally, "simple, uncomplicated happiness might cure her."

"You need to get rid of that messianic complex."

She spent the summer in an electric wheelchair provided by the do-gooders. "Look!" She would press a button and the chair would perform. I would hug her, wrapping my arms around a ghost.

"Any pain?"

"A pain in the arse." And she laughed with the pebbles in her mouth and a drip from her nose. She was incontinent and wore diapers, she told me with pride. She knew she was paying her dues to the human condition. A hairdresser had come and made her hair curly with a touch of green in it like a peacock. A local woman applied cheerful make-up. "Look at me now." She would cock her head sideways. "If I wasn't insane you'd fall for me."

"We'll never know."

"If you asked me to marry you I'd have said yes." And I would go silent. "It would have been a royal wedding. And a honeymoon in Gibraltar. Hold my hand." And I would squeeze her clammy little hand while she sighed with satisfaction. That summer was the sunniest in living memory. Her little house grew brighter. I would borrow a rose from beside the door and stick it in her hair.

"Never forget, I'm still nutty."

"Don't I know."

"And ugly, too."

"I've seen worse."

She spent all her waking hours in the kitchen. Nowadays we have rooms for almost everything, but no one builds a room to be sick in, much less a room to die in.

"I have something to show you." She was in her electric chair, a plaid shawl draped over her knobby knees. She was full of pain killers provided by the nurse, she would soon go sleepy and comatose; it was a way of practicing death a little at a time before nodding off for good. "Follow me." She loved to go places in that chair, negotiating doors, slapping the wall to stay on track. I followed her to the parlour, full of shadows and presences. A pot of artificial flowers sat sullenly before the fireplace. She opened a drawer and withdrew an envelope. "Read it."

The two pages were faded and stained: a much-used letter.

"Dear Evie," it began. And told her she should do herself a favour and forget about a certain Jack. Rather rude, I thought, and the handwriting cocksure with curvy flourishes. "Please destroy this letter after you've read it," Jack wrote. He should have known better. For nearly twenty years she had been reading it.

"So who's Jack?"

"I was young at the time," she looked at me sideways with her distorted old face. "I was all go. And fierce stylish. You should see my long hair down to my backside. I was too good for Jack. He was handsome enough but he had only one eye."

"Like you," I said.

"No, I had two eyes at the time." Dusk had fallen. The neighbour would be coming to put her to bed just as soon as I left. "I was a sight to see at that time in my life."

"It's time you forgot about Jack. He could be dead."

"Oh no, he's not dead. Look at the last line," and her nerves sent her body into spasms as often happened when she was excited.

"I shall never see the moon for the rest of my life without thinking of you," the last line said.

"We used to watch the moon. And to this day, when I see it, I know he's watching it – not all the time, I'm not that daft, but sometimes, I know, the two of us are watching it together. It's sentimental old shite, but that's life."

"So what happened your eye?"

"I stuck a fork in it."

"On purpose or by accident?"

"What's the difference?"

When her head drooped sleeping on her chest, I stole away. When the next month's moon came, I would look up through my bedroom window and think of Jack off somewhere, and wonder about him, and think of Evie making the huge decision to have only one good eye, like Jack. Or I might be in a crowd, or in the presence of some local lovely, and there the moon would suddenly be, a surprise, tugging at the tides, tugging at our lives.

That was the last time I saw Evie. I would like to be able to say her soul streaked across the sky like a long-tailed comet. All I know is, she died in the dark on a night our backs were turned.

The handful of people at the funeral included O'Lally. He shook my hand as if I were family.

"I'm glad that's over." I didn't ask what he meant. "You'll write an obituary," he added with belated magnanimity.

The *Midland Observer*, I knew, could have caused enough stir in the world for Evie to have taken heart and gone on living. I tried for days to write a few mighty lines about her, some expiation on behalf of humanity, but certain lives do not fit neatly into the scheme of things. I would look up at the moon and crave inspiration. If I could find the right first word, I might have managed it. Out beyond the moon was the rest of the universe, about which I didn't know a damn thing, except that there was a fifty-fifty chance of happiness there. Evie was surely yonder now and everything making sense. Yet the local paper wasn't local for nothing. It was more at home with football and politicians posturing. The inscrutable midlands shuffled along unburdened by Evie's story, while on moonless nights I waited for her to come back and give us one more chance.

À la Descartes

Picture, if you will, a tree-lined avenue curving gracefully for half a mile, its destination a mustard-coloured mansion crumbling under the weight of lost elegance. It was the hazy hour before dusk, when the day had given its all and was relaxing. The one looking out at the water lilies and beyond at the avenue was myself, Bartholomew.

A man came into view. Frankly I expected him – I'm above average in the insight department and enjoy premonitions, *déjà vus* and other epistemological irregularities. This fellow was on foot. He was carrying a plastic shopping bag held cautiously clear of his body the way one would carry eggs if one did not wish to break them.

As an author, I have tried in my own small way to add lustre to the human condition. I started ambitiously with a tome called *God Knows,* written in the first person. No one ever admitted reading it. Then came the brainwave and I wrote *Here Below.* With sensational, if I may say so, results. People everywhere, getting the picture, wanted to save us from ourselves. Rot, a lot of it, but the rest had merit: do good, avoid evil, get back on the bicycle.

Having provoked the populace into divulging, I felt a responsibility. Writers can't walk away from the mess they make. The resulting correspondence was stupefying as crackpots and others shone new light on the planet. From Plato's cave to the Bermuda Triangle they tortured me. Neighbours described neighbours breaking all ten commandments. Old curses were invoked, druidic spells paraded, rugby football and Wall Street derivatives brought to bear. Then popped up that man with the shopping bag, one Mossy O'Toole, who wrote a fabulous letter about the late Rene Descartes, who, as everyone knows, was invited by Queen Christina to emigrate to Sweden from his native France where he was already an exceptional philosopher. You may have seen his picture: a bony face with the hint of a snarl and the shifty look of a fellow who trusted no one and with good reason.

The pope was on his case for what might be heresy at a time when heresy could provoke an unhappy death. A stay in Sweden seemed to what the doctor ordered. But the Stockholm winter could be atrocious. Queen Christina, furthermore, was a fanatic and made him get up at five in the morning to talk philosophy. Descartes hated early mornings. In no time at all he caught pneumonia and died. That was in 1650. The Swedes, embarrassed, gave him a quick, quiet burial. The plot would thicken with the years.

One could argue ad nauseam whether it's cool for a man with tangled grey hairs growing out of his ears to wear diamond earrings in the same ears. Mossy O'Toole, in short, was not a conventional man.

"We're the Anglo-Saxon O'Tooles," he said at a certain stage. "We're to be found near Blue Ball not far from Tullamore. I myself am the black sheep of the family," he added with a hint of pride.

I, Bart, when not saving the world, am a confirmed bohemian. I'm not sure what this means but it seems to include a wide-ranging neglect of the social order. The mansion is a mess. Several Irish wolfhounds spread fleas from room to room. Rusty kettles, heaps of unwashed laundry and a yellow canoe are scattered across the drawing room. They have not been disturbed for a generation or more. The philosophy behind this inertia is to the effect that life is short and should be wasted only on essentials. I am tall and gaunt, by the way. If you wish to envisage me, envisage me as a cricket player dressed to play, something I have never actually done. I have cohabited for years with a willowy companion named Bella, an exotic person dressed in long draperies to the ground. Salt of the earth, apple of the eye, one soon exhausts the superlatives when she comes up for discussion. Like myself, she is bohemian. Thus, when a loud commotion came to the front door that evening, neither of us was in a hurry to respond. Bang, bang, the knocker went, while she doggedly read a book and I doggedly looked out at the lilies. On the other hand, we are all fascinated by interlopers and pining for surprises. While we are, for example, afraid of the grim reaper, we are equally afraid, when the occasion arises, to refuse to let the bastard in. So I let the bastard in.

"*Mon vieux,*" he said, something he said a lot. "*Mon vieux,* where has traditional hospitality gone?" He didn't look at me, as if he took me for a hired servant, brushing past with the plastic bag ahead of him until he deposited it on a table. "You must be?"

"Bartholomew."

"Oh, well, that's different. I bring you Descartes." He looked eccentric enough to butt heads with Descartes, something few do: in our day only a minority wrestles with the dreadful questions. He wore a bluish plaid suit, too big for him now, as if he had reached and then moved beyond that moment when human flesh begins to shrivel and disappear. Then the freckles across his face came into focus, miniscule blotches, each a separate imperfection. Those freckles were, furthermore, unevenly distributed, seventy percent, give or take, on one side and the remainder on the other.

Bella made broth. Dandelion broth, she claimed, added iron to the soul. I kindled a roaring fire while Mossy enjoyed a bath. There was a sense of occasion. As our guest talked, those freckles would move about his face, a universe of miniature moons and planets in their orbits.

"*Cogito, ergo sum,*" he intoned. "You don't need Latin to know Descartes said a mouthful." An evening breeze was blowing past the double doors from the orchard. The broth was laced with spices and the dregs of several tall bottles. The result was a mystical twilight, reminiscent of the evening the ancient Greek discovered Eureka, or whatever.

Descartes, so the story goes, found himself lapsing into the worst of all possible frames of mind: universal doubt. This had not been a problem since God knows when. Previously, when incredulity raised its head, litanies of saints joined forces with ancient pagans to make blind belief a *sine qua non*. Yet Descartes' demons demurred. Show us, they insisted. A whole world teetered, the only world we had at the time. And the trouble with doubts: when you give in to one, another pops up until they're everywhere. Soon the philosopher was wading in a cesspool of misgivings.

Still, he thought, if I'm thinking about it, whatever it is, I must at least be here.

"It was brilliant, *mon vieux*. Everything else fell into place."

"How?" Bella wanted to know.

"How what?"

"How did everything fall into place?" This is the kind of poky question no one wants to be asked, but Bella had a poky mind. A wolf howled in the distance, adding atmosphere; probably the neighbours' dog.

"If I'm thinking, I must be here," Mossy tried to explain. "And if *I'm* here, so is everyone else." Philosophically it was a limp old sausage, not one you could sink your teeth into. But the wily vagabond forged ahead. "When a dead man leaves ideas like that festering all over Europe, *mon amie,* there will always be someone to drag his memory over the coals – or am I mixing too many metaphors? And is that mead, by the way, in the bottle?"

"Wine, *mon ami.*"

"I have nothing against wine."

"It's made from the same dandelions as the broth," she explained. "Earth is winding down, old man, and the dandelion is your best bet. That and the roach are the obvious survivors in their respective categories. After humans have succumbed, it will be the cockroach drinking dandelion wine. Or vice versa." This aging girl, a nun in her youth, had spent life wandering from ashram to kibbutz to Amazonian jungle collecting nonsense. She had a great capacity for hope. She could see, down the road, a better life than life with myself, though she was vague about the details. This, by the way, was not such a startling discovery: I, too, could see ahead a better life than life with myself.

As the long twilight headed for midnight, Mossy asked if he could pitch his tent somewhere. This was a metaphorical tent and we pitched it on a section of terracotta flooring in the scullery. His only impedimenta, he explained, were a toothbrush and a pair of jockey shorts.

There was, though, one other impediment. Few relics create as much curiosity as a human head. Even the average skull: what a life it had, from the yowls of childhood to the hullabaloo, year after year, of facilitating what eye saw and ear heard, coordinating our days. I had been led to believe that one of the great skulls was in a box in the bag now looking conspicuous on the scullery floor. I nudged it with my toe. Whatever was in there was inert. It was mysterious. The world was always waiting for one Holy Grail or another. And like the lottery, I always thought I had as good a shot at it as the next one.

"I'm a troubadour," O'Toole said the following morning, "with no place left to go." Thus began further days and nights of claptrap as the three of us circled the skull.

"Here's what I'm telling you." Mossy was drinking tea made from a tea bag from his trouser pocket, a well-used tea bag, he said, that never made weaker tea than the week before. The followers of Descartes, in any case, asked the Swedes for his body back. When they dug him up, the French ambassador asked for the great man's finger as a relic – on account of the part the finger played penning the Descartes opus. "There is embedded in the human condition a hankering for relics," Mossy went on, "from Marilyn Monroe's underwear to Moroccan jugs. But body parts are priceless: Locks of hair or a tooth, but especially foreskins. Western civilization contains a vast treasury of foreskins. You'll find them in bottles and boxes, couched in velvet or in leather purses or ornamental reliquaries."

"Descartes?" I steered him back to the topic.

"Oh that. An attendant, seeing the ambassador take the finger, took the liberty of taking the skull. There was dancing in the streets, *mon vieux*, when Descartes returned to Paris. It was around the time of the French Revolution, so no one paid much attention to a missing head."

Yet a head is a risky factor to overlook. A skull is not merely a skull. No one would suggest, for example, that John the Baptist's was just a head sitting on a platter; or, later, just a skull. Once one got beyond the anatomy, one suspected another dimension. Such as being godfather, in Descartes' case, of the mind-body break-up.

Descartes' remains, it seems, rattled indiscriminately around Europe. Then a Swedish scientist, Berzelius by name, read in a newspaper that the philosopher's skull was for sale at a Stockholm auction. He bought it for thirty-seven French francs.

"That skull," O'Toole declared, "has been sitting for ages in the Musée de l'Homme in Paris." The freckles were going berserk as he piled one *je ne sais quoi* on top of the next. There was a notorious highwayman in that basement, also long dead. There was the odour of death, he said. He described the bewildered and ugly, the hairy and bald, the royalty and mountebanks – it was, after all, the museum of man, with an occasional nod to women. They were all dead. All except Descartes, whose *cogito* kept him from resting in peace.

"There's only one problem," O'Toole said after a week. He and the companion and I were sitting on the veranda overlooking what was once the family valley: trees of every pedigree basking below us, a fox looking for something to kill, a tractor groaning up a hill. I was growing sick and tired of Mossy, sick and tired of Descartes. Everyone said the latter's *Discourse on Method* was a powerful piece of writing, but I had never met anyone who actually read it, including O'Toole. Adding insult to injury, Mossy had taken over the scullery. A gaudy carpet appeared first. Then came items of antique furniture. A bird cage with no bird. A microwave oven. Only when I saw paintings of my ancestors on the scullery walls did I realise he was stealing from me.

The problem, according to Mossy: Descartes had been lost and found so frequently, that there were now, in addition to the Paris skull, four others.

"All of them Descartes?"

"Who's to say otherwise?"

It took a shameless rogue to insist the others were spurious and that the genuine article was lying on my table. But one further clue kept popping up: the philosopher's name was said anecdotally to be etched on the true skull.

"Is anything etched on your skull?" Bella asked.

This would seem the obvious moment for Mossy to pull his prize out of the bag. But that was not the kind of man he was. "Think about it," he stared at us confrontationally. "Descartes is the one who first announced the separation of soul and body. Don't you see?"

There followed a pregnant pause. Late in that pregnant pause Bella eventually nodded: yes, that she saw. And so did I. Nodded, I mean. I don't know why. Embarrassed, probably, not to know what the hell he was talking about. This embarrassment is surely the reason slipshod scholarship thrives in the world: no one speaks up during the pregnant pause.

Consider. One couldn't travel far in the arena of ideas without running into the soul. It got credit for most of our little victories in the past. How it achieved all this was seldom spelled out in detail because history was full of pregnant pauses during which doubters failed to speak up. At a certain point, therefore, it was assumed we all knew what we were talking about.

That was only half of the catastrophe. While the soul was spiritual and flighty, the body, a heap of gradually disintegrating molecules, was easier to nail down. It had, for example, hairs in its ears. How such a body and such a soul, apples and oranges if you will, could ever conjoin and get along together – that was one conundrum. How they could now drift apart, as Descartes suggested – that was the Rolls Royce of all conundrums.

I myself – don't forget – was on a mission, metaphorically speaking, to rearrange the furniture, to comb our collective hair, cover the embarrassing pimple, set the sun back straight in the sky. People now wanted safer cigarettes, cuter children, less dirt under their fingernails, more snow at the North Pole.

In such a climate of misgiving, all those skulls had a disconcerting effect. Second-hand heads, if you like, already the worse for wear. Sometimes there were a few teeth left. Often there was an opening where none was expected. No two were alike. And that were just on the outside. Each of the misplaced craniums was on a shelf somewhere, probably in a fancy box, brooding and waiting. With or without teeth. Definitely without the tongue, the eyeballs, the old familiars. No more hair. No more wax in the ears. No more ears. A finger once picked the nose. Spare a thought for the finger. Those bones once spat and winked, somewhere back along the road we came.

And another thing. Killing, once practiced only by a few, was becoming the rage. One worried that a higher power, if there were still one, might grow tired of us. The intelligentsia were befuddled. Writers hovered in vain over their computers, until my own *Here Below*, which had been translated into everything, reminded people that nearly everyone, given the opportunity, disapproves of killing and prefers instead to talk things over. For talking things over, though, one needs pros and cons. And, as my book pointed out, the great proponents of pros and cons were philosophers, of whom there were, I added tartly, precious few nowadays. This caused an outcry. Until, amid all the shouting, someone mentioned Descartes, and before I knew it I was locking horns with the ineffable Mossy O'Toole.

"We'll be having trout for supper," I said soon after, "with asparagus and the devil knows what. While we still have the long twilights, we might as well take a look at whatever you have in the bag." This little speech had a galvanizing effect. He went for a long walk in the rain. I could see him far down in the valley making up his mind. The modern world, he was surely thinking, was an old horse, tired, walking through abandoned meadows in search of a quiet place to die.

Supper: imagine three old wrecks like us gathered around a plastic table in the solarium. Small talk seemed superfluous. "We could try uplifting music on the machine," Bella suggested, dressed top to bottom in Carrickmacross lace. "Sibelius, anyone?"

O'Toole countered with the Clancy Brothers and Tommy Makem. Since he still had the skull, the trump card, Tommy Makem sang about the wild colonial boy and the jug of punch while we washed down the fish with dandelion wine. A moment came when none of us could think of anything further to delay the proceedings.

A robin was singing a warbly song outside as O'Toole opened the bag, a mere grocery bag once, now the focus of almost supernatural interest. The box, I could see, was made of ebony: black and shiny. The opening ceremony was surprisingly banal, no golden key or electronic whatnot. He just lifted the lid.

One would like to think, if the Grail is ever found, that it will be a sensational find creating fireworks on earth if not actually in heaven; orgy and ecstasy and bands playing. O'Toole's package was less demonstrative. "Go ahead," the breathless companion encouraged.

Even the Clancy brothers had fallen silent. Mossy lifted the lid delicately the way one would open a carton of eggs. There were no celestial phenomena. The skull, as skulls go, looked reassuring, typical. A mild, patient, skull. He picked it up without fanfare, without even the customary rubber gloves, and set it on the table.

We raised our eyes from the head and looked at each other. What could Queen Christina have seen in him? What could she have wanted to know at five in the morning?

"Doesn't look a bit like him," Bella said.

The mouth was gone. Gone all the things it ever said. Even if it never was Descartes', it was surely once a talking mouth. The philosopher used to have an aquiline nose. Gone now the way of all noses. The brow was furrowed right down to the bone. All that doubting must have done it.

His name was etched above the eye: Descartes.

That seemed to settle it.

Pagans

A brisk wind took shape until it was one of the dear departed. Alien energy ran rings around reality. Boulders sighed as the sun went down. World of fog and nervous briars. World of dolmens, memorials to ancestors who cherished friends and smote foes with equal abandon back when god was a thunderbolt. On fine evenings, the Pruntys could be found sitting on a bench and gazing at their own megalith not far from the back door.

"Dammit, Cornelius," Hazel fulminated in a twilight of vicious midges and her immense stomach growling. "Concentrate."

"I'm concentrating as fast as I can." Cornelius was about half the size of his wife. A wiry little former farmer, he wore a gaberdine raincoat to his ankles. His teeth were absent except for a few yellow survivors in the shadows. He had both money and inclination to invest in a mouthful of implants, but Hazel held strong opinions about how and when nature should be interfered with if at all.

The sun was known to get giddy before sinking beyond Scally's mountain.

"*Let Erin remember the days of old*," Cornelius sang in a rumbling voice. He could spellbind with old songs. He had a sunburned face that failed to tan on the farm that Hazel eventually turned into forestry where she planned to grow goblins.

"Hold on," he whispered. The evening tensed, disturbed only by a rapper rapping on Scally's television two fields away. "Wait!" Cornelius was on the brink of something. A suspicion of irregularity. "False alarm," he then exhaled, and the birds returned to singing.

"Moron," Hazel waddled into the house, her entire person bulging with disappointment. Cornelius concentrated harder. Familiarity had never blotted out awe. It didn't matter that for centuries the dolmen had been tampered with by local authorities or their prehistoric equivalents: in the old days, according to Hazel, giants could rearrange a field of dolmens before breakfast. Cornelius could sometimes espy his own forebears amid the hoary panoramas. Some might have a harelip or handlebar moustache, most carried spears. Nobody was ordinary in Hazel's world, everyone was fabulous. All you needed, she said, was karma to uncork the unlikely. He admired the way she defied conventional wisdom, which, she said, was all in the mind.

Calling him a moron, though, provoked murderous thoughts. Then remorse would set in. Life was too short already. Hazel was pathetic enough without a premature death, so was everyone. On the one occasion they came to blows, she had left him battered and blue in a two-fisted attack. Then she had gone on her knees, face disfigured with mud, tattooed arms clasping his shins, begging forgiveness. She was a practitioner of the big gesture. Whenever Cornelius looked back, life before Hazel seemed an insignificant waste of time.

Then it happened. The dolmen flexed its muscles in the dusk. It shook itself like a terrier in from the rain. It wasn't altogether dancing but it was fidgeting. The supporting boulders seemed to bump and grind in slow motion. Time stood still a minute or two. The capstone, which resembled a whale, levitated, hovered, making up its mind. Then, suddenly, the evening returned to normal. Except for one thing. The dolmen had moved a step closer to the Prunty homestead.

"Just as I expected," Hazel remarked. She had a moon face and greenish hair. "Those boulders are far from finished, they're getting ready for the future." Though only twice his size, she could eat several times as much as Cornelius, from potatoes to ice cream. The extra food created extra energy. She was a throwback to when women ruled.

The Pruntys were pagans. Hazel could trace her lineage, with only occasional gaps, back beyond prehistory. Cornelius had only lately stumbled on his new orientation. One summer, after a night of drinking, he found himself at daybreak driving past the Hill of Tara. It was the summer solstice and revellers were greeting the dawn. This struck him as inexplicably important. One of the cavorting druids was Hazel, thick as a tree, with wondrous hips that sashayed in primal display. They caught one another's attention. They clasped hands and danced.

"You're puny but you're game," Hazel greeted him.

"I'm drunk," he corrected her.

"Sober up," she said, "until I tell you the theology of paganism." She was wearing a pink petticoat and a saffron towel around the head. "You must have some compensating factor?"

"I'm searching for meaning."

"You came to the right place. This is the Stone of Destiny," her head nodded in the direction of an upright rock, around which the wild romantics were going delirious.

"It's nothing to write home about," Cornelius informed her. "There's a dolmen outside my back door would put it in the shade."

"And where is this back door?"

"It's a bit." He told her about the farm and living alone, about his liking for pancakes and weakness for porter. Centuries of instinct leaped to life within Hazel's heaving chest. Doors to and from the past were flung open. A courtship was instantly begun. He described the megalith's good points. "I suppose you'd like to see it?"

"Not until we're married." This was news to Cornelius, who nevertheless was impressed by paganism's no-nonsense urge to get on with things.

It was a small wedding: just the two of them and an archdruid officiating on a windy knoll in the upper field.

This turn of events caused a stir in the village.

"A wedding makes no sense without us gossiping," a villager justified their prattle. They gossiped like a Greek chorus, all that was missing was Greece.

"Cornelius and your wan."

"Ah, go on?"

"Aye, a pagan."

"That big wan?"

"Isn't that druids. Larger than life."

Country people, their roots deep in the soil for aeons, could sense when the land was going through a phase. They noticed the air more full of lilac. Cattle grew higher and wider. Rounder potatoes were found under stalks. The footballers won their first championship ever. At a more personal level, well-being was contagious. Old men returned to whistling in the fields and would sometimes dance in their own kitchens. Neighbours talked to neighbours to whom they had not spoken for a generation.

Attention was drawn out the road to Prunty's.

"They are what you might call the only variable."

"And don't forget that auld dolmen."

The Prunty homestead had come alive. A construction company descended to refurbish downstairs and added a few bedrooms. Hazel could be seen in a ballooning orange dress like an authentic druid, hammering and troweling. She drove recklessly around bends in the antique Volkswagen van, a relic of the hippie years. The countryside eyed them.

"A mosque, I'd say."

"No, that's the other crowd."

"Unless they're planning a clutch of childer?"

One Saturday, a B&B sign went up. The chorus chortled.

"There now."

"A pity none of us thought of it first."

"Sure, no one will come near them."

The B&B was quickly overwhelmed by tourists. Strange vehicles, with strange markings, created unlikely traffic jams.

"They're not from these parts."

"If they were from these parts, they wouldn't need a B&B."

"They're no tourists neither."

"Foreigners."

"Pagan anyway. Look at the haircuts."

When Hazel visited the village café for morning coffee, she was treated with civility. No one said a word.

"Have a nice day," she would say as she left.

"Oh, aye," they would respond.

On days when she didn't show up, though, they felt they had missed something.

"If anything happened to her, we'd regret we never knew her." A silence would fall, as if something were being overlooked.

Average bed-and-breakfast guests go to sleep watching television. Hazel's clients had other agendas. They converged on the megalith. They climbed over the stone wall that separated the dolmen from the Prunty homestead. They circled it, caressed it, took photos. The children played hide and seek amid the boulders. Yet something more solemn was happening. Those enigmatic strangers would sit on the bench for hours, brooding, waiting for some surprise, until darkness drove them indoors.

Soon a sign appeared beyond the stone wall. "Private Property," this sign said.

"He's a contrary farmer," Cornelius informed Hazel. On days like this he wished a little of his own meekness had rubbed off on his wife. He dreamed of a civility of which Hazel was incapable. He longed for a placid big woman knitting folderols and loving her neighbour as herself.

Instead, the status quo shuddered. And it came to pass that the wall, long taken for granted, refused to be ignored.

"That wall is crooked," Hazel was first to point it out. "Any moron can see it was moved." Any moron could see it did an unseemly zig and zag that left the dolmen in farmer Fawke's field and not in Cornelius' field where it clearly belonged. In an island sinking under the weight of stone walls, neighbours seldom discussed stones because everything that needed to be said about them had been said centuries earlier. Until, that is, Hazel arrived, wild-eyed and cosmic in aspect, and pointed out what everyone had tried to ignore–the dolmen had indeed been circumvented.

"It was years ago," Cornelius was nervous. "It's ancient history."

"Ancient history is all in the mind."

"And he has a shotgun."

"It's our dolmen," Hazel was in one of her preternatural moods.

The countryside grew thick. Talk grew intense. Fawke trundled heavily into the village café, the tractor still grumbling outside. He had a stainless steel leg from fighting in some war. He was a staunch Catholic, what was sometimes called a pillar of the church. He ordered a mug of tea. "Four tea bags will do." He was buried in thought for a while. The village waited.

"Our heritage," he said quietly then, "is under siege."

"It is," the chorus agreed.

"No one else does moving statues like us." He made big fists of his big hands. "Our crowd always had a monopoly on that until now."

Nostalgia entered the café and floated to the rafters.

"I saw it myself." A dozen of them took turns affirming they had seen one or another moving statue.

"We waited for hours in rain and hoar frost."

"The Blessed Virgin shedding tears."

"Aye, tears."

"That little turncoat sits out there in the dark," Fawke fumed, "and every morning my dolmen has moved further in his direction."

"It's the woman."

"You can be sure it is."

Being sure was the problem. Some said the dolmen had not moved an inch, others saw it galloping towards the Prunty place.

As summer rounded the bend into autumn, the parade of guests continued to frequent Hazel's Bed and Breakfast. They sat on the bench, sinister as crows on telephone wires. They talked foreign into their mobile phones. The children, afraid of Fawke's sign, sang incantatory songs from the safe side of the wall.

One morning, towards Halloween, Cornelius went out early to collect home-grown eggs for the guests. Fog lingered over the townland. You could see your hand but not far beyond. When his eyes grew accustomed, he saw a sensation. The dolmen was on the Prunty side of the wall. He approached cautiously and touched it. The boulders were covered in the usual lichen and the big fish drowsy on top. Beyond that, Fawke's stone wall was unreal amid the vapours, but he knew it was there.

"Get up," he said to Hazel, "until you see."

"Didn't I tell you," she redistributed her mighty person in the brass bed.

The B&B guests, alert for anything abnormal, poured out into the dawn. They caressed the monument, saying *ha*, they took photos, conspicuous in their yellow garments and haircuts, chattering like excited fools, while the children danced and went crazy amid the boulders.

Hazel emerged wearing purple and looking regal. The fog turned the early sun into a full bronze moon. People from the village began to appear, looking like silhouettes in ones and twos and clusters, astonished and watching. A dog barked in the distance. A donkey brayed back. Hazel mingled, saying quiet words to everyone. It was, the chorus said, otherworldly.

"We should have seen this coming."

"Weren't we the right eejits not to see it coming?"

They could hear Fawke before they could see him. Then his mighty tractor materialized through the fog, amplified and threatening. An exhaust pipe pointed at the white sky, a tin lid flapping. It approached in slow motion. It stopped beyond the low wall. Fawke descended awkwardly with his stainless steel leg. He reached back for the double-barrel shotgun. He climbed over the wall with difficulty, his grunting and wheezing could be heard. He stopped twenty paces from Hazel.

"That's a nice day now," he said.

At least, that's what some said he said. There was no agreement afterwards about what happened or who said what.

"Here's how I see it," Hazel is supposed to have explained to Fawke. God was for giving the world enough of everything – like an orthodox pagan she went back to first principles. Endless pears and plums along with bacon and cabbage. All the wine and lemonade, striped pyjamas and red sweaters. Black vehicles and any colour you want. All the bands and orchestras and stand-up comedians. All the hand-held electronic devices and rugby footballs. All the contentment. All the good looks. Elephants and every worthwhile animal. Wisdom and blessings like that, you name it. With justice thrown in. "And a sense of humour," she added. God, in this account, had plenty of everything, being god, thinking up new ideas and turning them into gifts and benefits. "Or at the very least into mysteries, like crooked roads or wet weather or exam results."

One day (Hazel continued) a crowd of newly-created people came along. "We could do with less," those early activists said. "There must be other places that need stuff more."

"You must be crazy," the creator was sweating from making the world.

"Fair is fair, god."

"Fine then," god said. "No skin off my nose."

"There has seldom been enough of anything since," Hazel concluded.

"That's not in the catechism," Fawke is said to have snorted.

"Easy now," Cornelius edged up to Hazel's side. In the event of a struggle, he had planned, he explained afterwards, to concentrate on the other's missing leg.

The locals were used to the fog lifting and paid no attention. The sun warmed the countryside. It picked out familiar details: oak trees, Scally's mountain, the bog road clogged with cars. They stood there like statues. It took a while to notice the dolmen because it was taken for granted. Then they noticed the stone wall, straight now without zig or zag.

Everyone went home, as they used to do in the old stories. But the chorus could not leave it at that.

"Ask her."

"No, you ask her."

"You have us wondering," one said, when Hazel waddled in for morning coffee. "Do you miss being like the rest of us?"

So Hazel, wise old sibyl, told them about the days of yore. She regaled them with blather about Manannan MacLir and Great-bladdered Emer. About mysteries that even today go bump in the night. The villagers grew to love her and her wild talk. Paganism crept back down country lanes after years in exile. A few admired the insane idealists who, in their generosity, gave away their birthright back when creation was, as Fawke put it, a pup. The majority, though, remained realistic and wished god had been allowed to create lashings of everything for evermore.

Time passed. The black shell of the B&B is still out the road. Fawke's headstone is a slab of granite protected by briars. Only the chorus survives.

"Mind you, it's not that long ago."

"Are you mad? It never happened."

Urban Myth

Even in our sophisticated age the winter solstice continues to play psychological tricks. Some solstice sensations beggar belief, yet people must decide for themselves because, deep down, such tales remain barometers of the sanity of the race.

But first the facts.

Most megaliths, even in Ireland, keep a low profile. Not everyone knows, for example, that the passage tomb at Newgrange has been brooding quietly for 5000, 200 years; already an ancient monument when Stonehenge was still an empty field. In the centuries that followed, the locals thought Newgrange was just an old kidney-shaped hill. Farmers would cart away stones to mend a mucky gap or build a pigsty. That was how they came upon a passageway that took them sixty feet into the dark earth where they found a fabulous chamber.

The chamber walls were carved by inspired ancestors in the early days of hammer and chisel. The passage was uncomfortably narrow because the ancestors on average were smaller than their descendants. Then someone noticed that at the winter solstice, on the rare occasions when weather allowed, the rising sun threw a shaft of sunlight down that narrow passage right into the chamber. This signified, everyone agreed, a miracle of architectural design. It also hinted at arcane riddles scholars never tire of debating.

People have always fallen head over heels for mysteries and secrets just around the corner. When word spread, after cars and cameras were invented, after progress created leisure and leisure created tourism, an indefinable energy attracted great crowds to Newgrange. Eventually these enthusiasts had to be organised. They checked in at a state of the art visitors' centre. Tour guides, versed in folklore, spiced their erudition with legendary Irish wit.

What throughout the year was mere tourism turned intense as the shortest day approached. Those in the know knew that cosmic bodies were extra active during the solstice. The sun was lining itself up and taking aim as it had done since time began. The moon's gravity was adding more tug, jogging sleeping psyches into fresh realizations. Year after year people responded to this fuss. So great the fervour grew, a lottery was needed to decide who would greet the sun from within the beating heart of Newgrange when the dead shrugged off mortality and insisted on being remembered.

On the year in question, just days before the solstice, the last tour of the afternoon, comprising thirteen souls, is a raggedy assortment so concerned with cameras and umbrellas that they fail to notice how the place is thick with spirit and reality coming unglued.

"Speedy now," Val is saying, "and watch your step." (He loves these people who, with only one life to live, are still prepared to spend an hour of it here in the distant past.) "Observe that stone. The triple spiral is found only in Newgrange. No, this stone here." It is useless. Some have gone ahead, others lag behind. The tour is ultimately about getting them in and out safely. He is a retired history teacher. He wears a yellow scarf around his head so that visitors will know he is their leader. He suspects the druids wore a headdress suspiciously like the yellow scarf.

Nearly ninety minutes later, the colourful turban reappears surrounded by satisfied tourists. Val counts them on the shuttle bus. He is one soul short no matter how often he counts. The others are oblivious of this brewing emergency. Some press a few warm Euros into his hand as they say goodbye. But Val feels a foreboding. Hard to believe, he is thinking, that the absence of one moron could make such a difference in the world.

"One didn't come back," he says absurdly to the director back in her wooden office. Roze is a prize piece of work from Coventry. Her curriculum vitae, everyone agrees, must be a beauty because she evokes the same emotions in the native Irish as the murderous Cromwell evoked in their forebears. Some compare her to frogs remembered from youth, some think dragons. Add to this a man's arms. She dresses in the same shade of green as the cabin attendants on the national airline, trying to be (as the Irish used to say of the better English) more Irish than the Irish themselves. On the other hand she speaks with that hoity accent which authorities, since the country went international, consider more arty than the native brogue.

"Well, you'd better go back and get him." It is so obvious when she says it like that, with authority, that Val is embarrassed he did not think of it. He knows the passage by heart, including every tight spot, knows when to stoop, when to pull in his already flat belly and advance sideways. If only the ancestors had allowed a few inches more. On the other hand, life is a tight squeeze. Wider and it would be like walking down Grafton Street: much ado about nothing. Val knows the ancestors well. He can see them making decisions about which boulders to put where. He knows the big hairy men and the small wiry men. Voices whisper old yarns. He tells tourists he can trace his lineage back to the original artisans of Newgrange. It is a privilege to give a decent tip to someone with such a pedigree.

The low lights are still on. Val sees a male tourist, a big old boy with mighty shoulders and a belly contoured like a reclining dome. He is sitting with his back to a boulder, knees up near his chest, looking at the floor in what can only be shame.

"Is this where you are?"

"Sorry," the fellow says without looking up. He is dressed in a serge suit, earth-coloured, and a tie adorned with autumn leaves. The hair is tousled like heather on a high bank. Mossy sideburns stretch down the sides of his face to where one would expect a beard. An umbrella rests against the rock beside him. "I can't," he says vaguely. "Claustrophobia," he utters the dread word.

"What the hell brought you in here with claustrophobia?"

"I didn't know I had it."

"If you just closed your eyes and let yourself go, I could drag you out."

"And wouldn't I know well what was going on?" A rustic, Val decides. But a better-class rustic, insightful. "Do you mind if I smoke?" the demoralized stranger wants to know. Val broods over him in sullen disapproval. "I waited for the others to go ahead, then I got down on all fours. It's my shoulders." He spreads them wide for Val's inspection. "I tried adjusting that rock – in case something had been overlooked. I can tell you for sure there is no gimmick. Do you get many like me?"

"Not many."

"Of course it's not the kind of thing you would broadcast." (He's so serene, Val is thinking, he doesn't know about the tyrant Roze out there waiting to kill him.) "I suppose there's no back door or anything?"

"Devil a back door." Val can see the wide man expiring within a year; the carcass in gradual decay;

the scattered bones in a thousand years. Meanwhile, ostentatiously nonchalant, the fellow lights a new cigarette from the remains of the old.

Outside, guides and others have forgotten to go home. There is a hubbub.

"Find Guard Rhone." Roze has big knees. Her comportment resembles the horsey side of the British royal family. Somewhere in her CV it surely says she is bold, decisive, does not suffer fools lightly, if at all. A dimple on one cheek saves her from seeming as ferocious as she would like. "Get him out," she explains to Rhone, a tidy, wizened man with a faintly purple face. "I don't care how. Cut him up in pieces and take him out in shopping bags. But only if you have to."

As Rhone enters the passageway, Val slips him two packs of Sweet Afton cigarettes. "I'm better going in alone," Rhone says when no one volunteers to go with him. He has no love of tight corners and often dreams of a room getting smaller and smaller until it becomes a nightmare, a room from some earlier life. Eventually, in the dim light ahead, the claustrophobe stands out like an apparition from the rocks of the legendary chamber.

"I hope this is not an inconvenience," he greets Rhone.

"Oh, no bother at all."

"You're the police, by the look of it?"

"Guard Rhone. And what do they call yourself?"

"Cadeau. William Cadeau."

"I suppose you haven't a criminal record or anything?"

"I am free of legal entanglements, if that's what you mean." They stand in the middle of the chamber and search each other's faces for answers without knowing the questions. Cadeau then looks meaningfully at the wall until Rhone's eye is forced to follow to where there is a dribbly, disorganised stain. "I couldn't help it."

"It couldn't be helped, then," the guard agrees.

"If we had a bucket or something."

"My instructions are to bring you out."

"I had no trouble getting in. Then something must have, let us say, raised the alarm. I mention this only because you're surely wondering."

"Here," Rhone hands over the cigarettes. "It's only sixty feet out as the crow flies," he finally says. "The secret is to think of your loved ones."

"Have you considered doping me or something?"

"There would be legal consequences. We're in the European Union now. People have so many rights, there's little anyone can do to help them."

Rhone emerges to find that what was only a hubbub has become a sensation.

"Put out the lights," Roze commands. "That'll move the fat fart."

They wait outside the entrance, a dozen of them, straining to see their man charging out of the blackness. But no spectre appears.

"This place is closed until further notice," Roze announces.

"Think of the publicity," her secretary, a malcontent known locally as Anarchy, taunts as she applies black lipstick.

"Hit the phones. Go to the website. Say there's flooding. Say weapons of mass destruction. We don't need tourists tripping over Rip Van Winkle. Find a blanket. But no food. We'll starve him out. One word to anyone and you're all fired." Roze strides to her VW Passat and in seconds is thin air.

"Heat up a pizza," Val pleads.

"And find a plastic bucket," Rhone adds. Along with the bucket he takes two blankets, raw carrots, bars of chocolate, bottles of water, cigarettes. He crawls from partial to total darkness. He has never seen a rat in Newgrange, nor even a mouse, but night is different, including unseemly sounds, including the unknown.

"Are you there?" he asks ahead once he reaches halfway.

"Jaysus, this is a fierce place," the other says.

"I brought you pizza. Bacon and mushrooms."

"I don't know about mushrooms."

"With extra cheese."

"I'll make it up to you, constable."

"I know you will." In the pitch darkness, he knows the stranger is in front of him, wrapped in a blanket. The tip of his lit cigarette intensifies when he drags on it, one small, fierce star in a vast, empty sky. Roze surely didn't mean it when she said to hack him up. "You could come with me. In the dark you wouldn't see anything to be afraid of." In a world full of terrorism, the grim thought strikes him, one terrorist could blow up all the history, all the dead bones. Maybe he is not such a fat man. Maybe he is padded with explosives. "Or are you not afraid?"

"Ambiguous more describes me. Danger all by itself is unfathomable. But then there's fear, a different fucker entirely, you don't even need danger to be afraid."

"Ambivalent. I'll put you down for ambivalent. You should give up smoking."

"I will, I promise." Such an ordinary fellow in spite of the sideburns and the fabulous head and shoulders taking up so much space in the darkness.

The staff disperses reluctantly. They are tour guides, security, secretarial, maintenance. They have been chosen from among millions, Roze tells them on good days. They would turn down positions at the pyramids of Egypt or France's Eiffel Tower for the rarer privilege of tending to Newgrange because Roze, though a bitch, is charismatic the rest of the time. Ministers and bureaucrats show up for photo-ops, but Roze embodies the rare, incomprehensible spirit of pre-history. Partly because she's neither pretty nor lovable, they suspect she walked over coals of fire to win this position of looking after old souls whose bodies were cremated amid mad pomp so long ago.

"What's it like?" she is abuzz next morning. "Is it dark? Is it cold? I'm going in."

"The smell isn't good," Rhone says.

"The minister is on to us."

"That surely means a leak," Val feeds her already healthy paranoia.

"We're at a crossroads. The minister fears we could lose the national identity. It's an argument there's no counter-argument for."

"In that case, you have no alternative." Val does not know what he means by this, or what the minister means. "Take Rhone for protection in case of foul play."

"I need to go alone."

"Bring a few cigarettes. Bring him something to eat."

"I hardly think so. We need to send a message."

"Kindness never did any harm."

She has sometimes loitered near the entrance. When no one was looking she would venture forward a metre or two before retreating with shortness of breath and palpitating chest. Claustrophobia never crossed her mind. The dead were and still are her issue. These are no ordinary dead. Not because they were once chieftains and goddesses, but because the descendants coddled them and put their bones on pedestals, never letting them be themselves. Every time she approaches the awesome monument she feels the departed right there on the other side of some frightfully thin membrane, one false move and one might be among them. She does not see them individually, as Val does, can't count heads because precise numbers mean nothing to souls. Yet they are not abstractions. Each has a face, beards for the men, tresses for the women.

Fear flourishes as she goes. Her body grows bigger while the passage gets narrower, nudging her. She knows instinctively when it's the point of no return and the only option is onward. Being intrepid, she gets her second wind and pushes on.

"Anyone home?" she calls when she's nearly there. An indistinct sound comes back, like a wounded animal from a field. The trick is to ignore the ancient sighing. The trick, as always, is swagger. "I have chocolate."

Here finally is the chamber that all the fuss is about. She knows she should be feeling more awe, but it's two days to solstice and the bureaucrats are going crazy and her job is in jeopardy. The first thing she notices, in the glow provided by her all-purpose pink phone, is litter; plastic bottles, scattered wrappers. She can smell the bucket. She thinks to be enigmatic, thinks to be threatening. She aims the pink phone and takes his picture in an exploding flash of light. He smiles agreeably for the camera but the photo has already been taken. From another pocket, but with the same hint of distaste, she takes out the chocolate bars and carefully hands them over like feeding animals at the zoo.

"Bill, is it not?"

"William, actually. William Cadeau," he says in what seems the original French. "Are you the person in charge?"

"I was until you came along." Getting himself in here, she now realises, surely involved a miracle, like a virgin birth. The only way he'll ever leave is bone by bone.

"Is that not a dimple?" Now he's inspecting her up close while his stale breath causes her to think toothpaste, to think toothbrush. "Fascinating," he remarks without being specific. "Something to sit on would be good," he adds. "And have you enough authority to get us, perhaps, a radio?"

"Why don't we just leave instead?"

"A cheap one will do. We don't need DVDs with Christmas carols. And while you're at it – I could eat a horse."

She sends out a text message. Val and Rhone eventually arrive with folding chairs plus two meals including mashed potatoes and gravy still steaming and for dessert apple cobbler covered with pale custard. The two newcomers squint at Roze in case she's a hostage. "That will be all," she says cheerfully, and puzzled, they go.

"I wish they had thought of a few beers," William says. "I have an insane fear of dehydration." He unfolds the chairs, places them a little apart. "I'll wager they're the first folding chairs ever sat upon in this sacred space."

"So," she says. "Tell me about yourself."

"I'll tell you the truth, madam, no beating about the bush. I come from Connemara, where I grew up listening to the ocean and tales of Grainne Mhaoil. May I smoke?"

"You may not." She is a keen student of authority, which can move mountains if handled with skill. "There are laws."

The cigarette is already between his lips and the lighter poised. They eye each other, sitting on their respective chairs. "Sorry," he says, then clicks the lighter and eases smoke up among the ancient memories. "Mine, madam, is quite a mundane story. I went to the big city and became a proofreader for a publishing house that specialises in Nobel laureates and former politicians. I discovered most of them wouldn't know what to do with a semicolon. So one spring morning I walked away determined to excel in some more agreeable milieu. I searched for years for a purpose in life. In desperation I thought – writing! It was then I grew the sideburns that I trust you already noticed. Until finally I found myself with the usual dilemma. I mean, what remains to be written?"

He unaccountably falls silent. (So the story goes.) This silence deepens when the timer back in Roze's office reaches closing time and the dim lights of Newgrange go altogether out. The two sit thinking, it is said, of one another. What they don't know of each other is admittedly wider and deeper than what they do. Yet they possess between them reserves of goodwill and imagination in addition to a desire to survive the present predicament for which neither has a name. They each develop a regard for the other: nothing like love or even affection, but what William might call rapprochement, or cutting through the crap as Roze would call it – blankets around their shoulders, their breathing palpable and eventually falling into an agreeable rhythm, his through that big mouth which has not yet found its toothbrush, hers through the haughty nostrils.

"I need to be going," she says all of a sudden. It may be she needs to use the plastic bucket but can't bring herself to do it. In the blackness there is that peculiar sound of feminine clothing.

"You could stay," he says superfluously. "I wish you would."

"You've left us in a right pickle, William," her voice trails as she goes. A silence ensues. Time passes in the inaccurate, spongy way time passes at night. Then he hears her returning – what else can it be? "On second thoughts," is all she says. Some say fear drove her back; others suggest it was *noblesse oblige* vis-à-vis this pathetic giant searching for the end of his own particular rainbow.

"We'd be warmer," he says, "if we moved closer together."

"You're an odd one, William." The pair redeploy the two blankets fore and aft and sit side by side. She eats chocolate, he smokes a cigarette, and they pass a plastic bottle of water back and forth. "I'll see you in the morning."

(How does anyone know any of this? It's an absurd question. Suffice it to say that if we passed on to posterity only the thoughts, words and deeds we could swear to, we'd be poor company with short histories. Verbatim conversations, in other words, are usually fiction.)

Out in the real world, tens of thousands have entered the lottery and a hundred have been chosen. There is no new war or scandal to distract from the solstice sensation. The media wax creative because Roze is either rescuing the stranded tourist or she's his hostage: two grand scenarios that get better when rolled into one. Terms such as Stockholm Syndrome get bandied about.

Bureaucrats have been dispatched from the city, but none has a background in whatever is happening. Anarchy, to her own consternation, tries to keep order. At last a text message arrives from Roze: "Outcome pending. Send food, a radio, batteries for everything, morning papers, coffee. Tell everyone Newgrange is still closed and yours truly is still in charge."

Such a message is ideal for speculation. Val is dispatched with the recommended items, including porridge and pancakes.

"How is everything?" he asks cautiously, observing Roze for any secret signal.

"Everything is fine, tell them everything is fine," she sounds too chirpy by half. The scattered blankets on the stone floor look surprisingly like an unmade bed.

"The minister says you need to be out by midnight."

"How does he propose we do that?"

"He didn't say." Sometimes so much needs to be said, it is impossible to know where to begin. "I'll empty the bucket, so."

"Thanks, Val. Remind me to give you a raise when this is over."

At some point the contemporary world is smuggled into Newgrange, namely a bugging device. It may be via a fake pack of cigarettes, or a harmless gismo casually dropped on the floor under cover of darkness. As frequently happens, the outcome is ambiguous and leaves room for conclusions that in time become folklore as a creative population strives to explain the inexplicable.

He excuses himself and uses the bucket. Eventually she does the same. This small ritual brings them closer together. "If we met on the high street or at the races," he says, "I'd never dream of telling you I had piles. Not in a million years." She says nothing. "Yes," he agrees with himself in a reflective way. "Smoke all you want," she says crossly when he lights up again. "Get lung cancer for all *I* care." The eavesdroppers, huddled at the visitors' centre, are at a loss how to understand such exchanges because the words never add up to reliable facts. Meanwhile the sun is coming around below the horizon at high speed and needs only favourable local weather to make a grand entrance.

"What now?" a sleepy William asks in the morning.

"There's only one way out." This unpromising remark ends any discussion before it gets started. There still remains the rest of the day, it is easier to postpone everything. They drink cold coffee from plastic cups, sitting on their chairs, his and hers by unspoken agreement.

(An odd conundrum refuses to go away: Roze's abdication. The woman everyone remembers should be by now an overachieving whirling dervish giving commands, issuing reprimands, asking terse questions, sticking her thick thumb in every dyke real or imagined. The little pink phone is all she needs to make her particular world go round, to put her bosses in their places and strike fear, mixed with admiration, in everybody else. This does not happen.)

"So who are you *really*?"

"I live in a lighthouse," he says. "Down the coast. Ships frequently came to grief there in the bad centuries." She looks at him with a sceptical eye. "A day came when, thanks to modern technology, the lighthouse was no longer needed. It was like a day the sun failed to come up. Stop me if you know nothing about fish." (She looks amused in the total darkness – light is no longer necessary to see he is growing on her.) "I knew where the fish were. Soon I had my own fishing fleet."

"May I have a cigarette?" (Out in the real world, eyebrows are raised.)

He puts two cigarettes between his big, cracked lips, lights them, hands her one. Her little phone is calling incessantly with the sound of a songbird. She ignores these interruptions. "I don't mind death," he says, "but I worry about spiders." Thoughtful pauses become part of their exchanges: embarked on a new adventure, neither wants to get ahead of the other. The day is moving on, the eve of the big sunrise. "White birds everywhere," William is saying, "soaring and diving. Dolphins flapping. Are you not getting hungry?"

She phones Anarchy, who says everyone wishes to speak to her, including Val and her relatives in Coventry and the minister and tons of reporters. "Tell them everything is going well," she reassures Anarchy. "Tell them it's very unprecedented." These are her very words. She asks for beer, toilet paper and roast beef, with mashed potatoes for William and boiled rice for herself. She snaps her little phone shut. "From in here you can tell the world practically anything and people will believe it." She speaks to him as to a trusted colleague, or a dear friend, with, yes, affection, and they look at one another and smile in sheer wonder.

Well-wishers are sending gifts: fancy food and survival guides and hand-made quilts. It's as if everyone expects something more to happen, some event bigger even than the sun shining through – some cosmic burp to give fresh direction to the humdrum. (For such soaring hopes places like Newgrange exist and those in the know know it.) Val makes several trips bearing gifts as the wise men allegedly did. He seems perplexed but faintly happy. He does not speak unless spoken to, and he isn't spoken to. The pair, meanwhile, listen to the crackling radio. The world, in a word, is agog. This is the most exciting solstice for thousands of years.

"Are there really dolphins?"

"Where?"

"You surely wouldn't lie, William, about every old thing?"

Come night, bundled up, they try to sleep, cheek by jowl but platonic as you like. Signals from the crackling radio rise and fall. They may be the sounds of unruly crowds outside or merely the earth flying through space with its usual whoosh.

"So," she asks, "what about that prestige publishing house with all the Nobel prizes?"

"Oh that."

Sleep is impossible.

Somewhere out there, he tells her in the wee hours, is the one book that needs to be written. Forget the fiddle-faddle that comes off the presses every day, piled into shopping bags, eventually eaten by mice and others before getting dumped in local dumps. All wasted words, all the semicolons and commas beating about the bush.

"You're just too – I don't know: would *lazy* be the word?" she says when he finishes explaining the life's work he can't bring himself to begin.

Eventually sunrise is only an hour away. Roze sends a text message: "May we expect to see the sun?" Negative, the word comes back. The usual drizzle. The minutes replace one another.

"Most darkness is assuaged by a glimmer of light," he says. "Even if it's only a candle a league away. But this particular dark is complete."

"William," she says, "you're such an old windbag."

"Be that as it may."

A suspicion of brightness mingles with the darkness. The two huddle together. She holds his hand (the story goes). The chamber grows brighter, vague and grey. Shapes appear. They become rocks, boulders, crevices. They become ancient carvings. Some shapes become the passageway to the outside, bumpy and narrow.

"Look," she says. The passage looks mysteriously bright – pale yellow creeping in an inch at a time. "I believe it's a ray of sunshine."

"What else could it be?"

They look in fascination at the sun shining on the stones, cheering up the tomb. No wings flutter, no souls cavort, as if the dead are sleeping late. The two humans look at one another. She hugs him, and vice versa, an extraordinary embrace. By the time they disengage the sunshine has withdrawn. William approaches the passage on his knees and stretches out a beefy hand to recapture that ray of happiness.

(History records that the sun never appeared that morning. There are pictures of cloudy skies and a record crowd dressed for wet weather rowdy under umbrellas. The archives are full of outrage over nebulous problems and persons unknown who hijacked the winter solstice.)

The crowds evaporate, leaving the catastrophe to officialdom to resolve. This calls for tact. A country does not want to become a laughing stock, a tabloid version of itself. There is an economic downturn and citizens are edgy. Global warming and corporate greed create a public mood eager for retribution. The last thing bureaucrats need is to look guilty. They argue back and forth between solutions and scapegoats. Symbols are the next best thing to the real thing, they decide, when the nation is, as always, at a crossroads.

Officialdom waits for a beep from inside. Some joke nervously. Beef sandwiches are hastily eaten. Scarves are wrapped tighter. Anonymous sources leak stories. The strategy, if it is not too grand a word, is to starve the bastards out.

The morning passes. When no text message comes, anxiety grows. If only Roze were here, some joke, she would know what to do. Roze wasn't the worst. A vacuum exists, a lack, and the beginning of melancholy for some opportunity missed. Someone grabs the initiative and sends Rhone in for a look.

There is no one wedged in the passage. There is no one in the chamber. There is no trash. The radio is gone, the folding chairs, the wrappers. Rhone emerges pale as a ghost.

While the media howled for tribunals to explore this national embarrassment, legend took its own more leisurely course. There was never a mention of foul play. Instead, William and Roze fled to a forest in County Cavan. If not Cavan, some county with a forest. They are, furthermore, happy there.

Inquisition

"Are we there yet?"

"Not yet." It was a game. In real life, Roger, twelve and precocious, knew everything. He was dressed in Barcelona colours because, he explained, soccer is the opium of the people.

She pretended they were out for a drive, like the song said, with no particular place to go. At any crossroads she could turn the Saab around and go home. Yes, a Saab, a car with attitude, not to mention price tag. That was Jill, her friends said, the contemporary woman who had left her foremothers in the dust driving breakneck to the next status quo.

"Hello, the Sugarloaf!" Roger saluted a perky mountain.

They were driving south from the city. The sun shone down on mighty new roads, on self-important hotels and ugly factories. Old churches that survived penal laws and famines now looked forlorn and in search of meaning. In the heyday of those churches, only a few years ago, Jill wanted to be a priest.

At a fork in the road she took the left. She still had options. The car slowed down but kept doggedly on. She knew every mile. Had she taken the right she would soon reach her parents' house, where she was once an only daughter. Because the parents were lawyers and wealthy, she was spoiled back then.

Leafy trees overarched the road. Around every bend memories jumped out. What Roger would call the best of times, the worst of times.

Over the brow of a hill the village was taking an afternoon nap. Her destination, if she had one, was at the far end. Soon there would be no turning back.

"Is this going to be boring?" Roger removed the headset of a small musical device.

"I hope so," she said. "I'll buy you loads of ice cream afterwards if you refrain from being obnoxious."

"Who, *moi?*"

Beside the church the squat stone rectory was brooding. This was where people came for consolation and strength in the bad years; where the cards were signed for masses that then ripped open the skies for God to come through with mercy and occasional miracles; where people came for a furtive confession when a big sin could not wait until Saturday. So much energy passed through here, so much atonement, even occasional joy. Whether God existed in heaven or not, he was certainly real here.

"I don't even want to know," Roger said enigmatically as the car eased to a stop.

The rectory windows needed paint. Wan yellow flowers bobbed about in the breeze. There were two doorbells. She chose the newer one. But the sound inside was an old sound, cranky and reluctant. Roger had assumed a respectful demeanour. She rang again. Priests' housekeepers were ancient history, they who once made the church's wheels go round. Roger threw Jill that look: they would be equally relieved if no one was home. Then the door opened. The priest held the jamb as if for support, looking intently into the sunlight. He appeared surprisingly drab in his black suit; she had expected him to be trendy and secular. Only the white plastic collar was missing. He was a canon now, a heavyweight in the diocese.

"Hello, Canon."

"Hello."

"It's Jill."

"Oh." He stood aside to let them in. He looked at the boy in puzzlement.

"This is Roger. My son."

"Oh," he said again. They were in a gloomy hall with a polished wooden floor. Doors lay ajar in every direction. He ushered them into a living room, light and airy. It was dominated by books: on shelves, on tables, on the floor. He had always been an ardent reader, a cultured man. The Christmas she was twelve, when her world was in turmoil, he had given her a set of Dickens. There was a picture of the bishop on one wall and an abstract painting on another. Even in summer there was a healthy fire burning. The three stood irresolute at odd angles in the middle of the floor.

"This is a surprise."

"Sorry," Jill said. "We didn't know we were coming here until we arrived."

"It doesn't matter," he said vaguely.

"This is Canon Doorly," she said to Roger, who stood ready to go along with whatever ritual might follow. But not even a handshake was forthcoming.

"Is there another TV?" There was a wide-screen set across the hearth from his black leather recliner.

"Only the one in my bedroom." The tone implied his bedroom was out of the question.

"He gets bored listening to grown-ups talking."

"He can't do any harm watching TV," the canon, upon pondering the implications, conceded. His face was flushed. "Come, boy, I'll show you." He led the way up the stairs.

"Shout, baby, if you need anything," she called after him. She scanned the room for hints of how Doorly was coping with the years. A photo of his mother was still in its silver frame. Overall it was a severe room. There was no way of telling a saint's room from a sinner's.

"You could have warned me you were coming," he came back angry. But Jill detected fear, too. She realized she was now taller than he. He would have figured in a jiffy that she was thirty-two. Would have seen at a glance that she had grown singularly attractive. The ample bosom would be new to him, but it was discreetly tucked away in a no-nonsense shirt. "What do you want?"

This generation did not happen in a vacuum, Jill realized, when she slowed down to take stock at thirty. Random considerations then danced in circles. On the whole the church helped preserve the race from falling into chaos. The world, furthermore, operated in news cycles. Today an earthquake, tomorrow a scandal: seldom did events grab people's attention for more than a few days. Minds jumped to the new, and the new was never hard to find. Then clerical paedophilia became the sensation that refused to go away. It was a stunning surprise that the clergy would come down from their pedestals to sin. Jill one day said to herself: now I remember. She had smothered the memories these many years.

Whatever you do, don't be a solicitor, her mother used to say. The mother wrote poetry on the side and had published two small volumes. The law, her father would then contend, is a noble pursuit and should not be belittled. He would tell her how Hammurabi got the law organized back in Babylon. After only a few thousand years the law had civilized the human race to the point it was now at. Making room for more transitory pursuits such as poetry, he would add slyly.

So she studied law at the university. While also pursuing such transitory pursuits as love. Which, she discovered, sometimes gave you a son you had not counted on. Life was hectic. While Roger's father hightailed it to Australia, law and love wrestled for Jill's soul.

She began finally to read the horror stories of clerical sex abuse. It was a worldwide scandal, but Ireland refused to be left behind. The buried memories were a surprise, like a page of a book skipped by mistake.

She read of others tortured by such memories, by guilt, by nightmares and dysfunctional lives. She had escaped all that. Or so she believed. Did it nevertheless affect her life? Ruin her without her even knowing it? Was she normal?

There were years of clerical cloak and dagger to decipher. Sometimes the names were withheld, sometimes blazoned in the papers. She found no mention of Doorly. She raked the Internet, and learned he had been moved around, but there was no hint of malfeasance. She made discreet inquiries of colleagues in the know. There was nothing sinister to report.

This created a dilemma for Jill. Let sleeping dogs lie, was a phrase her father used surprisingly frequently for a lawyer. Her mother the poet was less partial to this benign slogan. It would be easier to let the sleeping dog lie. As a lawyer she could make a case to nail him, but she wasn't sure it would stick in the court of conscience.

The absence of personal ill effects was beside the point. She was concerned for some wider equilibrium in the world. Her parents, for example, still admired the canon. Their house had been his home from home while he was their parish priest. Little did they know the extent to which he had made himself at home.

Most victims, it seemed, had gone to the guards with their complaints. Jill opted to write a letter. Dear Canon, she began, you may remember me. She did not threaten him. What, she asked, was he going to do about the past.

He wrote back that he did, indeed, remember her: "I am outraged by your wild accusations. If your imagination is playing tricks on you, perhaps you need medical help." He wrote about her "wonderful parents," from whom he still received a Christmas card every year. "Do you really want to break their hearts by dredging up girlish nonsense that never happened?" Then he softened. Indeed he remembered her well, a beautiful child. "Please write to reassure me that your letter was just a passing fancy, and all will be forgiven. I will, in the meantime, offer mass for your personal intentions."

Now I'm in a right fix, Jill thought. Now I have to finish what I started.

"What do you want?"

The face seemed no older because it had been an old face since first she saw it. He had a high forehead and small ears and the pale, thin skin of a man who spent life indoors, administering the kingdom of heaven from one or other of its branch offices. He had grey watery eyes she had not noticed twenty years ago.

71

The memories had returned gradually like wave upon wave on a shore. It had started when she was ten, playing games outdoors where nearly everything seemed natural and harmless. Then it moved indoors for winter. Him looking over her shoulder at the kitchen table, spelling words. Playfully wrestling with her when he volunteered for babysitting. He had been so patient, a peck on the cheek, then a sloppy one on the neck, until it was at least reasonable, if not inevitable, for them to climb the stairs, jostling and rambunctious. If no one talked about what happened upstairs, it must surely be because there was no need, it was taken for granted, what grown-ups sometimes did in private.

"For starters I want you not to deny it."

"Listen to me." While upstairs he had composed himself. "I could squelch you. Don't think I couldn't. Some people, and you may be one of them, think the church is a laugh, the church is finished. Not yet, it isn't." His face was in her face, intimidating, spittle at the corner of his mouth.

"Uncle Chris," she said. It was what she had been taught to call him. His real name was Christopher. "I wish you wouldn't talk like that, Uncle Chris. I'm not eleven now." Yet what if he could, even now, squelch her?

"Who put you up to this?"

"Perhaps we could sit down?"

"If you want." Jill sat but he remained standing, then started pacing. "Is it that you're hard up for money?"

"It's only fair to remind you, I'm a solicitor now."

"Even solicitors accept money."

He would be seventy now. Many paedophiles had grown old before they were caught, the papers said so. Many had died. Yet the church had never been more powerful. A billion Catholics and more. And not just numbers, clout. And not just political clout, moral authority. And, if the believers were to be believed, something divine, even today.

"Are you denying it?" He had spent a lifetime in authority, conferred automatically on the day of ordination. It was his stock-in-trade. The great advantage of authority was that it didn't have to be logical or legal. It didn't rely on right or wrong. It was impervious as the wind, autonomous as God. "Are you saying you don't remember? Don't you remember your red underwear? I didn't know the word at the time, and perhaps neither did you, but nowadays they're calling it paedophilia."

"It was you." He leaned forward, fire in his eyes, face flushed. "It was you throwing yourself at me."

"I was a child, Canon."

"Don't play the prosecutor with me. A little slut is what you were." The face was redder. Authority was slipping away and he had nothing to put in its place.

"Tell me this: was I the only one?"

The anger faded as quickly as it had flared. "Good God," he said, looking into the fire, "has it come to this?" He looked at her dully, defeated. "Look what you've done to me." He must have been in his late forties at the time, she figured, an age when he might otherwise be raising a family. Could it be I was sent by the devil to seduce him? "I wish I could say you were the only one," was all he said.

"I remember you used to give those sermons, fire and brimstone. Weren't you at least afraid of hell?"

"If only there were a hell." He broke down and cried, an unconvincing dry cry without tears, eyes closed tight and mouth twisted. In an instant he was on his knees in front of her.

"Get up," she ordered.

"I want to confess."

"That won't work, Canon. I'm not bound by the seal of confession."

"Where I'm stuck is, I don't believe."

"Don't believe what?"

"Any of it. Haven't believed it for forty years." A couple of big tears finally appeared, hovered on his cheek until he wiped them away with his thumb. "That's not an excuse – for what happened. Hell or no hell, I'd have done the same. Believers, too, have done unbelievable things, and God at his best has not been able to stop them from sinning."

"But the hypocrisy, Canon."

"That's what it was." He was slumped on the carpet, sitting back on his heels. "I've been waiting for something to happen. For a letter. Or a summons. From the guards or the bishop. I was afraid to pick up the phone. Afraid when cars stopped. I never thought it would be you."

"Sorry to disappoint you."

"Eventually I ran away." He looked up at Jill as if relieved to have someone to tell. "I was out for a walk and just kept walking. Headed for the West."

"Why would you do that?"

"I don't know, exactly. After a day's walking I was sorry I hadn't taken the car." He managed a smile at the memory. "The black suit was a giveaway. I had no money, so I stole what I needed. I got good at it. I thought of walking up to doors and begging, but couldn't bring myself. Even after I stole jeans and a farmer's hat I was sure people could see through me, that I was still a priest."

"A paedophile priest?"

"No. Whenever I felt like a priest I felt like a good one. I decided to be a wanderer on the earth. I would do penance. I made it to Lough Derg. You need money to cross in the boat, so I had to steal that. I didn't do any praying, because God was out, God was not available. But I did loads of penance, which you can do without God. Were you ever in Lough Derg?"

"No."

"There is surprising gratification in penance. Such as the sharp stones under one's bare feet. The diet was watery soup, I even skipped that. My guts were growling something awful. You could say I was mad, out of my mind. The thing lasts only three days, the pilgrimage, so I had to leave, but I turned around and went right back. I had a beard by that time, grey with streaks of black in it, yet I worried that someone might recognise me. If anyone did, they didn't let on. If you ever go, take an extra coat. There's a wind there that would go through you."

There was the sound of Roger upstairs. Getting restless, Jill worried. Then the toilet flushed. Roger was brilliant, he knew when to be a brat and when to be perfect.

"Mostly I lived under bridges. You'd be surprised how many bums are out there. They're decent once you get to know them, but they have to trust you." He was an ungainly heap by the fire on the stained fawn rug.

"This lasted about six months. But I remember them more vividly than my years in parishes. Small things like a fog over the river. I keep meaning to get up early to see that again. And red sunrises. Am I boring you?"

"So then what happened?"

"Then I came back here. One day I walked in the door and carried on as usual."

"What did the bishop say?"

"Welcome back, he said, or something like that. It's a different church now. The bishop is short on personnel, so priests can get away with nearly anything. Except child molestation, of course."

Everything is fine, Jill told herself, it's only surreal. For the most part life was continuous and even logical in a haphazard way, but smart people knew to make room for the surreal. One escaped going crazy by keeping a space handy for the extraordinary.

The canon rose stiffly from the rug. There were peat briquettes in an ornamental brass box and he piled half a dozen on the fading fire. He glanced at her. Wondering about the lie of the land, she figured. If he tries the smallest trick I'll yell and Roger will come to the rescue.

"Have you ever read the Russians?" He sat in the big recliner, leaning forward, wound up like a coiled spring.

"Not yet."

"One character, I think it's in Dostoevsky, tells about Christ coming back, to Seville as I recall, at the time of the Spanish Inquisition. He was soon arrested. Then one day the Grand Inquisitor visited Christ in prison. He complained about the previous incarnation.

"You weren't satisfied with the way God made us, he ranted. You wanted us to be better than human. We needed to have 'more abundant life,' to be 'sons of God,'" the canon inscribed the biblical quotation marks in the air with index fingers. "You raised the standard too high," he mimicked the Grand Inquisitor, "and ever since we have been forced to drag the bar down because of course we couldn't reach it. This, the Grand Inquisitor continued, has been the church's little secret. The hierarchy never told the people the bar was too high. Keep striving, the hierarchy said, while all the time the priests and bishops knew it was impossible." The canon paused, thoughtful, looking into the fire. "There is no hell, Jill. That's the good news. How could we be punished for failing to do the impossible?"

"That would be very convenient," she said. "I mean, for the likes of you." There hadn't been much anger to begin with, she couldn't let him talk her out of what was left. He showed no remorse. She would have granted him a lot of slack in return for remorse. He had instead created a smug theology for himself that would be easier to live with.

"So now you're back, the Grand Inquisitor said to Christ. I can't let you stir things up a second time. Something like that. Crucifixion is out of date, he went on. I'll have to deal with you in some contemporary fashion." The canon had always been suave. Her parents would ask leading questions and he would pontificate. That self-assurance, though, had evaporated. The windbag was an empty windbag at the end of his tether, grappling with old jargon that was no match for his needs.

"You need to turn yourself in."

"When the Grand Inquisitor finished his little speech, Christ leaned over and kissed him, according to the legend. I'm not sure what it all means. It may mean that love is, who knows, maybe more potent than the law," his voice trailed away.

"Mother!" Roger's knock on the door startled Jill. Then he opened it without waiting for an answer, which wasn't Roger's style. "Can we go now?"

"Wait in the car," she said. "We'll do ice cream," she shouted after him.

"The odd thing is, I never liked children," the canon said from the bay window. From behind she could see his bald patch. And the dandruff on his shoulders. Life was decay. He was not an attractive man and hadn't been attractive twenty years earlier. It would be some solace to have been swept off her feet by a more dashing type. She had to fight to keep the anger alive. If not genuine anger, at least an artificial outrage. Society had standards. People still had to cling to something. Something they could agree on. And they agreed overwhelmingly that paedophilia was the scourge of the day.

"I need to know what you're going to do."

"I think, suicide," he said as he turned around.

"I doubt it. You lack the courage."

"You have it wrong. I lack the courage to face the music." He crossed the room. From behind the photo of his mother he retrieved a plastic container of pills, held it out for inspection. 'They're the genuine article. Who would have thought it would come to this?"

"Go ahead. I can't let you blackmail me into saving you."

"I need time to prepare. Maybe make an act of contrition. Just in case – in case there's something. But frankly, as you suggest, working up the courage is the main thing. In the end I'll probably take myself by surprise. After a bottle of vodka to keep the courage up. Just pop them without thinking."

"If you don't do it by the weekend, I'll report you first thing on Monday morning."

He fondled the small container with forefinger and thumb. If only he had persevered under the bridges of the West: by the Suck, by the Shannon, by the Corrib. Doing penance until it killed him. Going hungry. Or freezing to death in January. A champion of pain. Or getting into fights with other bums, until one of them killed him, or until he killed one of them. Then he could go before a judge a self-respecting criminal with a pedigree old as Cain. She silently absolved him. Once a Catholic, always a Catholic: she remembered the words of absolution, they had played a significant part in human history. And he had, after all, confessed to her. It didn't matter that she had never been ordained, because the view of earth from heaven was different now. He could have redeemed himself. Made a run for sainthood. He could have become a legendary pilgrim, a patron saint before whose statue child molesters of the future would pray for guidance.

She backed away into the hall, closed the front door softly behind her. Walked briskly to the car.

"Don't look now," Roger said. "He's at the window."

"You must be starving, baby."

In an ice cream emporium painted purple they had hot fudge sundaes.

"He has a wide selection of videos," Roger said.

"So do you."

"Wake up, Mother. He's a pervert."

The afternoon sun shone on lazy fields. Sheep worked the light-green grass in one. Donkeys stood forlorn in the corner of another, the stigmatic cross on their backs.

"You know nothing about him." She drove slowly. Impatient cars rushed past, their drivers staring fiercely at her. "One morning, long ago, that man lay face down on the floor, up front in the cathedral sanctuary, with his forehead resting on a little cushion, that's how they used to do it. The bishop was there, and the clergy, and the organist was playing triumphal music. Because it was a great day, you see: the choir singing, and incense galore, stuff like that, and the families proud, down in the pews, they had waited so long for that day. But the crucial moment was when the young men, in a paroxysm of selfless idealism, told God, whom they could not even see, whom they could scarcely imagine – promised God that they'd walk courageously through life with heads high, marching ahead to salvation and the people following them, because all the people everywhere, since the beginning of time, have felt a strange something in their hearts, an odd little something, hinting, I don't know, that there might still be something, some secret – am I making sense?"

"No. But that's all right."

"So don't say – what you said about him. He might not be a hero. But no one can take away the promise he made down on his belly in that cathedral, long ago. In spite of everything he still has a chance for greatness, although he doesn't know, you know, how to go about it."

Back on the high road, the Saab gathered speed. A plane flew low towards the airport. Huge cranes stretched their arms over tall new buildings. Life was throbbing. Christ made a big mistake coming back during the Inquisition, but it would be a bigger blunder to come now, Jill thought, and people less ready than ever.

Burntollet Bridge

S he waits for him coming through the mist in the magic mornings. His head appears over the hump of a small bridge, bobbing, growing taller as it emerges from the city's ancient vapours. The head is always erect, the gait stately. It takes but one further factor to make him mythic or nearly: the rumour that, in his youth, he vowed to kill Ian Paisley. Something he has not yet done.

"Good morning, Moya."

"Good morning, Professor." The ten-minute walk to the university is the apex of her day. The routine started a year ago when she signed up for his philosophy course called "The Greeks." The spongy title allows him to pontificate on whatever he wishes. She brought herself to his attention by writing a satirical paper about the hylomorphic theory. He suggested they walk together so that his erudition could rub off on her. Students know the many meanings of this.

The first day they ventured forth, he ignored her, singing instead in a mumbling drone: Where do the flies go in the winter when the summer disappears? Into grandfather's whiskers, into grandfather's beard.

"Keep an eye on Socrates," he finally admonished. She has pondered this advice without success. He does not look at her, only at some imagined destination ahead. His face is more sad than heroic, distinguished mainly by the lack of any chin worth mentioning. The top of his head is barren and blistered as if corroded by pollution. He wears corduroy suits, clover green or rusty red, ideal, Moya tells her crowd, for a philosopher. If Socrates could get corduroy in Greece he would have worn it.

"So what about you, Professor?" Moya is a turn and uninhibited.

"What about me?" he feigns haughty puzzlement but a satisfied grin curls the corner of his mouth.

"Is it true you did time in Long Kesh?"

"Is that what they say?"

"That's not the half of it."

It took several mornings of leading questions to get the low-down. The Orange crowd, who, he said, represented the forces of evil, denied the people of destiny jobs and houses and, above all, respect. He presumed Moya was too young to know about that dizzy, yet now neglected, time. He told her of John Hume, Ivan Cooper, the People's Democracy, the whole nine yards. He too, he conceded, was there: agitating and upping the ante. His narrative was a mixture of fact and fancy but she could not call it boasting. Justice and goodness were making inroads until Ian Paisley emerged out of nowhere to torpedo destiny. "Spewing hate," the professor said. Moya waited for the legend to unfold, the plan to kill Paisley, but Fuddy, for that's what they called him on account of his real name being Duddy – Fuddy lapsed into silence, striding fiercely. She guessed he was in his sixties, but still fit, when he was in that mood, to kill dragons.

After Long Kesh, according to the rumours, he disappeared. Some said he buried himself in a quiet hamlet in England, but others believed he fled farther afield as Paisley rose from local malcontent to statesman. She'll get to the bottom of it, Moya promises her crowd, freckle-faced lassies and hard-cursing lads, drinkers and petty sinners perched, like herself, between ambition and idealism, the horns of every young dilemma.

The professor, meanwhile, is resting the Greeks and telling instead about the demise of Friedrich Nietzsche. On the latter's way to a local bistro, a horse is struggling to pull a coach while the driver beats it unmercifully. Nietzsche shouts at the man to desist. The mare staggers and falls. The philosopher throws himself down and wraps his arms around the horse's neck. "The poor, dumb beast," he laments, "look what you did." Onlookers separate Nietzsche from the horse, according to this narrative. Some are sympathetic while others jeer. "Where is God?" the philosopher roars. He grabs an unlit lantern from the coach and holds it aloft, searching. "We have killed him," he eventually concludes.

Fuddy looks through small spectacles hanging low on his nose, surveying the students, who can't be sure whether this is sublime or only a cod. When he arrived without fanfare a dozen years earlier, only a few signed up for The Greeks. But the legend of Burntollet grew, emanating from no one knew where, until a larger lecture hall was needed as one fabulous fact followed another. He reads now from the immortal *Ecce Homo*: "I fear that someday they will pronounce me holy, while I want only to be a fool." He directs a rare smile at the upturned faces and still no one is sure who is pulling whose leg.

"So what about Burntollet?" Moya coaxes next morning. She plans, when later she enters the real world, to be either a dentist for the money or a philosopher for the gas.

"We planned a march from Belfast to Derry." He is wearing a yellow tie and he is brisk, a step ahead of her – he has been waiting a whole generation for someone to ask this obvious question. "No violence – like King in America. We were eighty at first. No one thought it would be a picnic, so the lukewarm stayed home. The Paisleyites harassed us from the start. Eamonn warned us not to retaliate. We were testing justice and goodness to see if they still worked."

Moya has done research. He is not mentioned in contemporary accounts. That still leaves room for him to be there, even to be a hero. By the fourth day of the march the numbers had swollen to five hundred.

Not everyone could squeeze in front of the cameras like Bernadette. Just walking, the professor says, was wearisome. It sounds so pedestrian, ironic Moya thinks.

"He's an old bollocks," one says when her crowd gathers at night. "He's lonely."

"He needs a woman," another says. Faces look at Moya. No one wants to be naïve, especially children of the twenty-first century who look back at prehistory, namely the 1960s, and wonder how people managed in the days before sophistication.

"What?" Moya stares them down. She has hair black as a raven and pink, well-made cheeks and she is on the safe side of overweight. She is on the soccer team, playing right back, and has put at least one opposing player in the hospital. She is, above all, winsome and a turn. Everyone knows age is not an issue. Frantic age has frequently coupled with outrageous youth to goose the human condition for another go at carrying on.

"So what's it all about?" she asks on a morning of fluttering leaves. "Where is it leading?" He told her to keep an eye on Socrates and she doesn't intend to fall short of whatever he meant.

"Burntollet Bridge is just a few miles outside Derry," he returns to the scene of the crime. "Paisley held a meeting to stir up the old memories. A prayer meeting, he called it – he had a way with words. After that the Orange persons prepared an ambush. From a local quarry they collected buckets of stones and arranged them at twelve-foot intervals along the brow of a hill above the river. Other Oranges from Derry came out with clubs and iron bars. Around eleven we reached the bridge singing that we would overcome and give peace a chance. We were, looking back, a beautiful and inspiring sight. Not a gun among us. Am I boring you?" But he does not look at her, just marches ahead to Burntollet Bridge.

"Not a bit," she wants to hear about him and Paisley.

"A shower of bricks and bottles rained down as we reached the bridge. They came at us with cudgels and crowbars. Many of the marchers were knocked senseless, though no one, it must be said, was killed. Many were driven into the river. It was mayhem." It does sound boring, she thinks. Even mayhem doesn't cut it in an era of suicide bombers. The two have reached a rusty statue of the poet Yeats in front of the humanities building. "Have you ever heard of the Pass of Thermopylae?"

Since he never looks at her, Moya wonders how he even recognizes her in the mornings. "You don't need Thermopylae," she says. "It was a bad scene. You were, I have no hesitation in telling you, a hero. You were all heroes."

"Thank you," he seems grateful and wanders on singing lowly about how, in the winter, the flies hibernate in his grandfather's beard. "I wasn't always a fuddy-duddy, that is my point," he says over his shoulder.

"Don't worry, Professor. You're larger than life and that's a fact." Teasing him is like tickling the toes of stone deities on that Greek mountain.

In the classroom he tells about Xanthippe, wife of Socrates, "one mean woman." If Socrates was so smart, his critics asked him, why had he fallen for such a bitch? He married her to prove a point, Socrates told the smart crowd in that stony, old agora in Athens. If he could tame Xanthippe, everything was salvageable.

"Armageddon, it was Armageddon," he picks up the narrative the next morning. The challenge is to keep the old epic alive when the children of a new millennium prefer Batman, Spiderman, Real Madrid and whatever is on Twitter.

"Some say you vowed to kill Paisley?" There! It was out.

"I was down by the river. Stones and bricks were flying. I saw a girl in the water, one I had not noticed before. She was bundled up because it was January. A tall, handsome girl with yellow hair. Something hit her and down she went. The water was surprisingly deep, and icy cold, and dirty; it was, in truth, just a dirty, insignificant little river. At once there was blood on her. I was always afraid of water. I couldn't swim a stroke. But in I went – I don't know why, except that it had nothing to do with heroism. The water knocked me over, coughing and sputtering, but I kept on, I suppose because it was the right thing to do. But there was a sense of destiny as well, a silly concept only the young embrace. I was a coward all my life except for a few minutes that morning. The girl kept floating away, dragged by the dirty water. I believe I actually swam a few strokes until I grabbed her. You'd think all this would take hours but it happened in minutes, maybe seconds – time sometimes gives us extra when we need it. The girl was unconscious. Her blood was swallowed up by the river. I found my footing and dragged her out – I have wished ever since that I could have carried her in my arms. Eventually a burly RUC woman came to the rescue. I tried to protect the girl from this woman, whom we regarded as the enemy. The girl and I were inextricably linked, that was the point." He falls silent. "It may not be much of a point."

"You saved her life."

"An ambulance took her away. I never saw her again."

The university juxtaposes ivy-covered stone and sleek concrete. Bicycles are tied to lamp posts. Squirrels on crooked legs are inquisitive under fat trees. Moya and the professor drift apart without ceremony, strangers again until tomorrow. She observes him fondly, his bag of books making one arm longer. A wife would do something about the baggy backside of his trousers.

In the sunlit classroom he quotes Herodotus of Halicarnassus. This long-dead man was, in his own words, "preserving from decay the remembrance of what people have done." Moya thinks of the girl in the river, living on, old now, perhaps a grandmother. She has no way of knowing that, all this time, she has another existence in an old man's head.

"You may call me Fuddy. It won't come as a surprise." They are on the train to Dublin, dozens of them. It is a poorly planned conspiracy. A rugby international is one excuse for the trip, a Madonna concert another. No one is fooled, though. Ian Paisley is coming to town.

Newly ordained, long ago, Paisley created his own denomination to meet his theological needs and political ambitions. Such bold moves surprised friend and foe and got him elected to this and that until he became First Minister of a brand new Ulster. This did not make him, the kids agreed, the equivalent of a real politician or a pope, for example. Yet Paisley was taken surprisingly seriously by heads of state. The charade included invitations to photo-ops in Dublin, where hands were shaken and even hugs exchanged.

It makes sense that anyone who has ever threatened to kill Paisley would be of interest to the authorities if they knew.

In the city, the day spread wide in front of them, Moya's crowd drifts apart and comes back together in repeated waves of exuberance and anticipation. It's like hanging out with Lee Harvey Oswald that day in Dallas. It does not occur to anyone to take remedial action either to save the First Minister from Fuddy, or Fuddy from himself.

It is an afternoon event. The sun is shining agreeably and the Mansion House is in splendid form. There is a red carpet and a row of moss-green chairs on which the worthy will sit. The official business is the signing of some agreement about tariffs, but the real business is the handshakes and hugging. There are liveried officials for keeping order, but their primary agenda is to chat with strangers and lead the crowd in having a good time.

The professor is mingling. On closer inspection, no one seems to know him. Faces look puzzled, then smile when, presumably, he tells them his name. But after that they turn back to their friends. Fuddy's trousers seem less baggy. The corduroys are blue and red, the ensemble a quiet homage to the frequently vilified Union Jack. This is the kind of day on which Moya decides, not for the first time, that she will be a philosopher rather than a dentist.

Here at last comes Big Ian. He is in close proximity to the fussing Taoiseach. And others, of course. The great mouth is laughing, the mighty teeth polished. There is generous applause, so that one can not hear what the dignitaries say to each other. They move towards the podium. The speeches are mercifully short but the handshakes are interminable as pushy photographers take pictures. The politicians find all this attention intoxicating. Paisley goes the extra mile and hugs the wincing Taoiseach.

Others join in the handshakes. A procession begins, the great and good of North and South congratulating each other and vowing friendship. It's now or never. Moya feels a rivulet of sweat moving down her inside arm. And the professor does indeed move forward. He is inconspicuous except for the eccentric corduroy duds. He looks frightfully alone.

But the congenial disorder is interrupted by the liveried bureaucrats. There is no panic, nothing but bonhomie, but a nod from someone has indicated this is enough handshaking for now. Poor, dear Fuddy is in the wrong place in the queue, cut off; Fuddy, who only wants to let bygones at last be bygones – what else could it be without a gun?

He stands bewildered. Once, surely including that day in Burntollet, he was lightning and decisive, fast on his feet and possibly debonair and life was making sense. Moya presses forward and takes him by the arm.

"Be a gentleman, Professor, and buy a girl a cup of coffee."

"Excellent idea." But he stands looking after Big Ian. It took a lifetime to get this close.

"You have no weapon, I suppose?"

"Sorry. No weapon," he says apologetically. "We were all against violence," he adds over coffee and a tiny chocolate biscuit. "I wouldn't want to spoil that now."

He is jovial on the journey home. He has a shopping bag with a few newly bought books and, in a further paper bag, a bottle. The students, who have bottles of their own, tease him.

"Can we see the gun, Professor?"

"You could have given him a belt in the mouth anyway."

They drift away on the rowdy train, leaving him alone with Moya. The head lolls forward in uncomfortable sleep. A rival train rushes in the other direction, wakes him befuddled. He smiles bravely. He glances at the brown paper bag but opts for courage instead.

"It was a great day, Professor. And it would never have happened without you. You and all the marchers back in the glorious days, all the injured and even the dead. You made a difference."

"I can't stop thinking of her. That gash above her eye is bound to be still there. Apart from that she was very like you."

"I'll take that as a compliment." But Moya remembers she had yellow hair and was tall. There are other differences. The other girl was at Burntollet Bridge. Few can say they were knocked senseless into that dirty water. "Would you not go and look for her?"

"The worse luck might be to find her. An old woman now."

Silence falls. Where, Moya wonders, did they all go? How could it be so important once and now only a historical hiccup? The stones so willfully piled for battle are scattered about or in the river and maybe some never got thrown. Archaeologists of a future millennium will find cudgels and iron bars and piece together a fragment of history. With the help of footage from old archives they will reinvent people who were there. But the real people will be gone like water under the bridge.

Strangers

This old house has been abandoned for a generation. Thatch clings to the rough rafters except for what has fallen rotten into the kitchen. Two small windows squint like cracked spectacles at a startled horse and whins on a hill. Lumpy stones show traces of whitewash. A door, red paint peeling, hangs by one hinge. Su goes click, click; excited, picking her way amid sheep droppings. When she looks again through the viewfinder there is a talking donkey coming through the doorway, so of course she shoots it.

One day she went to Dublin for a dental appointment. She passed a gallery featuring photography. The pictures begged to be noticed. Not that she liked them – they were slick and shadowy but did not show reality as Su saw it.

"I suppose they're abstract?" she said to the emaciated girl behind a computer.

"Exactly. They're the next big thing."

"I could take photos you wouldn't believe."

"I'd love to see you try," the other said without sarcasm.

Su had already missed her dental appointment. She visited several camera shops until she found a man she liked. All she wanted was a digital camera, fully automatic. Digital, the man agreed, was the next big thing. "Just point and shoot."

"But will it, if I want it to, nail what is really there?"

The man could not guarantee this because, he said, "reality is a son of a bitch."

"You're honest at least," she said and paid him.

Now she is back in the rattley car, driving leisurely until a tree in a field practically waves at her. She eases to a stop, closes the door quietly, the camera strapped around her thin neck. She creeps forward, scarcely breathing, because there are people up the tree. She guesses half a dozen, though others could be hidden amid June foliage. They smile at her, strike poses. She shoots them up and down. She waves back at them. What they're doing up there is nobody's business.

"Lions and tigers," she says to Blue, who waits panting in the car. He's called Blue, she tells people, because of his colour. When they point out that the dog is really white, Su smiles: "And what colour is the sky *really*?" Blue has a big dog's head for thinking and talking back.

Su is nearly thirty now but looks as young as she feels. She is willowy, and toothy in front, with weightless bronze hair. Her clothes seldom fit that odd classification some call style. "Jeans my arse," she will say if the subject comes up.

"Shame on you," Anabella will say.

"You have to think about it," Su will respond. In the matter of dress she likes the word *couture* and says it with an exaggerated accent, her rubbery mouth uttering vowels the French would die for. She wears dresses down to her ankles. These hide the fact that she wears no knickers. Su seems eccentric, but so, she would say, is everyone. "Eve wore no knickers," she would say, "Adam neither."

"So how did it go?" Anabella asks.

"Well. It went well. People everywhere I looked. They all want to be shot."

"Don't I know." Anabella has never seen any of the people Su sees all the time.

Three years after her own parents left her orphaned, years spent in foster care and misery, Anabella's parents adopted Su. Anabella was two years older than Su and has remained that way. She cherishes Su and is cherished in return. They live in the deceased parents' house. Su goes to school year after year because she never seems ready for the world.

"I'm slow," she tells Anabella.

"You're deep, that's all," Anabella explains.

When she had enough pictures taken – her portfolio, she called it – Su took them on a shiny CD to the Dublin gallery. The emaciated girl could not see the same images Su saw. "Is it a wall?" She didn't notice the boy and girl on the wall, children, Su explained, of a lesser god. No one could see a talking donkey in the doorway, nor the people in a tree, nor the bodies floating in a lake – even Su had to admit they were strangers.

A day came when the school authorities called Su into the office and told her they had taught her all they knew.

She had taken every course twice and some more than that. The other girls loved her, while the boys loved looking under her dress to see Tipperary.

"But I know next to nothing," she told the school principal.

"You know more than you'll ever need," he explained. "Most of what we teach here is overrated."

The principal's revelation gave her confidence, she could march through the world knowing enough. Yet employers failed to see that her sagacity was equal to their needs.

"You were cut out for photography," Anabella, indomitable and big-hearted, encouraged her. "Put an ad in the paper." Thus she was hired to shoot a wedding. The newlyweds complained that many of their relations were missing from the pictures. Su did, however, notice a stranger in several photos, on the extreme right or left or ducking behind some in-law.

"Don't you see him at all?" she finally asked Anabella.

"Not a bit of him." Romance had eluded Anabella. She longed to be waylaid by a man, preferably a stranger, because she disliked every man she knew.

After the wedding debacle, Su abandoned commerce and embraced art. A professional photographer was expected to stick to the facts, but an artist was better off crazy. "Talent is tricky enough," the generous Anabella said, "but genius is sublime." Art was necessary to keep the world from going insane, Su guessed, but you couldn't force it on people, especially when they were getting married and had enough troubles already.

Through the winter and into the spring Su haunts this country town in search of surprises. Point and shoot and wait and see. Wet houses stand shoulder to shoulder and radiate when the sun comes out. Bank managers throw money out the windows of solid banks. Vegetable shops sell bicycles and the parish priest sells vegetables in the graveyard. Inquisitive townspeople peer through brick walls. Little girls jump in puddles and splash. Little boys call Su nasty names until she snaps them and hands them over to the law. Toothless old men pull in their bellies and smile, in their wild imaginations they are still twenty-six. Puffs of green clouds grow agitated, butting heads across a yellow sky. It is an ideal time to be an arty photographer. The world is begging to be noticed before it dies. In such metaphysical matters you can't fool Su.

"When will we see?" people ask her on the street.

"Soon," she promises. She plies the computer with dexterity and turns out a new portfolio. Anticipation mounts. "Lions and tigers," Su goes and the blue dog goes bow-wow in this exceptional household. If art needs to be daft, the world has beaten a path to the right door, she tells the talkative dog. The galleries, though, reject her every time.

Yet artists by definition are too stubborn to give up. The first million pictures might be failures, Su tells Anabella after a bout of bitter sobbing, and the million and first might be a Michelangelo. She takes to the streets again, follows the river on which the town was built, a tired river now, shoots shadows at noon and the night moon dodging chimneys.

A man, she notices, is appearing regularly in the pictures. He is down by the river in the small hours and frequenting High Street in the afternoon. Su dashes off in the noisy car to explore him. Even when he fails to appear in a photo, she suspects he is hiding amid bushes. He's a surprisingly small man, not much bigger than a big dwarf, broad at the shoulders and carrying a large, noble head with curly hair glistening. He has, if the photos are correct, a ruddy face and is formally dressed in black with pinstripes. He does not look at the camera, as if pretending to be in the scene by accident.

"He could be dangerous and up to no good," Anabella warns.

"Don't I wish he was dangerous."

She stalks the apparition who seems to lead a frantic life. He spends hours in offices, in the library, in courthouse or clinic, never staying long and soon on the move. He talks to everyone, shaking hands, looking up into faces, yet his feet are restless in the black shiny shoes as if they were late for another engagement. Then a pat on the back or a quick handshake before he gets into the purple car and drives importantly to the next rendezvous. There is always someone waiting at the other end, shaking his hand, always in good cheer. There are frequent forays to a café for coffee or the pub for a pint.

She asks people, who all agree his name is Raphael Bang.

At last he walks towards her from the far end of town, bushy eyebrows arriving ahead of the rest of him, black moustache spread like wings ready to fly. It is a kind face and Su goes click, click. At a hundred yards he looks thirty, at twenty paces he looks forty, close up he must be all of sixty. He is wearing a red tie, and Su can tell you that red does to a photo what mustard does to a stale sausage sandwich.

"We meet again," he says. He is so cheerful, not a lugubrious bone in his body. The accent sounds foreign; probably, Su thinks, from over the water.

"And vice versa," she says without knowing what she means. She fiddles with the camera. "Look," she shows him his photo on the little screen.

"I look like Charlie Chaplin." Only an aficionado would know that the shillelagh he twirls so handily was a *sine qua non* the great comedian would not have been caught dead without.

"That was not my intention." Su has never heard of Charlie Chaplin.

"We're only an experiment," he says. "That's what I have figured out so far. The creator practiced on earth before going on to do his major work elsewhere. Next time we'll do coffee," the restless feet are already pointing him in a different direction. "Snap me as I go," he says, and she does, as he makes a game little leap in the air and throws a leg sideways just like the legendary clown.

"God is only practicing," she tells Anabella in the evening. "We're a work in progress to see how we work out. Then on to the next round. On the moon or out there."

"Don't trust him." Life has taught Anabella a hard lesson or two. "Don't forget the man who sold his soul to the devil."

"Who did?"

"A man. It happens all the time."

But Su knows it would be dead easy for Satan to sell Anabella a bill of goods. Despite the wise head on her shoulders, the heart insists on being heard. They have slept in the same family bed for nearly twenty years. "Not that we're lesbians or anything," Anabella pronounced firmly when the subject came up.

"But sometimes we pine."

"Everyone is lonely." A devil with a cure for loneliness, the girls agree, could have all the souls he wanted.

Now it's brilliant July. Summer must be captured because it is fleeting and then slow to return. Su goes after flowers. Bumble bees loiter and pose for the camera. Birds ditto. And always when her mind strays, strangers. They look coy, tickling the real world.

"Fabulous," Anabella says, though she does not see the strangers. "That must surely be art."

"Art is useless," Su is tired of the photography going nowhere. "All people want is a washer and dryer and a car that won't rattle."

Every day now Raphael Bang makes an appearance, hurrying, chatting, taking over the town. At the end of the day he's in most of her photos, including marching into the sunset doing his sideways hop like Charlie Chaplin. Discreetly she enquires about him. He is an entrepreneur, people say. Or a wheeler-dealer. Beyond that, Su bumps into the usual wall: what is the truth *really*?

"Breakfast, perhaps?" he suggests on the phone. They order pancakes. Raphael, polite, talks about trivia. "Did you ever hear of Plato, then?"

"Never did," Su spreads strawberries over the pancakes with her index finger.

"He was a goalkeeper for some team. It may have been Chelsea or Shamrock Rovers. I suppose you were never in New York?"

"Not once."

"That's a lovely dress so early in the morning."

"Guess which of us is not wearing underwear?"

"I don't know. You maybe?"

"How did you know?" Even as she cackles with delight Su knows that if she were smarter, Bang would be talking about weighty issues like life and death and taxes.

Weeks pass. Raphael Bang is totally proper, always solicitous. "I have a secret," Su eventually says. "Look." She shows him one of her pictures.

He looks at it, head sideways, one eyebrow up. "A blackbird?" he says as if he suspects a catch.

"It doesn't matter. Look at this one."

"It's the statue of the dead IRA man."

He can't see himself in her photos. She can't, therefore, tell him about the strangers. This is a setback. Like Anabella, Mr Bang was somewhere else the day they handed out imaginations.

"In the chain of being I'm somewhere between perfection and a mouse," he explains. He picks up the shillelagh and gives it a flourish. When he says complicated things like that, Su feels privileged to know him. And Anabella seems hopelessly eccentric when she warns he might be the devil.

"An exhibition," he says another day. "It's time."

"People are blind," constant rejection has corroded Su's optimism. "They couldn't see a fart if you flew it in front of their faces."

"We'll see," he twirls the stick, sending excitement all through town. He becomes more busy, more ubiquitous, shaking hands with all sorts, from the high to the mighty to bartenders and cattle dealers. He throws the shillelagh ahead of him onto the passenger seat and does an illegal turn with screeching tyres.

"The audacity," Anabella scolds.

"He's somewhere between God and a mouse," Su explains.

Within days posters appear in shop windows and on bulletin boards. Su's First Annual Exhibition, they announce, will be formally opened by a luminary from Dublin. The pictures on the posters, taken from Su's CD, depict local buildings: the church, the library, semi-detached houses. "And not a soul to be seen in any of them," she complains to Raphael Bang. "We're sunk."

"Incorrigible lass," the mouth grins just south of his thick moustache and he takes Su's hand in the town square. He darts around town making arrangements. A mighty banner stretches across the façade of the museum: Su smiling like a celebrity.

"And me little more than a moron," she says to Bang. This is the culmination, she thinks, though she's not sure what the word means.

"You could at least wear underwear," Anabella admonishes before the big evening. "You'll be in the public eye."

"It will be our secret," she hugs dear Anabella, bulging in all the wrong places.

"No one will bother to show up," Anabella then says with satisfaction.

There is just a dribble at first, because in this town it's not fashionable to be on time. Some are strangers, others acquaintances. Some arrive walking, others in posh cars, many from afar. They talk quietly the way sophisticated people do. Su, instructed by Raphael, mingles, carrying in her hand a narrow wine glass with nothing in it. The pictures are a wonder: big monochrome prints in black frames; others in living colour; slides clicking in a streamlined machine and bouncing off the wall.

"Why would this fellow waste his time on someone like you?" Anabella, on her third glass of wine, picks the inopportune moment because the question is driving her bonkers.

"Isn't that what a mystery is?" Su says. "When you don't know what's going on, and it making no sense?" More and more she has the impression, since Raphael Bang appeared in her life, that her sagacity is gradually surpassing the sagacity of Anabella, dear Anabella, whose main asset is loyalty, a tawdry and thankless virtue on a glitzy evening of champagne and beautiful people. "Why are you not happier, Anabella, and this my ship coming in?"

Bang meanwhile is beaming, looking after everything, turned out in black with a red bow tie, hugging strangers, nodding instructions to caterers carrying trays. He is at home in this elegant milieu, doing what he was born to do. Now the people are pouring in. The buzz is louder, excitement rising, friends meeting old arty friends, glasses tinkling.

There are further surprises.

"Look," the people are saying. "Look at that donkey in the doorway."

"And over here, look at those people up a tree."

"A dog flying and fishes riding bicycles, these photos are unbelievable, yet there they are, and that old fellow peeing down a chimney."

"They can see *everything*," Su is ecstatic. She runs off and hugs Raphael Bang.

"Who are those persons anyway?" the guests are agog shaking Su's hand.

"They're strangers," Su says, "and that's the truth."

"They're absolutely awesome." Her new admirers hug her, because artistic people are huggers, gregarious and gracious; there would be no wars if it were left to them to run everything, no death or taxes either. They reach with thin bangled wrists for another glass of white wine from the tray. There are snacks on pine tables. The town should do more of this, everyone agrees. Kind words are said about Bang. "Who knew he could pull off such a stunt?" They listen respectfully to the luminary from Dublin, though they are eager to get back to the photos and snacks.

No one notices that not everyone sees the same strangers in the photos, or in which picture is the dog, the donkey, the ambitious cow jumping over the moon. Art, the luminary is saying, depends on what you see.

Anabella sulks on a plastic chair, sure the devil is in the neighbourhood looking for bargains. Mr Bang approaches her, the perfect gentleman, and whispers something amid the noise. Anabella's knurled face turns dark. She points a finger and he looks, but only the two know what this is about. Su is sad that Anabella can't find it in her heart to leap up and do an old slow dance with Raphael Bang.

The townspeople are telling Su of the wild things in the photos such as they never saw in real life: not just the church but the bishop up a yew tree; not just the IRA statue but pigeons dropping droppings; not just pigeons but curlews and clucking hens. Out-of-towners wonder out loud how this ordinary town could have been transformed into such an art Mecca. Discerning buyers grab up favourite photos in a flurry of spending while Mr Bang stuffs cheques into a deep trouser pocket. Elegant gents line up to shower Su with compliments.

"In the chain of being I'm somewhere between the cat and mouse," Su explains.

"It's a conspiracy," Anabella can no longer contain herself. "He's paying you all to believe it."

But Raphael Bang, always ubiquitous, is quickly on the scene making everything reasonable. "Sometimes life boils over," he says. "The status quo sails quietly along for ages, and then for no reason at all erupts like a volcano, before returning to normal again. That's what Su's pictures are about." He puts his short arm around her shoulder and the local media push and shove to take pictures. The guests are charmed even as they wonder what Mr Bang means, that thing about the volcano.

It is all hours before the party is over. The wine drinkers are most reluctant to go home. Others double back for a further peek at Su's photos. "Extraordinary," they say one last time. Raphael steers stragglers towards the door. He offers Anabella a ride home and she defies probability by accepting it.

"Someone put them up to it," she says again to Su in the haunted hours before they sleep.

"Did you not even see the donkey?" drowsy Su asks.

"Donkeys don't talk."

The next day returns the town to normal. The big banner still stretches in front of the museum, sagging now because it has no more surprises. Locals discuss the intense and scarcely believable night. In another day or two the town is divided into those who were there and those who were not. The former have no way of explaining to the latter what a mighty experience they missed. You had to be there, they all agree. Some coax others in to see the photos. But it is no longer the same. There are just houses or trees or flowers, grand in their own way but no longer – people can't find the word – no longer alive and a little crazy. The frenzy that took over the town that night is gone. The mystery has returned wherever it came from. Some who were there sigh with exasperation. These privileged ones compare notes, refer to favourite photographs, chuckle at remembered oddities. Gradually they realise that others do not remember the same details. They put this down to the unreliability of memory – and there was so much going on, they're so happy they were not among those who missed it.

A few days pass like this before anyone notices that Raphael Bang is missing. He is usually most visible in the evenings but no one has seen him. The guards are notified. They prise open his back door. Word spreads.

Next morning, while others search his usual haunts, Su searches the town with her camera. He had a way of appearing just before she clicked. Or he would be, for all practical purposes, invisible, only to appear when she downloaded him to her computer. He'd be terribly dignified and important, she was confident, keeping the status quo in order, or he'd be grinning from behind a rose bush or doing his Charlie Chaplin thing. She shoots until the camera runs out of memory. Raphael fails to make an appearance.

"How could he and he, dead?" Anabella's tone implies that Raphael Bang's death is the logical conclusion of everything that has gone before.

Everyone has a different version of what occurred. He was found under a holly tree out the road. He was found face down where the river is shallow. He was sitting on a bench just keeled over. No, there was no gun – why would there be a gun? No, we ourselves didn't see any body.

The guards are cagey. But inquisitive, too. They come to question Su. When did she last see him alive? What was his state of mind?

"I'm deep but I'm slow," Su pleads, "but one thing I can say for sure is that his state of mind was first class."

"Was there a special relationship between you and Mr Bang?"

"There certainly was."

"Was it intimate?"

"Oh, intimate? Oh, it was."

"Stop torturing the girl," Anabella comes to the rescue. "She didn't do it."

"Do what?" the guard asks.

"Do what?" Su asks.

She searches the town for new pictures to take, drives out into the country. She focuses on unlikely places, up trees, down wells. She is no longer looking for Raphael Bang. She is looking, rather, for the others, the quiet population that became her friends, including donkeys and old men and handsome lads.

They no longer appear, as before, out of nowhere. There is only the photo of a well or a bungalow.

They lie side by side in bed. Anabella is snoring.

It wasn't Anabella, Su says to herself. How could it be? It was life's way of boiling over. She sees Raphael Bang clear as daylight shaking hands with some, kissing elegant women on their painted cheeks. She sees his shiny shoes impatient to be moving on, rushing to some appointment and the tyres screeching. She knows he is stirring up some new town, giving it ideas, preparing it for the volcano.

She puts out a hand and touches Anabella. "They saw. No one put them up to it."

"Whatever you say." Anabella turns over.

They were his people, Su thinks. He brought them to life, looked after them. When he gave them assignments, they were happy to oblige. This included pigs and goats, who never get chosen for anything, but scarce people as well, eccentrics, the unpopular and odd. She nudges Anabella again.

"Are you awake?"

"I am now."

"They're still here if we could only see them."

"Don't I know."

Troubles

Dark shadows shuffle back and forth in a disorderly pattern. They're a mile from town, then down a lane, outside a house. No one enters or exits. It's November and the withered leaves are falling. Up closer, the shadows are men, four of them fiercely smoking, or is it five? Their heads are bowed and silent as if for some ancient ritual. The sun, going down reluctantly, keeps them under surveillance.

Inside the house, a family of four observes from the shadows.

"Maybe you should go out to them," the mother says. The father does not respond. "That's four days now."

"Five," the daughter, Yvonne, eleven, corrects her. "I'll go out."

"Shut up, you," Aaron, thirteen, fires at his sister.

The TV is silent, flickering in the dusk. The mother lifts the phone, considers what to say, or to whom, puts the phone down. It's twenty minutes now. She wishes for a swashbuckling husband, then feels guilty. She vows not to let another day pass without telling someone about whatever this is.

"It's him," she whispers. "It's Hambone." A household name. "I'd know him."

"What's the difference?" he answers uselessly. She loves her husband, usually a character but now paralysed by fear.

"I'll go myself," she grabs a pink cardigan.

"You'll do no such thing." The father wears an abused blue sweater with stains. His eyes are liquid and his face shiny as if sweating. He slaps the floppy hat on his round head, shrugs, looks at the television as if for direction.

"Are you sure?" The mother has second thoughts.

"No, I'm not sure." He should lighten up, she thinks. She would go out laughing and haranguing the bastards for having nothing better to do. The three watch the father going nervously through the little gate.

"I say we move to Australia," Yvonne says.

"Not tonight, baby," the mother is the brave one. For no obvious reason she grabs her compact, applies hurried make-up, then a pale lipstick and smacks her lips, then a hand to her hair. Then asks seething Aaron: "How do I look?"

"Not funny." At school he gets into fights.

The father hesitates by the road. The ghosts stop walking, gather in an untidy cluster. "Isn't that a grand evening," his eye is on Hambone, if that's who he is.

"A grand evening, surely," Hambone agrees. He's formidable, with big bones, big features, he is said to be a monster. Though you'd never meet anyone who actually knows him. Or where he comes from. He may not even exist. "You're looking well."

"Could be worse."

"Aye, you're looking fit. What do they call you?" Hambone finishes a cigarette and starts a new one, standing desperately close, standing sideways and not looking at the other.

"Ah now, I'd say you know me." The low sun is winking through the trees. Beside the road the dog is stretched. That's why he didn't bark.

"No, I insist. I don't know you."

"You'd be strangers, then?"

"That strikes me as a trick question. Wouldn't you say, lads?"

The other four, looking glum, nod. "It's insulting," one says, probably the right-hand man. They smoke with fierce intensity as if sucking blood out of life.

"No insult intended," the father says amicably. "Why would I insult you?"

"You tell me." The right-hand man refuses to be mollified.

"Dammit, I'm famished," Hambone says. "I'd give good money for a mug of tea."

"You said a mouthful," the other man says. "I'm starving."

"We can fix that," the father forces himself to be jovial. "A sup of tea is no bother."

"A fry maybe?" The right-hand man is gangly and his open shirt shows a hairy chest. He is wearing sunglasses. "Anything less would be unsuitable."

"Sure, a fry." The father is still jovial. "There may even be a few beers."

"No beer," Hambone, already opening the little gate, stands aside to let the father go first. "We never drink on a job."

"What job?" It is hard to keep alarm at bay.

"You have a suspicious frame of mind." Hambone withdraws a mobile phone, scans it, puts it away. "We mean you no harm."

"I know." It is said cheerfully. "Why would you?"

"You said a mouthful there. Why would we?"

One stays behind, sitting on a plastic chair.

"Tea for everyone," the father says with authority coming through the door. There is a hint of vindication: nothing would do her but to go out to them. She is in the kitchen, the kids close. He notices the lipstick, can't understand it, she must be out of her mind.

"And something on the pan," the right-hand man is enthusiastic, rubbing his hands. "A few rashers and free-range eggs, like." He makes himself at home from the living room to the kitchen, picking up photos and putting them face down. "A tidy family. And yourself, missus, must be the handsomest woman in the county."

"I won't stand for that," the father tries to take charge. "Show a little respect."

"Well, listen to *him*." The man turns on the father. "Only paid your wife a compliment."

"You did not," Aaron says.

"Not what, son?"

"Not a compliment."

"Did you hear that?" The man is still wearing the sunglasses. "I could blow your brains out, son. Splatter them on the wallpaper. If you had any brains."

"Get on with that tea," the father nods to the mother knowingly. "Are there any fresh eggs to go with the rashers?"

"No problem." She makes quick moves, to the stove, to the fridge. Everyone has crowded into the kitchen, drawn, it seems, by the food, or by the woman. She pushes past them. "Set the table, Yvonne."

"There's a fancy name there," the man feels Yvonne's behind.

"Hey, you," Hambone shouts at the man. "Hey, there, don't do that again."

"Or what?"

"Or I'll shoot you."

Things fall quiet. Yvonne helps getting bread, getting the condiments. She is confused. This evening may even be normal. This may be something that happens all the time, but children, protected, don't notice it until they reach a certain age. She places plates of rashers and eggs in front of each stranger around the table. There is none for the father, none for the mother. When the edge has gone off their hunger Hambone cheers up.

"I tell you, lady, I hadn't a fry like that for years." The mother does not respond. "On behalf of everyone, thank you. That's all I'm saying. Isn't that right, boys?" They reply with grunts. Hambone has long, untidy hair for a man his age. "We could be friends if it wasn't for the circumstances."

"What circumstances?" the mother asks without looking at him.

"See? There you go again. Making mountains out of – I wish I could get to know you better, maybe have an exchange of pleasantries." They light cigarettes all around the table and smoke fills the kitchen. "Here, sit down."

"You got your fry," the father speaks up. "You should go now."

"Which way is the lavatory?" the right-hand man asks. The mother points up the stairs.

"I can see you don't like him," Hambone is amused. "And neither do I." The man can be heard prowling upstairs. "A savage, is what he is. A butcher. I wouldn't tell that to everyone, and your good man there seems harmless, if things were different we could be friends."

"What things?" the mother asks.

"Things? What are you talking about?" He is high-spirited, manic. "I'll tell you something, lady. You're a lovely woman. Himself is lucky to have you, but I don't know what you saw in *him*." Hambone laughs and looks around at the faces. The right-hand man descends the stairs with excess clatter. Hambone stops laughing and says to the father: "We only want to know what you're up to."

"I don't know what you mean."

"Don't know? Don't insult my intelligence." His face turns red and angry, an unruly face that the rest of him is unable to control.

"I wouldn't want that."

"What?"

"To insult your intelligence."

"We're friends, then?"

"Whatever you say." Yvonne has begun to cry. Her shirt sports a Mickey Mouse on the chest. Aaron, anyone can see, would risk killing Hambone. The mother is alert, scarcely breathing. The other two take turns upstairs. After they flush the toilet they prowl about.

"Are you happy, lady?" Hambone asks.

"I'm grand," she is cheerful. "Why wouldn't I be?"

"Grand, so." He looks her up and down with admiration. He is restless. "It's quiet here. And you so near the border?"

"Why wouldn't it be quiet?" the father's voice has grown smaller.

"Still, it would make you wonder." Hambone gets to his feet, stands in front of the mother. He holds out his hand and she shakes it without knowing why. He is slow to let go. He smiles at her and she smiles back gamely. "We're only having you on," he says.

"Having you on," the right-hand man echoes.

"We could have a party?" he still holds her hand.

"Maybe some other time."

"You'll never look as well as tonight."

"Leave her alone," the father jumps up, knocking over a chair. "Get the hell out of here," his face is red and moist, his chest heaving. Then his innate timidity douses the anger. "For God's sake, go and leave us alone," he pleads. "We're not in any organization."

"Organization?" Hambone is astonished. "What organization? Are you saying you associate with undesirables?" He takes the mother gently by the arm. "In that case, lady, we have no alternative but to question you."

"Stop it!" Yvonne cries and strikes Hambone repeatedly with her little fists. Aaron jumps up in similar fury. One of the silent men flings him back in his chair.

"Aaron," the mother yells. "Don't do that, baby. Be good, all of you."

"What are you waiting for?" the right-hand man asks Hambone.

"You're right," Hambone is resigned to whatever needs to be done. "Can't do it in this madhouse, though. We'll need to go upstairs where it's quiet."

"Upstairs is good," the man confirms. A seriousness has set in.

"Don't," the father pleads.

"Your cooperation is appreciated," Hambone says to him soothingly. "Sit down now." He eases the father into a chair.

"Everyone, be good," the mother's words are full of concern. "We have done nothing," she is even cheerful. No one answers. No one looks as the mother ascends the stairs followed closely by Hambone. The footsteps grow quieter when they reach the carpet. Everyone listens for where they go. Where can it be but the bedroom? No one looks at anyone else.

The father jumps to his feet again, lunges at the stairs. "Come down from there or I'll kill you."

"I know how you feel," the man blocks him. "I'd kill him myself if I could."

"Mammy!" Yvonne screams.

"Shut your mouth," Aaron shouts to protect her.

One of the silent fellows has his brown boots on the table. The other turns up the volume on the television.

"Louder," the first one says. They look like brothers. One wears a wedding band. "You could take tea to the moron outside."

"Take it yourself."

"Shut up," the right-hand man shouts. There is a talent competition on TV, several finalists getting a last chance to win.

"I need to go," Yvonne says. "To the toilet."

"No, you don't," the man says.

"I'd say, the dancer," one brother says to the other.

"I'd say the one sang *The White Cliffs of Dover.*"

Whatever is happening upstairs is drowned out by the songs.

"I'll bring him tea," Yvonne says, still sniffling.

"Who?"

"Him outside."

"Brave girl," the man says. "You have more courage than your da. If he was a man he'd be up above killing those two."

"I have money," the father says. "I'll pay you well if you go up now and kill him."

"That's a terrible thing to say." He turns to Aaron. "I have news for you, son. For the rest of your life you'll regret you didn't do something."

"Don't listen to him," the father says quietly to Aaron.

"He wants you to be a coward," the right-hand man taunts.

Above the singing there is a noise upstairs. One of the brothers, teased by curiosity, turns down the volume. There are cigarette butts on plates, in cups, stuck in slices of bread.

"I told you, the dancer," one brother says. A floorboard creaks above.

The mother steps from the carpet to the wooden stairs, followed by the heavier step. Those below see her sandals, his heavy boots. Everything raises questions. Her face is neither battered nor bloody. Hambone looks relaxed. The mother looks pleased. Aaron appears bewildered. If his mother is so happy there may be no need to kill anyone. The father is turned to stone. If the mother is happy he can't be blamed for the action he fails to undertake.

"That was satisfactory," Hambone pronounces.

Yvonne screams. The father puts an arm around her.

"Shut up," one brother says. The other brother turns up the volume again.

"Turn that down," Hambone says affably.

"Everything is fine," the mother is eager to restore harmony. She looks exactly as before. Her hair does not appear disturbed, nor her clothes, no sign of blood, no sign of kissing. "These men are leaving now," she smiles at Hambone with a toss of her head.

"Very satisfactory," Hambone repeats, pleased that everything is going well.

"What is this about?" the father asks.

"We come in peace," Hambone says. "We come to remove any suspicions that may or may not have surrounded you. Some day you'll appreciate what we're doing. Have you been out at night?"

"What of it?"

"It all depends on where you go and who you go with and what you do and why and, ah dammit you're not a stupid man, you can see where all this is leading."

"I never told him anything," the mother says. But she is not angry. She wants peace. To Hambone she says, "You promised."

The headlights of a car flash along the wall. "Go out and help the moron," Hambone says to the brothers. They go, shuffling, reluctant. No weapons appear, perhaps none exist. Hambone looks at each face in turn. "All the traffic, it's like a bloody airport around here." The car outside growls back to life, eases away. The brothers return.

"Guns?" Hambone says abruptly. "Sit down," he adds. "Why the hell is everyone standing?" Yvonne sits on her mother's knee. Aaron is squeezed between the two brothers. "Look at us," Hambone says. "People can get used to anything." He is the only one standing, flexing and restless. "Guns?" he repeats.

"No guns," the mother says.

"I was asking himself. Bombs?"

The father shakes his head at the ridiculous question.

"And the queen?"

"What queen?"

"Is there more than one?"

"What about her?"

"What about her?" Hambone is growing jolly again. "Do you pray for the lads?"

"What lads?"

"Could you sing Roddy McCorley?"

"I don't know that one." The father looks steadfastly at the floor.

"Do you know 'The Sash My Father Wore'?"

"Don't know it."

"You're a dead loss. Stand up."

"I'll stand when I like in my own house," the father remains seated.

"Please, Willie," the mother pleads. "Do as he says." The father stands. The brothers are grinning. They admire Hambone after all. Their grins are identical, eager for whatever comes next.

"If you go now," the mother says, "we'll all swear we never saw you. We don't know you. Nothing happened."

"Isn't she a beauty?" the man says.

"I'd like to facilitate you," Hambone says to the mother. "But it looks suspicious. That thing about Roddy McCorley. And everyone knows the Sash. You'll have to come with us," he says to the father.

"Please," the mother says.

"We can still be friends," Hambone says. "If we meet on the road, or in some town, it will be as you say, like tonight never happened. If you ever need a hand, I don't know, someone in trouble, whatever it is, you have only to get in touch." The brothers have taken their places beside the father. "It was nothing herself told about you," Hambone explains to the father. "She was the soul of discretion."

"Stop it," Aaron makes a feeble last try.

"Atta boy," the right-hand man pats Aaron on the head. "You'll need to be the man of the house for a while."

"Nothing bad is going to happen, baby," the mother says to Aaron. "Nothing bad, Willie," she tells the father.

"I'll be back in no time," the father says. He is cheerful for a moment. "We'll clear this up, I'll be back in no time."

"In no time," Hambone repeats. "And the fry was grand, missus."

Willie sits between the brothers in the back seat. The right-hand man drives, Hambone beside him. The moron has disappeared.

Through the back window, in the bad light, the father waves a cheerful goodbye.

"He was smiling," Yvonne says inside. "Why was he smiling?"

"He knows everything will be fine," the mother says. "He's more amazing than you think."

"So why are they taking him?"

"First they'll torture him," Aaron says quietly. "And then they'll kill him."

"Not on your life," the mother stops being busy and sits with the kids at the table. "When those bad men are not paying attention, your father will turn the tables on them."

"He'll pluck their eyes out," Yvonne says.

"Only if they ask for it. Your father would prefer to let them go with a warning."

"He'll bury them alive," Aaron says. "After cutting out that man's tongue."

"He'll give them a piece of his mind," Yvonne softens.

"And then bury them alive," Aaron insists.

"And before we know it," the mother's eyes are shiny with admiration and love, "Willie will return, your daddy, brilliant and fearless, but acting low-key and humble. And he'll say not to worry, it was all about nothing."

Emily's Fault

Emily waited patiently in the middle aisle.

Bill Kilbride longed to reach out and touch the coffin. It was much too spacious for Emily; she could twist and turn in there with room to spare. Only twenty and gone without goodbye. If she moved over, there would be room for both of them.

Bridie Kilbride knelt beside her husband. Her eyes were fixed on the flickering sanctuary lamp. In thousands of churches the red light announced God was home and looking after the world. The church never backed away from this mighty claim, never pretended under pressure that the light was only a metaphor or a symbol. Martyrs died unenviable deaths rather than turn their backs on this vague but sublime hunch.

Bridie waited for the light to go out. It was typical of sanctuary lamps to seem always on the point of extinction.

The priest placed a hand on Bill's shoulder as he passed, nodded solemnly to Bridie. Earlier in the world, there would have been shrieking and ululations, people's untamed expression of their incomprehension and loss, but now it was the undertaker's job to package the emotions. The priest sprinkled holy water. Everyone assumed the soul had gone home on an earlier flight, the holy water was to soothe the spirits left behind.

The homily mixed the divine and mundane. Spare a thought for the parents of this only child – you all know Bill, probably bought a sofa in his shop, and your children were likely taught by Bridie, and Emily, everyone loved Emily. The priest had unruly hair like sedge in a bog, his face sallow and rutted.

Near the back, among the casual mourners, was Roddy Coyne, everyone aware of him. Bill Kilbride resolved to kill Roddy Coyne after mass. Then doubts set in. Had he the sheer courage to do it? Would the diminutive Coyne, at the vital moment, look him in the eye and have more of whatever it took to prevail? In any case it would be a sacrilege to kill so soon after mass. Or was this just an excuse for being spineless? Bill's thoughts ran haywire, strangling each other. He would do it, somehow, otherwise he could never again walk upright on the earth.

The priest said God was good despite sometimes doing inscrutable things. But how can this be, Bridie went over the priest's head and asked God. Creation was great before, everyone said so, mile-high mountains and water lilies and Emily rushing happily into the future, but not any more.

The congregation, led by the priest's hoarse voice, sang 'Be Not Afraid'. There was much comfort amid relatives and friends. The church cherished its people. Humans had come a long way and religion was among humanity's highest accomplishments.

Despite the palpable love, though, there was a hole in the story. Somewhere during the mass, Bridie, without fanfare, stopped being a believer.

The coffin was wheeled to where the hearse waited and the good people came forward with condolences.

Emily had driven to a concert in Dublin, where the accident happened. She lived on for a night and a day, floating in and out of consciousness. She would come back briefly and talk to her distraught parents, but she was not the same Emily.

The media were spare about facts. The driver of the other car was unhurt, the papers said. This other driver turned out to be bigger news than Emily: a county councillor from an important county, one of those unaccountably wealthy men distinguished for fundraising.

Some people think nothing is true until the media report it. One has only to put an ear to the ground, however, to realize that Ireland is constantly talking to itself. It talks in whispers when it is not scolding and shouting. Talks in half-sentences and incoherence, backbites and winks and nods, profound or gossipy, frantically and constantly, saying things one seldom reads in papers.

Roddy Coyne was drunk as a lord that night, the countryside was saying. He came at reckless speed out of a side street without stopping or looking. Emily slammed on the brakes, which meant that she put her car, at the crucial moment of impact, directly in front of Coyne's Mercedes.

Witnesses emerged to tell their versions: the damaged body gone off in an ambulance, the "little fart" in his mustard suit throwing up his arms in frustration. The guards smelled a stink but it was impossible to look the other way. Coyne failed the breathalyser test with flying colours. It was damned awkward, and he with a meeting to attend. Sure, the guards said, by all means make a few phone calls. A chief inspector appeared. But even God would get sued in a case like this. Eventually, that is, after the grief receded. Do everything by the book. Oh yes, absolutely, be at the funeral.

"I can't tell you how sorry I am," Coyne elbowed his way to the church door, the hand extended to Bill Kilbride. He had a healthy pot belly under a grey suit. Now was the time to kill him, high noon. Bill could strangle the bastard before anyone intervened. But something had happened to the world. Civilization had brought people to a point where we did not kill, if at all possible, in front of other people. Bill was big and slow and soft. Common sense fought with emotion inside his head. No matter what he did, justice would not be done while Emily remained dead. The hangman's rope was history.

There was not enough evidence to hang Coyne in any case. Except for the effrontery. Talk in the countryside was that Coyne considered himself the victim. The law, though, did not consider arrogance a crime. The law's hands were tied. That was why people sometimes took the law into their own hands.

"Be off with you now." Bill Kilbride refused the outstretched hand.

"Thank you," Bridie said at Bill's shoulder, not in gratitude but dismissal.

Coyne's face was one moment a show of sorrow, the next a mask of resentment and defiance.

"Have it your way," his tight mouth said as the extended hand slowly withdrew.

I didn't lay a hand on him, Bill thought. I let Emily down. And then he thought: Emily wouldn't want him killed, that wouldn't be Emily. And then: shite, there never was a chance in hell I'd harm him; I haven't it in me, a cowardly bollocks like me. But I'll see that he gets a good stretch in jail. Though that's not likely, either. Killing while drunk is of small account nowadays. A few years and he'll be out. Then I'll deal with him. I'll beef up my anger in the meantime, work on my courage. Some night I'll take him out to the graveyard to visit Emily.

"Bill," Bridie nudged him. There were hands to be shaken, thanks to be muttered. Eventually the hearse inched away. "Do you think she's in heaven, Bill?"

"Of course she's in heaven."

"I don't believe any more."

"What do you not believe?"

"Any of it." It was the worst time to tell him, but she risked it – in case he might be able to make everything clear. Bring God back to life.

"Don't say that, Bridie. Not now of all times."

"All of a sudden I could see that a good God wouldn't do this."

"Have you told anyone?"

"Don't worry. I won't let us down."

They eased their way past a gable of old stones that was once a church. Bridie could see a mile of cars along the narrow road behind them. All the good people. If God didn't make the world, it must be people who did. But if people were it, they had a long way to go to perfection, starting with drunk drivers.

"Do you think he'll be here?"

"Who?"

"That little man." If he had offered her the condolences instead of Bill, she would have taken his hand.

An open hole in the ground awaited Emily. She would have been fascinated. *For me?* she'd say. Her cousins carried the box over tangled grass. Mourners took up positions amid askew headstones, everyone surely sparing a thought for their own turn later. Bridie would have gone down into the grave and swapped life with Emily. Yet at this terrible moment all she could think about was scanning the crowd for Coyne. If he shows, she thought, maybe I'd shake his hand and forgive him. Such a generous gesture amid all the pain might kindle some spark of meaning. Even without God there was still room for some redemption. But Coyne didn't show.

The parents talked and sometimes cried but nothing eased the pain.

"I've been thinking," Bridie said one day. "That little man would walk free if we said the word."

"Why would we do that?" They were returning from the seaside, where Bridie would sit on a rock, a shawl around her shoulders, and try to take in the ocean. But the ocean was too wide and restless.

"I think she knew what she was saying in the hospital."

"Most of it made no sense."

It was all my fault was one of the things Emily said. "With a look in her eye," Bridie recalled, "as if, as if." Bridie, that night, ran in search of Bill, but they found Emily asleep again when they returned. She would open an eye and make some seemingly coherent statement. Bridie and Bill would coax her, but the mysterious fragments hid more than they revealed.

"Unless she saw things more clearly," Bridie said. "What if she wanted to let that man off?"

"Why would she do that?"

"I don't know." Emily had twenty years to make her impression on earth. It was a smudgy impression – just one of billions who stopped a day and moved on. There was a temptation to make her a myth or a saint, to turn her into a cause. But what would the cause be? *It was all my fault* was a scant philosophy to build on.

If the church was the most impressive building in town, the courthouse came a close second. Slabs of cut stone outside and polished marble inside hinted broadly that this was a lasting city. Religion promised justice for the long run while the law offered solutions for the mean-time. While not as tardy as eternity, the wheels of justice turned slowly, almost reluctantly.

Bill parked his Volvo beside the Volvo of Donal Harkin, solicitor, struggling up the steps with a gnarled cane in one hand and his briefcase in the other. A long, lean man, he wore white suits and bow ties and had cultivated a hint of an Oxford accent. He, too, had listened to the countryside and learned that Coyne had a history of drunk driving. Once he hit an elderly woman in Tipperary and got off by blaming the woman for recklessly disembarking from her bike on a steep hill, though the story was bound to be more complex than that.

"No new developments?" Harkin glanced at Bridie, a lawyer's nightmare. He wanted to nail the defendant and Bridie wanted to acquit him. Maybe. The best he could extract from her was indecision.

Coyne's solicitor had been approached. Coyne's defiance had only been confirmed. Which was irrelevant, according to Bridie, if Emily really had a last wish.

"She doesn't go to mass anymore," Bill sought the moral high ground.

"What did they do before there was mass, Bill?" She took his big hand in her hands. "Do you think, sometimes, they might have done the right thing anyway? There must be times, even back then, when they didn't act out of revenge. Maybe sometimes they surprised everybody and did, I don't know, the kind thing, I suppose."

"Is that what you want?" Bill asked Bridie.

"I don't know."

So Harkin, taking no chances, had filled his briefcase with arguments.

It was not like the court cases on television. It was informal and even disorderly, with constant whispering and terse talk in small groups. If only the little man would come up to her, Bridie thought, and hold out his hand again, and say again he was sorry, that would do it. They could all go home. She and Bill didn't need a fortune in damages, it would be making money from Emily's death. She had it in her to embrace Roddy Coyne, do him what would surely be the biggest favour of his life.

It was not working out like that. Several lawyers surrounded Coyne, surly and shifty and taking care not to look at Bridie. After Harkin made a quiet statement, Coyne's lead lawyer went on the attack. He mentioned *outrage* repeatedly. It was not clear who had committed the outrage but it presumably wasn't Coyne.

Gradually the proceedings became surreal, as if taking place in a foreign language. Bill and Bridie sat side by side while Harkin attended to the case. At lunch time he assured them it was still an open-and-shut case. Overnight there was optimism bordering on cheerfulness. Bill was called in the morning. His testimony was over in a few minutes. No one gave him an opportunity to express outrage or mourn Emily. He returned shaken to his seat and Bridie squeezed his hand.

After lunch, Bridie looked down from the witness box at Roddy Coyne, who looked at the floor. It was his last chance to come forward with outstretched hand.

"Please tell us your name," Coyne's lawyer asked.

And she told him.

"And your address?"

"I want to tell you about my daughter Emily."

"Your address, please?"

"Before she died, Emily spoke to us."

"Later," the lawyer said. He looked down to Harkin for help. Harkin stared back. He seemed almost amused.

"She said it was all her fault," Bridie said.

"What was?"

"The accident."

"Who said?"

"Emily, my daughter."

The judge made an intervention. It was not as dramatic as interventions in the movies, more a mumble in the direction of Harkin.

"Let her have her say," Harkin said with clear resolve, almost triumphantly. Having failed to forestall this moment, he seemed elated to embrace it.

"Go on," the judge muttered.

"*It was all my fault*. That's what Emily said. Before she died."

"Go on."

"That's all."

"I hope you're not mad, Bill."

"I'm not mad."

"Can you take me to the ocean?"

So he turned the car around and pointed it at the coast.

Case dismissed. The judge added mouthfuls of legalese but basically he meant everyone could go home.

"I never looked at him but I could see that sour little face. I saw the big ears taking it all in. I couldn't see inside his head, but you can imagine. His jaw dropped, I saw that clearly. *It was all my fault*, I said. Something must have stirred inside him. In his head. Or his heart, I don't know. Remorse or something. I was so sure he'd be happy. That he wouldn't be able to hold himself in. I even thought he might come rushing up and give me a hug. And shake your hand, at least. And maybe get all sloppy and sentimental and want to be friends forever after. And I thought, maybe, I could do that, though I don't know about you – it's different with men. Then I watched it sinking in. The meaning of it all. It seemed to take forever for those fat solicitors putting two and two together, you could read it on their faces. Do me a favour, Bill. Don't drive so fast."

Bill slowed down. A few white clouds were high in the sky. They were in no hurry. The world had time.

"Then all the hand shaking and smiling when they realized. Even Coyne – that begrudging little grin, and thanking the lawyers and kissing his dumpy wife. He seemed to forget he had me to thank. Or Emily at any rate. But I think it never crossed his mind. I thought, he'll be moved. He'll recognise goodness. He'll realize the world is still generous and it's not all graft and making money. He'll come over, I thought, and I planned to hug him even if it killed me. Emily would have approved, wouldn't she, Bill?"

"She would."

"Emily believed in disinterested love. I never heard her say so, but disinterested love is what this was about. Giving the man who killed her a clean slate. If you're only going to live to be twenty, and you want to leave something to be remembered by, a legacy, you know, I can't think of any better way to be remembered than this. She might even be a saint. When you think about it: we could have fought that case. And won in spite of Coyne's fat solicitors. And got a nice settlement. And put that little man in jail. But the world would never know the calibre of person Emily was."

Bridie sat on a pocked boulder. The ocean came up and talked to her. The ocean confirmed her most cherished opinions, over and over, threw wave after wave against rocks that always seemed to prevail. But the waves would win in the end, Bridie knew, and some future day, after she was gone and forgotten, the shoreline would be transformed by that same indefatigable sea.

Bill, meanwhile, walked on the sandy beach, his footprints making a mockery of the well-ordered sand. Seagulls flew in untidy patterns. He wished he could fly like that.

A year later, as Bridie sat by a turf fire, Bill set the newspaper in front of her. It said Coyne had been drinking and driving again. Even for a drunk he seemed to have hard luck. This time he hit a toddler, who was expected to survive. Bridie waited an hour before she was ready to speak.

"We shouldn't blame ourselves for this."

"Of course not."

Soon after dark on an evening of drizzle a car pulled up alongside Roddy Coyne walking home.

"Step in," the driver opened the passenger door.

Coyne, surprisingly readily, did so. It may have been thoughtlessness, it may have been mistaken identity. Too late he realized the driver was Bill Kilbride.

"Jesus Christ," Coyne said.

"We're going to visit Emily," Bill told him as they moved into traffic.

Family

Sodom and Gomorrah and now Dublin.

On a hair-raising Saturday night, youth prowls in small groups like wolves. They are dressed scanty for summer and gaudy for sex, or it may be vice versa. Many wear the spiky mane. Some sport blood-red plumage. Girls with puce lipstick insist on being seen. Spectres cast shadows, jive and yowl. Cell phones are *de rigueur*, less for communication than strategy. Incoherence and bedlam are ubiquitous as the hot breeze. And everywhere bottles. Booze is the engine driving the night. Yet beyond the bingeing this evolving breed is in the grip of some other spell – in search of something none of us can name.

These are not snap judgments. I have been here before. I, too, am searching.

I follow an old gent around a corner that he negotiates with difficulty. We fade from the bright street into a dark one. I want to shout a warning to turn back, but I have been rebuffed already, and even an old man can cut you up if you step in his space. An occasional wan light squints down. Predators are fewer here, but more vicious. It is pointless to tell the old duffer about danger because it is only an opinion until something happens. In this case it takes the wolves about three minutes to find him. There are five or ten of them. Their shadows separate and come back together in loose cohesion. These, too, talk and laugh, but in a more suppressed and sinister fashion. They seem exceptionally young, several of them girls. They converge with fascinating inevitability and rain down blows and in no time he is on the pavement.

I circle them, keeping my distance, until I am a shadow in a dark doorway. He never makes a sound. Down on the street, he's harder to hit. Some settle for kicking him. A girl with pointed shoes kicks him in the face. A young lad kneels on his chest and hammers away with quick, small fists.

I could risk it. Could step into the street and shout at them to stop. Throw in a few curses to frighten them. If I had the voice for it, they might come to their senses, be ashamed, slink away and become good citizens hereafter. Or they could turn their attention on me. Several carry bottles that could crack one's skull, but my bigger fear is a broken bottle carving one's face. Even at that, I am all too aware, I could stand up to them, lash out with flailing arms while strength and courage lasted. Inflict a little revenge on behalf of the old man. Take the hits. And the cuts of a knife.

Not having me to cut, they have to use the knife on him, a sickening first stab, then stab, stab, several times, I never saw a human stab a fellow human before. The old fellow is not dead, or he would not shudder and lurch each time he takes a hit. He seems to look at me, but that's only imagination, only guilt. The young wolves are slowing down, scattering. This dance is over. They do not bother to search him. It's an oversight, I think incongruously. He might be carrying a gold watch, an antique of some value, with "All my Love, 1960" inscribed under the lid, a treasure he might have clung to in all kinds of turmoil and now surely was buried deep in the pocket of his wretched brown coat.

A couple of youths, runts of the pack who could not get near him while their betters were getting their kicks, bear down for a couple of parting shots. They curse the heap in the middle of the street, needing to be mad at him because why else would they kick him?

To the best of my knowledge that old man is my father.

I saw him on O'Connell Street a week ago. Kept my distance. Observed him for signs, not knowing what to look for. About that height. About that age. But finally one searches for something more remote and inscribed in the genes.

He was sitting in a doorway. Last week. I passed up dozens of other wrecks, using instinct as my guide, and settled on him. He with the brown coat. A sweater under it even in this summer weather. And the shaggy beard struck me as the beard I thought I'd have if I had a beard. Up from the doorway, he weaved between vehicles, several times avoided getting killed. He put his hand out for money, a week ago, a feeble gesture without conviction, without success. I walked into his path so that I could drop coins into the feeble hand. No word of thanks. I wanted to call him a thankless git, but that would be only the beginning of what I'd call him. I said not a word. Looked into his eyes for a clue. They were sick old eyes. He won't, I thought, even see the lorry that kills him. If only he were singing, I've been thinking all week, or was boisterous in some other manner, as if he were happy, then let the lorry hit him and make the happiness permanent.

Tonight I found him in the same or an adjacent doorway. He's a stay-at-home hobo, then. And here we are.

What kind of man would not rush in to rescue his old father? A healthy big man of forty-three with a smooth face not yet rutted by either laughter or tears, wearing collar and tie under a grey suit such as we bankers usually wear. And a mobile of my own in my pocket in case of mishap in this unfamiliar terrain. In a laughable effort to blend in, I am wearing, over my thinning hair, one of those peaked caps with the logo of some oil company inscribed up front.

I didn't rush to the rescue because I didn't know for sure he was my father. Some will find this explanation inadequate but that's not my problem. Yes, there was something about a scar, but a scar means nothing on people like him. I could have asked his name, but names likewise mean nothing to such people. Finally, if I were sure he was my father I might all the more willingly have thrown him to the wolves. Then there is the further fact that I am petrified on this street. Life, in short, is complex.

"Hello." It is a comical greeting as I risk moving closer. "Hello, can you hear me?" He is in the foetal position, insofar as the battered body will allow. It is common, I believe, for certain animals to curl up like this for protection. That must be blood reflecting the light. "Hello, are you alright?" I am down on one knee. Now the suit will have to go to the cleaners. There is not a stir from him, nor a sound. I move in for a better look at his face. He seems in his seventies. My father would be sixty-seven, of that I'm sure. But then, one must allow for living.

I touch his hand, feel for the pulse. I know nothing about medicine but there seems to be some faint motion there. The hyperactive mind wonders would I go on with this if I knew he was a stranger. For now it's a hypothetical question and I am one of those cagey, bureaucratic types who seldom waste time on hypotheticals. It's different when one knows what one knows. Up close, he smells bad. He would smell bad whether he were my father or not. I am constantly glancing around, meanwhile, not wanting the thugs to come back. And not wanting to be seen in this situation by any chance acquaintance. Not that it's likely, yet coincidence plays unbelievable tricks. The night is still full of energy, and the music defiant. A few have stopped to stare. Their interest, I think, is not in the beaten-up man, but me. I resist the urge to tell them he's my father. Or that he's not. Be cautious, my inner self says. No good deed goes unpunished. I wouldn't be the first to get sued for being a good Samaritan. Which I am not.

It takes only seconds to think in circles, holding a hand that maybe once held mine, maybe slapped me, a calloused farmer's hand for grasping a spade, digging spuds.

He groans a surprisingly strong groan. I let the hand go. Call an ambulance, I order the bystanders. Then pull out my own mobile and call the emergency number. Because it is the crazy hour in the city, the ambulance is here in a jiffy. They bundle him in. I am prepared to play dumb but no one even asks. So I ask where they're taking him. To the hospital, they say, where else?

One day in 1969, after the hay was saved, my father cycled off without explanation and returned towards evening with a new Morris Minor. The following day, he drove off in the Morris Minor and came home with a David Brown tractor followed by a neighbour driving the Morris Minor in second gear. I was eight and my sister Peggy ten. We kept our excitement mute because everything has a reason and we could see none for what was happening, and neither could our mother, asking questions and getting only cagey answers.

The day after buying the tractor he cycled off again and never came back. If I knew he was going to do it, I would have paid more attention, and so, I'm sure, would my mother. I would have observed whether he was wearing a starched shirt and tie as he did on Sundays. I would have remembered the things he said that morning. Did he throw a dash of water on his face as he usually did before going to the town? Did he drop any hint that I failed to pick up? Did he wander the house taking a last look at the familiar contents, or at us? Did he walk the fields, out of sight, jotting things down in his memory? What did he say to mother? She could not, ever after, remember, or if she did she kept it locked up. If he took a bag with what he might need, I failed to notice as I saw him swing his leg over the sturdy bicycle. The only thing missing when he was gone was the gold watch. If there was anything else, she refused to tell us children. She had given him the watch, with the rare word *love* inscribed, and found solace in the fact he remembered to take it when there must have been so much on his mind.

I regretted for years not running down the garden to see which road he took. It seemed absurd to be cycling when the Morris Minor sat idly behind double doors in the barn. When evening came, Peggy asked where he was.

"He'll be back shortly." A vague wisdom came to me that day, so that I never asked my mother more than she was willing to tell. She filled the house with false cheer

145

and watched television with us. When it became dark she finally phoned, talking low. Peggy and I looked at each other. What surprise will he bring today?

Early in the morning she took us to search the farm. Then she left on the bicycle, warning us to be good. She came and went and phoned by turns, worry building. The years have played tricks with my memory. It was maybe a week before the guards came. She kept hope alive longer than was likely. Her sister and others were in constant attendance. Once it was in the local paper, everyone knew, especially at school.

It was a year before she would touch the Morris Minor. She had already returned the tractor.

"He was providing for us," she would say when Peggy said she hated him. I, with my new wisdom, kept the hatred locked up, saving it for some reckoning that would come to pass.

"He disappeared into thin air," mother would say when she had to say something.

"Where did he get money for the car and all?" Peggy chased the loose ends.

Mother would go silent. She hired a man to help on the farm, then sacked him for stealing. Eventually she bought a tractor of her own. Neighbours spoke well of my father if the subject arose. As time passed he was mentioned less frequently. I wished he had died. That way, there would be a funeral and an end to it. Sometimes I wished he came to a bad end. Because of my advanced wisdom I had no trouble with options, whether to shoot him or hold his head under water, but I never thought of getting a gang of hoodlums to beat the tar out of him in Dublin.

As the years passed and we grew into adulthood, the space he left gradually filled with gossip that grew until it turned into legend. Word would trickle back that he was in Baltimore or Chicago. That he was a successful tycoon or else in jail. A skin had to be put on those stories to keep them fresh. That's where word of the scar came from. There was some mighty conflict in New York or Texas, with echoes of John Wayne, the storytellers ignoring the fact that the twentieth century was nearly over.

I felt obliged to tell mother. To protect her, I thought. Once a laughing woman, she had become stoic, a solitary island in the parish. "People have to be talking," I said. I myself had assumed a similar stoicism and inhabited an island of my own, one on which the sun seldom shone.

"I don't want to hear about it," she said with finality. So I didn't tell her when word came he was spouting philosophy at Hyde Park Corner in London; or working miracles on the sick in Toronto. Eventually the legends brought him back home, dressed up like a scarecrow. He would, in this telling, take up positions in trees at the far end of our farm, and weep there for some great sorrow. No, the teller did not see him personally. No one ever had a story from the horse's mouth.

I stand by the pool of blood and watch the flashing ambulance nudge its way through the revelry. I could go home now and never tell a soul. I feel sorry for the old man but he won't keep me awake at night. I used to pity every hard case until I realized that at any one moment there are dozens or hundreds getting stabbed or shot, and finally I decided I couldn't pity them all. So now I change the subject, dwell on something more cheerful.

The trouble is seeing their faces. I should never have bent over him, giving him some hold on me. Not that he's my father.

There's no chance of a taxi, so I walk to the hospital in the small hours. Away from the revelry there are quiet streets asleep.

I lack the usual compass in my head that gives others a sense of direction. So I wander around the hospital in search of a badly stabbed derelict. I bypass the front desk, ridiculously afraid of arousing suspicions. I look much too respectable for the mission I'm on. I could say he's my father, but I wouldn't look the part, or he wouldn't. I could tell them he's William Dolan, known locally as Liam. This, too, would pose a problem if it's not who he says he is. My advice to people: if your kin is dying, make sure of their names. (Just look at me, making a little joke under these incongruous circumstances.)

I like to think I'm at home in banks but almost anywhere else I'm at sea. So I buttonhole a fast-walking woman, a nurse or orderly.

"Can I help you?" So many people ask that question, ours should be a better world overall.

"An old man," I say, pithy and professional. "Several stab wounds. I'm here to represent him." Whatever that means. "May even be dead." I must have heard clipped talk like this on television.

"Wait there a minute," she points to a bench. This is too easy. Unless she's gone for someone to evict me. The last thing one needs is what the papers call an incident. If she raises any fuss, I'll just walk out and never come back.

"Come this way," she says. "That the one?" She points through a window, and I nod. "He'll pull through," she says.

"When can I talk to him?"

"Not tonight." She has a foreign accent.

It didn't take the doctors long to do whatever they did. He is looking up at the ceiling with his mouth open. His placid face does not seem surprised by the events of the night. This may be because he's used to it, does it all the time. Gets stabbed, I mean. The face is battered, but not as badly as one might expect. Worse wounds are doubtless under the blue sheet. Not a chance he'll look through the window and maybe wave and say, "Rory, begod, I'm glad to see you, come in and we'll have a drink." (I need to desist from this levity before I make a fool of myself.)

"Thank you," I tell the nurse. I want to hug her, but even I know better.

Mother makes rhubarb pies when there is rhubarb, and apple pies the rest of the year. When I visit at weekends she feeds me as if saving the world from hunger.

Then, a year ago, she started talking about the past, and the wall she had built around those grim days began gradually to come down.

"He hated farming," she said out of the blue on a Sunday morning over a bed-and-breakfast kind of fry.

"Really?" I didn't ask whom she was talking about.

"He wasn't very good at it." She herself had, the whole countryside agreed, become a top-notch farmer. Though she stayed aloof she never became odd. A man from Poland does the heavy work, although she can still drive the tractor or give a bullock an injection. The Pole lives in the attic, but there has never been a whiff of scandal. The Morris Minor long ago was replaced by a red Toyota she treats with loving care. "I think he found farming boring." She began to tell me stories, at first remote as if he were a stranger, then gradually with what seemed like affection.

"He always wanted a tractor. Farming would be a breeze if he had a tractor."

"Did he never drop a hint," I risked asking, "that he might, I don't know, walk away?"

"Not that I noticed."

A week later she returned to the subject, never mentioning him by name.

"He loved you and Peggy."

"If he did, he kept it under wraps."

"He would go into the room and watch you sleeping." She had no dramatic revelations. She just knew he loved us. My own view was that the guilty bastard was wrestling with his conscience as he searched for courage to walk out on us. "And he tried to teach you football. He wasn't very successful at that, either." Again the unaccustomed smile appeared. After nearly a lifetime she seemed to be learning to relax.

"I hated football. But if he had stayed, I'd have been a footballer." "Don't I know."

I phoned Peggy, who confirmed that mother was going through a phase. Peggy, since she married and had a few children, had softened, wanting a grandfather on our side of the family. I, for my part, decided years ago that I was not a marrying man. This left me at mother's mercy when she finally had time for her personal crisis.

"Those rumours," she said, "do you think there's anything to them?"

"What rumours?" I was on my guard.

"That he's back. I don't live on Mars, you know."

"What makes you think he's still alive?"

"I just know it." It was the weakest and also the most convincing answer she could give. For a person of financial disposition, if I may say so, I place unusual reliance on insight and premonition.

"So what exactly have you heard?"

"That he walks the roads dressed like a beggarman."

"Has anyone seen him?"

"Not anyone I know of." She might even be a little misty-eyed. Love and hate ran wild through the world, and much depended on which was having the upper hand on any particular day. Our own family history was getting on in years. What were once emotions, including fierce ones, became only memories lapping on the shores of our receding lives.

"Do you think you'd know him if you saw him?"

"Why wouldn't I know him?"

"He wouldn't look the same. He mightn't even be the same."

"Something would be the same." She left it there. I understood her to be saying she would still recognise what she loved about him in the first place. She would never do it in so many words, yet she was asking me to find him if I could.

I walk cream-coloured corridors to where, by what can only be fate, I find the foreign nurse. She fails to remember me until I mention the stabbing, the old man with a beard. The beard is gone, she tells me, but the stabs are still there.

"You're an angel," I say to her, and touch her bare brown arm, a gesture wildly at odds with my usual reserved disposition.

There are two of them to a room, on their backs. This is how the human race comes home to roost, in from the caves and fields and hovels, this is definitely progress. I feel giddy with unaccustomed emotions, I need to be cautious. The one by the window is fat and beaming.

"Isn't that a grand day now," he says. Outside his window it is already dark. He'll die on a grand day, that man, because isn't every day? I nod to him coolly. Must not send misleading signals, I am already out of my element coping with this other fellow.

The stuck poor bastard is not beaming but looking straight up with his mouth still open. But he doesn't fool me. He's thinking at the speed of light. Considering angles, wondering about outcomes. He looks younger without the beard. But not necessarily like my father. If he had a scar before, he has several now. I insert myself between the two beds, my back to the beaming fellow, cutting him out of the conversation in case it ever gets started.

"And how are *you*?" I say to the fallen hero.

He makes an incoherent sound. All my life I would have taken that sound at face value. I grew up with a liking for mathematics. Sums were unambiguous. A hundred was a hundred and a half a half and a Euro just that. There was no room for argument, and no need. Such disciplines as poetry or history, by contrast, were mushy and unstable, a whim could blow them in a different direction. But now I am unaccountably losing that old self-control. There's something awry here. He can talk if he wants to talk, the old fart. He's street smart, he's playing a game.

"Feeling any better?" I try again.

The head does not move but the eyes follow a slow orbit in my direction.

"I was there – do you remember when you were attacked?"

"Keep at it," the big fellow prompts behind me. "He can talk if you keep at it."

"Can you show me where they stabbed you?"

And he does. Pulls back the sheet, opens the pyjamas. His gaunt old body is a map of sores and slashes, red and purple and some still bandaged. His eyes are on my face to watch my reaction. I should, by the way, have asked mother what colour of eyes to be looking for. It may seem odd that I don't know, but I'm willing to bet most people don't know the colour of their parents' eyes. The face as a whole is a bigger enigma. Every face on earth is different, even those of identical twins. But there are enough similarities to fool many of us much of the time. In short, I have no conviction about this unfamiliar face. And as for the body, there are fewer clues, a few nondescript ribs, an uneven scattering of greying hair. Could be any chest. No reason on earth to pick this one out for special consideration, much less filial affection.

"Ask him what his name is," the big fellow tries again.

"What is your name?"

"Don't know," he says, or seems to say. But since he looked at me he has not stopped. I wonder what he's seeing. If he's truly my father he'd have to be a bad basket case not to make some connection. Are old memories perhaps beginning to crawl through his addled brain? Of me on my little bicycle. Of Peggy on his lap. Of mother in bed.

"Are you feeling any pain?"

"Yes," he says. The brain is definitely working. He's an old fart. He's nothing to me.

"Do you think now, will Tipperary win on Sunday?" the big beaming fellow wants desperately to connect.

"I'll tell the nurse," I say to my man. "She'll give you a pill." I feel no pity. He's a stranger, who, by the way, didn't become such a wreck as this by leading a noble and upright life.

Three evenings in a row I return, worried lest he be moved elsewhere or dumped back on the street. I bring chocolate and he is able to eat it. Mr. Sunshine in the next bed asks for chocolate, too, and because I am confused I bring him a Toblerone.

"Any pain tonight?" I ask my own fellow.

"None at all," he says, working the chocolate. "I'll be out of here soon," he is suddenly a talking machine.

"And where will you go?"

"We'll have to wait and see." He's cagey. An imposter or my father, the brain in my head sways like a pendulum; or maybe the imposter and dad are the same thing.

"Why don't you come for a visit," I suggest to mother at the weekend. "One way or another, you'd know at once."

"I will not," she responds lightly as if I had made a joke.

"And why not?"

"He made his choice."

"You mean, you think it's him?"

"I didn't say that." Yet she asks so many questions it is obvious she wants me to continue the chase. I wonder about all the secrets she's not telling. Might she be the culprit? Men usually take the rap for being unfaithful wretches, but it is not unknown for women to have skeletons of their own hidden away. I look at mother now with more curiosity if not suspicion.

"May I come in?" I say as I poke my head around an ajar door in a nursing home named Evergreen.

Back at the hospital, I did not exist, least of all as this man's kith or kin, so when he went missing I did not risk being inquisitive. But the angel with the round brown arms winked at me, slipped me a slip of paper with the Evergreen address, while I slipped her a Toblerone I was foolishly taking to the big mouth from Tipperary. I'm certain she isn't a nurse at all, but some angel from beyond the usual parameters; I hope she doesn't drag me back to religion.

"Come in," he says, but I'm already in. He has a room to himself, state of the art, painted blue, and two big sunflowers in a picture. My first thought is who is paying for this? I am, the taxpayer. This is what's wrong with the country, easy come easy go. And real flowers in a jam pot on the window sill. The taxpayers didn't do that. Can there be somebody else seeing him? For a moment I resent this, as if someone were after his money. Giddy, did I say?

"So how do you feel?" He looks too healthy to be in bed. But he may be a different story under the blanket.

"What is your name?" He is wearing plaid pyjamas, and his wisp of white hair is neatly combed. He is propped up on two pillows as if expecting company.

"Rory Dolan," I tell him. Though uninvited, I sit on the chair. I eye him for any flicker of recognition. "From Kilboyne," I mention the old townland. In case he got one knock too many on the head, the memory may need to be jogged. At the hospital he avoided eye contact when conversations turned personal, took refuge instead in the cracked ceiling, but now he has eyes only for my cracked self. "I suppose you never heard of Kilboyne?"

"Can't say I have." He seems more coherent than before. If he's so coherent, though, and never heard of Kilboyne, it's time for me to go home.

"You never told me *your* name."

He waits for several pregnant moments, gazing at me, confused or maybe planning some strategy. A little colour has returned to his cheeks. He has a kindly old grandfatherly face. It's not the one I remember but there's so much water under the bridge. He taps the side of his head with his little knuckle, tap, tap, as if to say he can't get in.

"Would it be Quinn?" At the bank I play underhand tricks like this on suspect clients. I don't like myself for doing it, but life is not neatly scripted and one is forced to improvise. He is looking through my eyes into my mind, searching for the answer I want. Not finding it there, he taps his head again.

"Would it be Liam Dolan?" It is not that impetuosity got the better of me, impetuosity is not my strong suit. I need closure on this outrageous episode so that I can return to my orderly life. "William Dolan," I elaborate, I have it rehearsed, let there be no ambiguity.

"That's it," he says. His eyes are full of eagerness. A man who has been away a while is rejoining the human race and glad to be on board again. This revelation ought to make me happy, or even the opposite, but it does neither. It leaves me wondering. Maybe memory came back or maybe the street-wise old geezer is betting everything on one big guess full of ramifications.

"And where are you from?"

"Kilboyne."

"What was your wife's name?"

He taps the side of his head.

"Any children?"

"Two. Two children."

"And their names?"

"Rory." He thinks a while and taps where the brain should be. I know the experts have ways to deal with the likes of him. Scans and such. Wires hooking his head to his heart and then into their computers. They know what questions to ask to catch him out. But I don't think they have ways to deal with the likes of me. The brain will always be leaping ahead and concocting new what-ifs in a world where all the people are mysteries.

My sister, on the phone, says forget him. Mother says it definitely isn't him, then asks all the questions one would ask about a long-lost husband. On my next visit I tell the director of nurses I am the old man's son and hint at a shady past. One might expect her to be suspicious, but she treats me like some prodigal son. The world is an unlikely place.

He shakes my hand. I give him the chocolate. Sure, I know the old story about Pavlov's dog. I'm nobody's fool. Pavlov wouldn't know where to begin with this one.

"How are things in Kilboyne?" he asks.

"Fine." I'm even happy to see him. "The meadows will soon be ready for cutting." It is all silage now, from what I understand, but I suspect he's not up to snuff on silage.

"Which fields?"

So I tell him what I know, mention fields he might remember, mention neighbours by name. I have been storing up gossip from my mother. I quizzed the Pole about the farm. It's too early to tell him the house he walked out of has been replaced by a bungalow. Sometimes he lapses, and that's when I wonder is he a fake father of my own making.

"Do you remember Peggy?"

"Well, of course I do. Are you talking about your sister?"

Who could argue with the logic? And what he fails to remember can be excused because of the lapsed years and the drugs and beatings which must have left his brain wondering what was real.

"Tell me, now, were you ever in America?"

"Oh I was. Worked for the sanitation department."

"Where was that?"

"Omaha, Nebraska." It should be easy to check it out, a fax to Omaha. Unless he lived under another name there. If he's an imposter I should hand him over to whoever is in charge of imposters. But more likely I won't. What would we do without rogues? Not that he's one. Today he's a humbug, but tomorrow he'll be my father again. It has more to do with me than with him. "It's near Chicago, Omaha is," I can scarcely slow him down now. He's looking so well, I hope they don't dump him back on the street. Or worse, try to fob him off on me. There must be regulations that protect me against this sort of thing. "I used to go to the baseball," he is saying. "The Kansas City Royals and Chicago Cubs." And he pauses, searching through his memories. It seems genuine and not an act. Not many in Kilboyne would know of the Chicago Cubs. Could it be he made the right move once, took a cruel risk and saw some of life? "But all the time I'd be thinking of the fields of Kilboyne." Aha! Just when I'm warming to him the suspicion creeps back. The old fart is saying what I want to hear.

"What was your wife's name?"

"How is she?" he ducks the question. I tell him she's still alive, it seems a good place to start.

"I think you're a fraud," I say then. "Otherwise you'd remember her name."

"You mean Helen?" he asks as if I'm the one confused. It is a turning point, I think, until I recall how easy it would be for a con man to put two and two together and find her name. So I take a sweater from the shopping bag because his narrow shoulders seem cold, but basically I just need to give him something. I give him a radio because the TV is not working. I give him instant coffee because he fell in love with coffee in Nebraska.

"In the diner," he says. "A diner called Lena's Place." There is no Omaha accent, another cause for suspicion.

"Where was that?"

"In New Jersey. Did you hear the one about the New Jersey hillbilly with the short arm? He had to use the other arm to wipe his ass." He laughs a quiet, wheezy laugh. A sly sense of humour is emerging, taking bigger risks every day.

"You're a character," I say in my pathetically uptight way. Yet even I feel loose on good days. Especially when I abandon the inquisition and take a leap and believe him. All this has become surprisingly time consuming. The nursing home is an hour's drive from the city, not to mention time wasted buying cakes and oranges. I'm neglecting my work. Then there's mother, who complains I'm spending more time with "that man" than with her.

After a two-day hiatus he's up and sitting in a chair listening to my radio, I know damn well it's for my benefit, and ditto the new sweater, he's a fraud.

"How's your mother?"

"Do you remember that tractor you bought her?"

"I don't want to talk about it."

"If you don't talk about it, I'm walking out on you." So he sits there looking out the window. I opt to let him sweat. I'm searching, as always, for some shadow of the face I knew before he rode away. "Are you holding back some secret about my mother?" He looks at me with some kind of stoic resignation. People have been sitting dumb like this before judges since the beginning of time. "Am I your son or not?"

"Well, sure you are."

"In that case, you'd want to hug me, surely, or at least shake my hand."

"It's not up to me." He looks out the window at the sky. "It's up to you."

"What kind of car did you buy her?"

"A Morris Minor."

"That could just be a guess," I say eventually. I have picked up his habit of mulling over every word before risking it.

"You told me yourself, last Friday week, that it was a Morris Minor."

Peggy is visiting mother. They gang up on me. They never see me anymore, they say. That old renegade is breaking up our family. The words float about the kitchen and I'm the only one sees the joke, such is the change that has come over me. But if I lose my job over him, I'll strangle the old bastard for good.

"Come and see him," I invite them.

"A lot of good that's done *you*," Peggy has gone cynical.

But mother has gone quiet.

I am trying to reconstruct his interrupted life, to see he gets a pension or something. He's in tolerable health for a physical and mental wreck. I have friends in offices who can get him some sort of identity. We could throw him to the guards, who would soon decide who he was, or at least who he was not. But I'm not ready for that. I bring him Swiss roll, which mother confirms her husband used to like. One thing I do not bring is booze. I peer under the bed in case he might have bottles hidden. So far so good.

Since I can't think of any other name, and neither, it seems, can he, I am using Liam Dolan for the moment, my father's name. If he's not my father, I venture to think my father wouldn't mind. We are negotiating unexplored territory. Europe has been transformed into a mighty bureaucracy, but even Europe has no clue which Dublin drunk, if any, is my father.

Mother is on the phone practically every evening, asking questions. She says she's trying to protect me. Still, when I tell her yarns about him, I detect the bitterness dissipating.

One day, back then, we were in the garden and I asked him could we have a donkey. So he took me on his back and galloped all the way to the road. A week later he came home with a donkey. He told me this and I in turn told mother. I sing down the line snatches of old songs he used to sing to me, such as 'Paddy McGinty's Goat'. She goes silent on the phone, and I pile on the detail, putting in a good word for him, how he always told me and Peggy to do what mother said. It never rained during those years, I remember, and we would help him with the hay and afterwards we would go fishing in the shady stream. Mother asks questions, trying to catch him out, but I am never short of an answer, I, who previously had the most arid imagination in Ireland. Yet in real life I have no recollection of a donkey.

"But mother, he won't bite you."

It's summer and she's trying to buy me back with rhubarb pie.

"He did it before."

"It might not even be him."

Through the back door I can see the old house in which he grew up. Slates have fallen off, exposing the rotted timber. The windows are sightless black holes. That house died the day he cycled away. To think I saw him go and didn't stop him. Didn't even shout goodbye. I could have said, hold on for a couple of years. No matter what pain you're in, be a man and grin and bear it for Peggy and me if not for mother, in a couple of years we'll let you go. You old bastard, I could have said to his back when he kept on pedalling with his head down. You'll be sorry, you old bastard, I'd say to the poor bastard who must be suffering something awful and afraid to look back.

Mother is now making a salad in the house I built for her with the first money I scraped together, mother with a regal bearing in spite of all the hours on a tractor. Something died in her, embers at last turned to ashes. But what do I know? I don't know what she never told me. The fields stretch into the distance, climbing to the horizon where a few clouds are mixing purple and copper. All my life I never noticed nature. I'll have to be careful not to go soft in the head.

"Sit over," she says. The salad is the price I pay to get at the pie.

"Answer me this. If you knew for sure it was him, would you agree to meet him?"

"Sure," she says after some thought. "Only, I'd have a gun in my handbag." The words are threatening but there is a charge in her voice to the effect that a little excitement might be welcome at last.

It is Sunday afternoon in a quiet town. There remain only a few cars outside the superstore. In the sleepy square an ancient stone cross holds up a broken arm. A quick shower trailing a rainbow has moved on towards Dublin, leaving the sun to dry the cobbled stones.

Peggy's car comes slowly around a corner as if looking for the wooden bench. Mother gets out, as does diligent Peggy with paper towels to dry the bench. Mother, dressed in black, sits at the end of the bench while Peggy drives away.

"That's her," I say to the boyo sitting beside me in the car some distance away. "With the handbag," I add, because I am in my giddy mood, but he knows nothing about a gun in the handbag.

"I don't know what to say."

"You'll think of something."

"I'm not feeling too good."

"This is your last chance." I can, when I wish, be imperious as any banker. "If you are a fraud, you still have time to say so. I won't kill you, I'll just beat you up like they do in Dublin." But he is more afraid of the woman on the bench than of me. I have decided to adopt him no matter who he is. I think he thinks I'm his son, even if he's not the father who cycled away. It will be gas if mother comes out of this saying he's a fraud so she didn't need to shoot him for abandonment.

He looks humble walking across the square. And with good reason. It's a big day for him. And for mother, too, I suppose. Some will say it's unfair to put mother through this. I agree. Unless, of course, he's the man who left us thirty-five years ago. Something has to be done about that.

She remains seated. He slows down as he gets closer, one tentative foot in front of the other, dressed in white shirt and perky yellow tie under the neat blue suit I bought him. He's gauche as hell, and why wouldn't he be, a bum until recently. One might expect him to try the traditional handshake. A hug, on the other hand, would be going too far, though with a gauche guy you never know. We'll talk about this in years to come. I wonder what we'll be saying.

He sits down at a safe distance on the bench, leaving room for two people between them. They're looking at each other. Now they must both know.

Odd One Out

"This thing has no brakes."

"Shut up, they'll hear you."

"They never flew in a son of a bitch like this."

The SOB to which Sven refers is the penultimate space shuttle about to blast off from Cape Canaveral. Few are chosen to visit the International Space Station. The rest of us eventually grew accustomed to the launches and hullabaloo, so we seldom stop to ask what is in fact going on. This is part of a greater inertia: civilization, no longer able to keep up with our complicated lives, focuses instead on sport and celebrities in an ocean of mindless trivia. The dire consequences cry out for attention.

"Specifically in the matter of slipping the surly bonds of earth," Sven says now, "our betters feed us urban myth and flying saucers and ET on the bicycle. We're adults and tell ourselves we don't believe a word of it. But occasionally we suspect there's no smoke without fire. In good times we ignore the smoke because there are tons of distractions. But in times of malaise, like now, our imaginations throb and we worry."

It seems ridiculous that NASA would tolerate such jibber-jabber. One reason may be that the cutting edge and the absurd are more akin than anyone suspected. Another possible explanation is that the bureaucrats simply don't hear Sven because cause and effect are out of kilter.

Ordinary people know next to nothing about what goes on in such exotic milieux, that's the whole point.

It is surely no accident, then, that in our current throes suspicious stories are circulating. They coincide with the end of the shuttle program. As if to say: now it can be told.

So here's *Discovery* (if *Discovery* it is) on its final voyage. There are three astronauts on board: a Russian female (a cosmonaut, to be politically correct) named Olga; a fighter pilot named Bruce who survived Afghanistan; and tawny Sven from North Dakota. This last is the big mouth suspected of spilling the beans.

"If a thing can go even half-an-inch faster than 186,282 miles per second, then the sky is the limit," he rambles on while steam dribbles from vents and white clouds keep their distance up above and a multitude of television cameras wonder will all those nuts and bolts hold together or will a stray spark torpedo another dream. Sven is referring to the recent discovery by physicists at CERN that neutrinos sent flying from their home base in Geneva to the Gran Sasso laboratory down the road in Italy actually travelled 0.002 per cent faster than the speed of light. This would be no big deal, except that scientists always insisted nothing could go faster than light. Einstein, the granddaddy of all scientists, based his theory of special relativity on this rock-solid understanding. One can't blame Sven for being concerned.

"I'm starving," he says.

"Later," someone tells him, it is not clear who, because there are voices everywhere: earth has developed a fierce need to talk, though no similar need to listen, which is why so many sounds wander the globe in search of a willing ear.

"That neutrino arrived in Italy 60 nanoseconds ahead of the light. That's not much. Sixty billionths of a second, give or take. And admittedly there was an allowed margin of error of ten nanoseconds. Though it might have been twenty. But my point is, if you can do even an inch faster than light, you're off to the races. You're in a time warp in no time. You scarcely have time to phone home and tell them you're entering a black hole and there are no brakes."

Some suspect this is the sort of bull astronauts talk all the time, but, as already stated, we have no way of knowing.

The outward journey, once the initial thrust and vibration are out of the way, goes without incident. Olga has been to the space station before and is blasé. Bruce, the hardened fighter, still has that gift of understatement common to heroes. "Wow," he says, before they get very far.

"Tell me about it," Olga's syntax is similar to that spoken in New Jersey.

"Look at that planet," Sven says. "That's some planet. Look at all that space," he babbles on. "I can see North Dakota. That must be Fargo. Looks like a big turd with the lights on, it's Fargo for sure."

"Relax, Sven," the Russian purrs in her condescending way. "It gets better."

"Awesome," he insists. Yet Sven is not just a loudmouth. An anthropologist, he is not typical of NASA's hard-core scientific explorers bent on finding water or other elements to explain where we came from. His brief, rather, is human nature, with particular emphasis on future interplanetary exploration against the day when earth will be too small for all of us. "Hey, Houston," he intones, "if it's all right with everyone I will now eat a sandwich."

Houston shrugs, knowing he's incorrigible, and approves the sandwich. The three float around inside the paper-thin skin of the speedy spacecraft, pressing buttons, reading dials.

"I can't wait to see Mossy," Sven says.

"Good old Moss," Bruce affirms. There are five at the space station up ahead: Russians and Japanese, an American (Moss) and a French fellow experimenting with the right side of the brain. Four are men. One of the Japanese is a woman. They are admonished not to think in terms of nationality or gender, but human nature, in spite of the hype, is still beset by traditional patterns. Time, by the way, takes on a different perspective out here. Forget sunrise and news cycles and how Wall Street and the Oakland As are doing.

"Did you see that?" Sven is sure something extraterrestrial has just flashed past the window. "Houston, there's debris out here."

"Nothing to worry about," Bruce assures Earth. Yet Bruce knows it needn't be big as a bus, it could be big as a toaster. Then the hole in the cabin wall would be toaster-size, enough to put your leg through. Think of the slurpy sound of getting sucked into the void. And what do you think about as you go, what plans do you make?

A moment comes when the ISS is visible ahead, the most advanced machine Earth has produced after billions of years of striving. A machine that itself has never been on Earth. "It came into existence in space," Sven explains. "As the planets did. As the stars did."

Even Olga is impressed, taking pictures, making foreign noises. "They'll be glad to see us," her voice is almost emotional. "It gets lonely out here."

The docking, once so delicate, has become routine after more than a decade of to and fro. The crews meet at the intersection of the two spacecrafts. There is elation and even affection. Vast hugging takes place so that photos can be sent back to earth. The nations that, strictly speaking, own this vehicle need to be reassured that certain objectives are dealt with. Such as peace and prosperity, the old imponderables.

The five from the host machine, their fat space-suits discarded, are in their stay-at-home duds. Everyone talks at once, amid backslapping and stale jokes. Yet common sense is not ignored. Keep an eye on the vehicle. Make the routine moves. Listen to Houston. Murmur back. The ISS will circle the home planet and be back hereabouts in ninety-one minutes, awesome.

"Hey, Moss," Bruce greets his friend. "How you been?" In the end it comes down to trivia. How you been? Nothing sensational, there's enough of that already. They are a tight community. They know the risks, the consequences. They are among the most talented of their generation, each almost a Copernicus or a Christopher Columbus or an Isaac Newton. Sure, there are occasional tensions and contretemps, the typical drawbacks, but up here (if here can be said to be up) such hiccups are not even a fly in the ointment.

"Bruce!" Sven whispers before an hour has passed. "There are six of them."

"Six what?"

"There's supposed to be five." Not everything they say can be heard in Houston, obviously, because the voyagers can turn themselves off. "Count them," Sven insists.

"I counted. There were five."

"There's a woman."

"I know."

"No. There's another."

Outside, the cosmos stretches for unimaginable miles amid quarks and every kind of galaxy. One might expect highly-educated humans, the only verifiable brains in all that space, to be able to count to six, or is it five? The trouble is assumptions. The trouble is doubt. As if minds had run ahead of their owners.

"Is it some joke, Sven?"

"I'm an anthropologist, Bruce. I'd know a woman."

As they mingle, Bruce finds himself obsessively counting. Three newcomers and five from before, now you see them, now you don't, because the space station is spacious and designed like a maze. Outside, two Soyuz spacecrafts are attached awaiting potential emergencies, because, out here, crises are the enemy.

"Olga! Did you notice anything odd?"

"Did *you*?"

"There's an extra person."

"Who?"

"I don't know."

"Not so loud."

"I saw her with my own eyes," Bruce now comes floating. The atmosphere is conspiratorial, voices muted. No one knows whether Houston knows. With the exception of Olga, who might as well be from New Jersey, the Americans are not ready to confide in foreigners, especially the Russians: dour types passing gas and playing chess. The Frenchman, meanwhile, is on a trip of his own, the left side of his brain interviewing the right side. "She's no astronaut, she looks fishy." Bruce is confused.

"Could it be she's here for the guys?"

"Prostitute, do you mean?"

"I wouldn't use the term. Not out here."

Earth's best brains wrestle with the data, the implications. Context is vital. After a painfully slow start, humans picked up momentum a few thousand years ago. They learned to grow potatoes, invented the wheel, made flying machines. But long before that, if the folklore is accurate, they designated certain women to be available, as Sven says, for the guys.

"So who's available for the girls?" Olga huffs.

For several days the three newcomers perform the tasks mission control dictates. They are vigilant. The extra person doesn't behave like a hooker, but what exactly does that mean? Everyone is integrated and made to feel at home. Bonhomie and jest make the daunting work tolerable. And anyway, who's to say which is the extra person? Presumably the one not introduced when *Discovery* arrived. Unless she just happened to be in the loo at the time.

"I'm Andrea." She soon breaks the ice, normal as anyone. "I'm pleased to meet you."

"Pleased to meet *you*," Sven responds. "You're an enigma for sure." She seems friendly, an ideal human being. "Tell me" – once the ice is broken Sven is keen to resolve the anthropological angle – "how long have you been here?"

"Here?"

"On Earth?"

175

"This isn't Earth, silly." She is adorable in her teasing way.

An enterprise as huge as the ISS could never have succeeded were there not a great seriousness behind it. Every question has been asked – prompted by a previous question, developing into reams of rationales, logistics, metaphysics, going deeper and deeper, higher and wider, going back to Plato and Parmenides and even Adam and Eve, then leaping forward to Einstein and Hubble and, yes, the Tea Party and your uncle Jack. Whatever it is, we're all in it together. What you see looking out the space station window is seen in the light of all the memories and imaginations and ambitions and fears and funny bones of the race. But right now the issue is: does this woman, if she is a woman, belong?

Sven says to her as they hang out after eating beef and vegetables squeezed from plastic containers: "Did you ever hear of Blaise Pascal?"

"Is he a baseball player?"

"The eternal silence of those infinite spaces terrifies me. Pascal said that. Not the baseball player, another guy. Were you ever in Cincinnati?"

"Is this a trick question?" But she is not a bit defensive. Not exactly the girl next door, though the girl next door is not what she used to be. Females, for obvious reasons, never wear skirts in the space station, but her jeans and striped shirt look suspiciously like they came from Gap.

"You're an odd bird and that's for sure."

So, as if reading his mind, she tells him, without prompting or coaxing, that she's from a distant planet named Clickety-Clack. She pronounces it in her own quaint tongue, with a clicking sound amid amazing teeth, causing Sven to wonder is her dentist truly extraterrestrial or could he be just a little Jewish man from Florida. The quandary is: what makes a woman undeniably human? If she knew Cincinnati, or could give you the low-down on Pascal, that might mean only that she had done her homework.

"DNA might do the trick," Sven suggests later to Bruce.

"They may not have DNA out there."

"Out where?"

"On Clickety-Clack."

"That's true," Sven concedes. It doesn't escape him that two humans can't have a logical conversation unless they agree to agree on certain fundamentals, in this case Clickety-Clack.

"Pascal's head was up his ass," Sven pursues Andrea. "There are no silences out there. Too many stars banging into each other, there's bound to be noise, clanging and thundering. It's like trees falling in the forest: don't tell me they're silent because no one any longer listens to them. Is there really a Clickety-Clack?"

"Is there really a Fargo?"

"So how did you get here?" Unlike humans encumbered by gravity, the astronauts float about, bump into one another, turn and return.

"You wouldn't believe me if I told you."

"Try me."

But just when one of astronomy's great secrets is about to be revealed, Moss comes barging in.

"A word with you, Mossy," Sven then says. The two glide down a plastic corridor at 17,239 miles per hour plus whatever speed they are gliding at (because in this instance they are gliding in the same general direction as the space station).

"I know what you're going to say," Moss says. "So don't even bother."

"Is she from Clickety-Clack?"

"Is that what she told you?"

"Don't mess with me, Moss."

"Here's the score," Moss says. "If you tell people there is an extra person on board, they will be sympathetic, because this is a humane environment here. But afterwards they will think differently about you. If you tell it to more than one, they will, behind your back, tap their temples with the index finger, like this, with a knowing grin. Your career, in short, will be over."

"Do the Russians know about her? About her getting on the wrong flight, I guess, about her being, I don't know, a spy or a mole on a secret mission, you tell me. Has no one talked to her?"

"Everyone talks to everyone around here."

"And Houston?"

"We're from the USA, my friend, the greatest superpower ever conceived, of course Houston knows everything. Here." He picks up the clunky old phone, a Russian phone, but it still works. "We live in the most open society on earth, old buddy. Freedom of information and do you want fries with that? So tell them what's on your mind." He holds out the phone and it floats in the space between them.

"What should I say?"

"What do you want to say?"

"And what will *they* say?"

"They'll tap their temples with the index finger. Like this. It's distressing to think about it."

"I'm not distressed."

"I know. You're Sven."

"That I am." They look at one another for ages, at first defiantly, then wearily, until it seems one of them might fall asleep. The phone floats away.

There is work to be done: circuit-breaker boxes to be inspected; computers to be booted; dandelion seeds to be planted in little jars. Sven doubts whether these are the tasks for which his anthropological training has prepared him. Yet there is no blueprint for flight to Mars and especially beyond. Whatever happens next must be pure invention. Like creation out of nothing. It is a tall order. And the others, he is confident, have not one inkling among them. In a nanosecond of self-doubt, he wonders in his poetic way whether Earth's reach might be exceeding its grasp. He ponders those unaccountably left at home who might have kept catastrophe at bay. He thinks of poets, billionaires, a bishop or ayatollah, an honest man or woman. Above all, what is missing is supervision. Someone to take the place of God for the short term. There is neither politician nor judge nor jury here, no army or navy, no referee or bouncer. Under the loose circumstances it was inevitable that a bureaucratic screw-up would cause someone like Andrea to be left behind on an earlier mission. Or someone wasn't counting the day that one space suit too many slipped into the shuttle in Florida. Or, equally likely and more intriguing, an alien spacecraft came sidling up from far away as if it belonged. The pilot of such a vehicle had only to say, here's Andrea as per our earlier arrangement. How do you explain that to Houston, back in the land where many don't even believe in global warming? The answer is, you don't explain. You work things out. You talk in circles and expatiate in riddles until you are all vaguely agreed that Andrea is a good sport, Andrea is doing no harm, she somehow belongs, but don't, for heaven's sake, tell any of this to the media or the taxpayers or, just to be sure, to Houston.

Andrea grows more beautiful with each passing day, a transformation for which anthropology has not prepared Sven. Yet proper decorum is maintained. He waits for a revelation, a hint.

"I'm stuck here," she says one day. Obviously she can read his mind. "My limousine doesn't stop here anymore."

"Are you getting old?"

"What do *you* think?"

"I'd say you're in your prime."

Then he has what back on earth is sometimes called an epiphany. If one can, as the scientists say, travel faster than light, one can gain ground on the passage of time. This gives one an advantage over those who do not travel as fast, namely nearly everyone. Even Sven knows his knowledge in this area is imperfect, but imperfect knowledge can be an advantage. It leaves more room for hope, for taking chances, for arriving, on good days, at more positive outcomes. He does not know where any of this is leading, and that's his greatest advantage – if he knew he might lose heart and turn back. Out here on the edge of beyond, failure is acceptable and pusillanimity a liability. He does not know whether he is thinking metaphorically or realistically, and worries only about falling into a crack between the two. Finally, there is the difficulty of reaching the speed of light before one can go beyond it.

"Tell me about yourself." Modern science prefers hard facts to mysteries. "Did you live in a house out there, or in some more advanced format?"

"Does it matter?" Her great mistake, even humans know, would be to tell all. Ignorance lures us on, why else would we care what is around the corner or over the hill? Andrea, if worry is part of her make-up, may worry that, once this hairy-chested American learns all about her, he might be disenchanted and walk away.

"Well then, how do they make babies?"

"The same way as here." There is clearly a twinkle in her eye. Sven can see her mind ticking over. In addition to knowledge there is ignorance. In addition to ignorance there is incoherence and its first cousin ambiguity. And behind all that lurks a huge indefinable hankering. People are surprisingly the same whatever planet they come from, Sven is discovering. They crave romance as Sven does. This often leads to babies, the imagination lures him on in an intriguing way. Babies can be cute, Sven has always heard, but here in the middle of nowhere what do you do with the diapers? Without an adjusted paradigm, romance would be a crock. He considers by turn a tiny boy, an infinitesimal girl, and worries that in either case the incipient person would be a misfit the length and breadth of the cosmos.

It is but a matter of days until *Discovery* must depart. In the meantime space walks are taking place. One of the Russians, wearing fat gloves, makes adjustments while everyone talks in an undertone or not at all. Houston murmurs amid static – NASA seems so far away. Earth is blue and green below, pulsating with activity one would never suspect from far out, and beautiful, though you cannot see North Dakota from here.

Andrea is seen to be playing her part. When the crazy machine is cruising at great speed (though nowhere near the speed of light), she is the life of the party, if it can be called a party. Yet, when there is a television broadcast, she is never in the picture.

This absence makes sense only if science, nay knowledge in general, is doing a somersault. Sven can't help wondering how often people fail to show up in photos. Can some opt out of being seen by the naked eye? Are there people out there, are there people all around us, just waiting for the right moment, for the perfect opportunity? Does NASA know about this? Does anybody (other than Sven)? There may be a population we see and another we don't. Counting will have to be reconsidered. Now that certain items can move faster than light, all the old thinking needs to be rethought.

"Did I ever tell you," he asks Andrea, the two of them hanging out, "about the mountain I climbed in my youth?"

"You never told me." She is a better listener than earthlings (unless she is an earthling).

"This was Mount Olympus in North Dakota, a mighty hill. At the top lived an old man. His face was lined and he had no clothes worth mentioning. He survived on an occasional dead rabbit or an eagle that might fall from the sky after flying too high. But he was cheerful and undaunted. Never complain, never explain, he would say."

Sven longs for her to open up and tell yarns about the fantastic people she has met and how the sun rises over her home town, if it does, and whether there is rain or beer or dogs or cats on Clickety-Clack, if there is such a place. He wonders do they wear clothes or pay taxes. Anthropology has always been timid about the thin line between wonder and nonsense. He would be a laughing stock if she should turn out to be from Texas or, worse, North Dakota.

"I have something to confess," he says the following day. "There is no mighty mountain in North Dakota." Pause. "So I never climbed it."

"No old man?"

"Not on Mount Olympus. But I've met old men like that, great old fellows full of vigour and wisdom and, okay, bullshit. I wanted our planet to be interesting – just in case you were never there."

"You still don't believe in Clickety-Clack?"

"If *you* do, I do."

The five are going home, the three are staying: that's the story on Earth. With the demise of the shuttle program, numbers are about to be cut back. No one mentions the extra person.

"Well, Mossy? What are you going to tell them?"

"Are you kidding?" Moss looks the other fiercely in the eye. "Think how it would sound if we say we have, I don't know, an extra body, I guess, an extra human, out there on the ISS. You know what people are like. What are they going to say to CNN? What are they going to tell congressional committees?"

"Speaking as an anthropologist," Sven says, "I know she came from that planet."

"What planet?"

"So you're going to say nothing?"

"I don't know what you're talking about."

There is no more reassuring sight than the space shuttle kissing the space station goodbye and rounding an invisible bend for home.

Higherarchy

Earth is in the doldrums, smothering under the encrustations of history: plastic bottles and crud, global warming and bad thoughts. Those who knew better always headed for higher ground, from Moses to Martin Luther King. Up there, you can still catch a whiff of the pristine blast that gave galaxies a kick in the arse the day of the Big Bang. Croagh Patrick, in other words, is more than a pious superstition.

Fiacra, an archbishop, grunts with satisfaction, agreeing with himself about the sublime. For five thousand years, pilgrims made this annual trek, thinking to avoid hell. But even when the hierarchy let hell lapse, Croagh Patrick lingered. We're still searching for our lost selves, Fiacra decides; they must be up ahead. At the statue he takes off his shoes, ties the laces together and hangs the ensemble around his neck. The trickle of pilgrims going up envy those coming down. A few of those going up, though, are already turning back, the faint-hearted. One face is vaguely familiar.

"Aren't *you*…?"

This particular tenderfoot would prefer not to be noticed. Ralph is not his real name: the new bishop of somewhere down south, who caused a stir blowing in from Rome, where, the scuttlebutt said, he had once been headed for greatness if not the actual papacy.

"Dammit, it *is* you. Congratulations. You'll do a great job. Ralph, isn't it? I meant to drop you a line. Are you settling in? And did I by any chance see you turning back there? Going back for a stick, I'd say? Here, take mine. Forty-two years I've climbed her, I could do it blindfolded. You look puzzled. Ah, I get it. You don't know who the hell I am. Fiacra. The archbishop. I know. Ancient. Should be locked up years ago. I sent in the resignation but no one had time to reply. Sorry. I talk too much when I'm nervous."

Fiacra extends the hazel stick. Ralph fails to see Moses or any of the great climbers. He sees an old fool, droopy and bleached under a red woollen cap. He can't know that the dandruff-grey sweater was discreetly stolen from the Vincent de Paul charity shop. He takes the outstretched hazel stick. He fingers it and cleaves the air with it as if making up his mind. He smiles the ingratiating smile he was taught in the Vatican's diplomatic corps. He makes the huge decision to embrace again the quaint Irish Catholicism he thought he had shaken off for good. He falls into step beside this chattering old goat, all piss and vinegar and was that not a fart he heard?

"There's no need to remove the shoes," Fiacra is saying. "Sometimes I think I only do it to show off."

"Ah, feck it," the younger man becomes practically reckless. He sits on a boulder and removes the shoes. "Pleased to meet you, Archbishop," he holds out his hand and they shake. He is middle aged, still young for a bishop. His designer sweater is a far cry from the Vincent de Paul.

"Call me Fiacra. The other doesn't suit me." They walk and stumble along while a sluggish cloud departs the mountain heading for Westport. "You think you're making progress; then you look again and she's farther away than ever. Some say she moves."

"I wouldn't doubt it." Ralph squints at the askew pyramid pointing remorselessly to heaven. From the purse strapped around his waist he takes a pair of sunglasses.

"It's a nice day anyway." This innocent remark is followed by a silence, by the unspoken. "A man like you," Fiacra then says. "On a day like this?"

"And what about yourself?" Ralph counters.

"Ah, I'm history. He wouldn't be interested in me."

After years of promising, the pope has agreed to visit Ireland. Though not as Catholic as it used to be, the entire country is in pandemonium, the authorities bowing and scraping in that familiar way. Except these two. It's enough to make one wonder. "I suppose you're not a molester?"

"Devil a bit," the bishop laughs, more amused than insulted by this rude rustic.

"Me neither." He is a few feet in front. "Let me know if I'm going too fast."

"All that pomp and hypocrisy bothers me." Ralph is a handsome man, the hair still dark and ample, and Rome has bestowed on him the tanned complexion women love. "The media vultures and asinine speeches: I've been there and done that."

Sometimes it's the lumpy boulders; most of the time it's the sharp stones, the sliding stones, the tedium. "His Holiness never liked me. That's why I'm here today."

"Jaysus! He knows you well enough to dislike you? I'm impressed."

"It looks like we're halfway there." Ralph changes the subject. "Are you not starving?"

"I am if you are."

"I have chicken sandwiches."

"And I have bacon." Fiacra burrows in the rucksack. "This is a delightful outing." Benches are strategically placed. He brushes off bird droppings with a mottled hand. "You forgot to bring a beverage, am I right?" So they share Fiacra's bottle. "You worked in the Holy Office, I suppose? You must have powerful stories?"

"I'm bound to secrecy, of course."

"Ah, go on. There's no one but ourselves."

"Those Vatican officials," the bishop shakes his head halfway between disbelief and admiration. The stories are bursting to get out. "When they lock up their offices."

"Yes?" Fiacra's role is to make Ralph feel good about spilling the beans.

"They have enormous iron keys to their office doors. Some are eight inches long, antiques, you know, some tarnished and rusty from surviving all kinds of weather since the dark ages."

"Begod!"

"They slip the key into the trouser pocket, under the long black garb with red or even purple trim. They shuffle down long corridors. They pull out a smaller, shinier key, kept in the other pants' pocket, to enter their hallowed apartments. Cardinals are by definition the most intriguing. Each has a black briefcase, which he puts under his bed after extracting certain documents. He will make phone calls over the weekend, often in several languages he learned when he was a seminarian and no good at football. The ambitious young man survived, back then, by learning German or Greek. And when his more athletic colleagues boasted at supper about a goal scored or saved, the budding cardinal quietly reflected on irregular verbs."

"You're having me on!"

"So, on Friday nights they go to their favourite restaurants and consume unimaginable amounts of spaghetti and meat balls, with just the right wine, vintages stored under dust since the days of the Borgias."

"Go on, go on."

"Names get dropped at those dinners. The following week letters go out, with red wax seals in some cases, telling the recipient, your goose is cooked, come to headquarters for a dressing down, because here next door to the chair of Peter we know what's what."

"You don't mean it!"

"By Saturday night it's a different scenario." Ralph too is having a delightful outing. "The old boy is studying his documents, wearing a silk robe he received years ago from a pastor in Illinois. Sometimes there is a knock on the door, and a handsome young monsignor arrives to help with theological minutiae. These intellectual encounters can go on into the night. Sometimes they take a break, and sip a little vino, and the old man produces the iron key. He lets the other finger it, which the younger man does with much reverence and with longing. Eventually they put the key back in its place under the pillow. From that moment on, things will never be the same. A shiver has run down the spine of mother church, and the future has been shunted a little, though it may be twenty or forty years before the Holy Ghost comes home to roost."

Refreshed by the grub, the two pilgrims forge ahead. Ralph's mobile comes to life, a few bars of Gregorian, but the words are lost on the wind.

"Turn that thing off," Fiacra admonishes. "In case it drowns out some deeper message." The islands of Clew Bay are glorious below. "This could be a great world yet." Their feet are bloody. One had to be tough to survive in the church. And when decadence occasionally got a grip there was always a Francis or another daredevil to resurrect hardy old God again.

A plane flies over.

"Do you think that could be him?" Fiacra wonders.

"It's going the wrong way."

"Unless he's backing in." Silence settles, and exhilaration in the inspired air. "What does he think about, Ralph, when the pomp is in full swing and the monsignori exchanging one pointy hat for another?"

"Hard to say."

"He's thinking what's for supper, if you ask me. He's thinking about some old thing, when he was young maybe, some incident that comes back to haunt him. And you know why? Because he's still a member of the human race." The two heads are down. The damaged feet leave behind occasional smears of blood. "Do you think, does he ever, pardon me now, late at night?"

"Oh, I wouldn't think so."

"For the glory of God, don't you know? Why else would he, at his age?"

"You have an inquiring mind, Fiacra."

"In the gutter, is more like it."

"There's no need to be so self-effacing about everything." Boulders above threaten to pulverize them. Ralph is moved to magnanimity. "I remember once, at a convivial gathering in Rome, I heard an influential cardinal mention you by name."

There is a pause until Fiacra can't restrain himself. "So what did he say?"

"It wasn't so much what he said. It was the fact that, at that moment, you were on the mind of this eminent man."

"But what did he say?"

"He said he had received a letter. He didn't say what it was about. I, of course, presumed it was favourable."

"Why would you presume that?"

Ralph has no answer. Another plane flies over, going the other way. "That's him for sure. He's taking the scenic route." The silences are awesome, coming from so far away. "Did God really make us, Fiacra, or was it vice versa?"

"Either way, he has a lot to answer for."

From the summit, lesser mountains can be seen amid shadows. A few pilgrims murmur together and drink from their bottles before returning below.

"Now what?" Ralph ponders whether to tell his new friend that, try as he may, he can no longer believe any of it.

"If you have a prayer, go ahead and say it." It is obvious to Fiacra that the new man is unaware of the wild cosmic tug. "Then you might as well head for home."

"What's your hurry?"

"Oh not me. I think I'll stay."

"Ah, Fiacra, don't be ridiculous."

"Something may turn up. Do you remember when there was no four-minute mile? Then, all of a sudden, there was the four-minute mile. A breakthrough, I suppose you'd call it. A new beginning."

"I can't force you, Archbishop, but I'd be remiss, when I get back, if I didn't report you missing."

"Fiacra. Call me Fiacra. And if *I'm* ridiculous, what about – you know – all that stuff about sparrows? He opted to be a laughing stock." He produces a bar of chocolate from the rucksack, breaks it, hands half to the other. "You'd be on solid ground, Ralph, if you could spread your wings and defy the way the wind is blowing."

The bishop looks around for help. There should be Red Cross, someone in uniform, but they're all below attending to football matches.

"So what do you plan to do?"

"If I knew I'd tell you. Honest. But if you come back tomorrow, and I'm not here, you'll know we came to the right place."

The Ronan Chronicles

1. Pascal's Wager

Every morning, out of the blackness, a hint of brightness would appear – impossible to say when one gave way to the other. After that, it was only a matter of time until the world was up and running.

Ronan looked at his watch. Not yet seven. His pyjamas sported a white stripe like a jailbird. His large, angular head hinted at a big, bony body under the blankets. The chemo had taken the little hair that was left at eighty. But the blue eyes were alert like lights on a dashboard that showed the motor was still running.

"Good morning, Malachy." He had volunteered to double up with Malachy, who had not spoken a word for two years. "Another foggy one, I'm afraid. Did you sleep well?" He always threw in a question in case a miracle happened overnight and Malachy might be bursting to talk.

Down the hill was the river – which was why this was called the Riverside Nursing Home. He could see the water reflecting the bronze sky. The wall was still there, if it was a wall. And where the wall met the water, a boat, if it was a boat.

Someone shuffled by on the corridor. From the distance came a clatter of dishes. "I'll will you all my worldly goods, Malachy, if you'll just say a few words. Or better yet, sing an old song." He scratched his groin. He could stand himself no longer, reached for the mobile.

"I need to urinate." He knew Nurse Starski was on duty.

"Good morning, Ronan," she said affably. "You know how to urinate. Or shall I walk you through it step by step?"

"If you would, please." But she had cut him off. He eased himself out of bed, sat for a minute to check aches and pains. He had only one crutch, which he used under the right or left arm depending on the spur of the moment. The television set was still asleep on the wall. The wardrobe had a mirror attached, in which he refused to look at the remaining tatters of his ego. Malachy's side of the room was crowded with plastic tubes and medical instruments. There was a cheap print of a clamp of turf by Paul Henry on one green wall and a calendar on another. It was a hard room to love. He phoned Starski: "The senior occupant of 244 is moving out. Malachy wishes to be excused."

"Leave me alone, Ronan," Starski said.

In the dining room, Benny and Sara were already eating their bran flakes.

"You're late," Sara said. She had lost her dentures years ago and no one ever thought of replacing them. She was in love with Ronan and told him so whenever she could pry him loose from Benny, who in turn was in love with Sara. The three of them stuck together, Benny said, because they were the only intellectuals left in the nursing home.

"The sun came up again," Ronan announced as he attacked his porridge.

"It's tireless, that sun," Benny said. "That's several times this week."

"You're looking debonair, Ronan," Sara said, "you must have slept a sight." She had spilled the milk and it dripped from the table into her lap.

Meanwhile, other residents were wheeled into the dining room. The walls were green like the bedrooms and kissed in places by the sun. The toast arrived. One girl brought coffee and another tea. Life seemed ordinary, Ronan thought, yet every time the sun showed up it instigated enough intrigue to drive the world out of its mind. He pulled out the mobile and dialed expertly with his thumb.

"This is Ronan O'Day – don't hang up. I need to go to confession…"

"What did he say?" Benny wanted to know.

"He didn't say anything, he just hung up."

"By the hokey," Benny's laugh sounded like a hiccup. "If I was you I'd report him to the bishop."

"It's no use. The bishop is running out of clergy and the few who are left have forgotten how to hear confessions."

"Sure don't I know. I never bother myself."

"You're looking debonair, Ronan," Sara returned to her theme.

"Did I ever tell you about Pascal's Wager?" Ronan asked.

"Tell it, Ronan," Sara coaxed.

"Just between ourselves, Pascal's Wager is why I need confession."

"Go on," Benny encouraged.

"Do you believe in God, Benny?"

"Well sure I do."

"And have you proof?"

"I don't need any – I got along grand without proof until now."

"A God that might send you to hell?"

"Oh I'm going to hell for sure," Sara said with enthusiasm.

"Blaise Pascal," Ronan held up the cup for more coffee, dumped an extra spoonful of sugar into it, feeling expansive, an intellectual among intellectuals. A world of nostalgia drifted up from his days at university when athletic young men and mysterious girls solved ancient enigmas in cafés down Dublin's side streets on evenings that had no end. "Blaise Pascal was a philosopher, you see."

"Ah, go on," Sara said.

"One can't be sure God exists: that's where Pascal came into the picture. Aquinas' five proofs, Anselm's ontological argument, when it comes to real life these are only old wives' tales." He lit a cigarette. "Here's the crux of it. God either exists or doesn't exist. If the chances are fifty-fifty, you might be tempted to take a sporting chance and live the risky life. But you'd be on thin ice. Because, if you backed the wrong horse, hell might be waiting on the other side."

"You're a genius, Ronan," Sara's head was lolling, her eyelids drooping.

"So if one met God over yonder, with heaven in his right hand and hell in the left, a long-lasting hell full of burning and regretting, one could, to say the least, be in a fix."

"So long as there's a toilet there, I won't mind," Benny said and shuffled off.

"But if one has wagered on God's majestic existence," Ronan focused his full attention on the sleeping Sara, "then one can face the future with equanimity. If, at the heel of the hunt, we find no one there, we won't have lost anything. We'll just have darkness, which, under the circumstances, won't bother us. But if God is indeed among those present, why, we'll be glad we bet on a winner."

Sara opened one eye and smiled.

"But there's a catch, Sara, old doll. If we bet on God, we have to stick with the straight and narrow. Don't bear false witness. Put money in the poor box. Go to confession when lust raises its head or we want to kill a neighbour."

Several crows were perched in the trees beyond the window, sullen and watching. They knew a lot from observing people. Certain crows were said to live ten thousand years and Ronan thought these might be worth listening to. Later, maybe. He removed the mobile from his pocket and put the robe around Sara's sleeping shoulders.

Back in room 244, it took an hour to dress. "It's not us, Malachy, it's time that has shrunk since we were young." He dialled again. "Is that Riverside Radio? ... This is Ronan O'Day – don't hang up…Am I on the air?…The priest refuses to hear my confession.…" But Riverside Radio did not want to know.

The carers had changed Malachy's sheets and topped up the liquid in his plastic pouch. Short of a miracle, he would never eat another fried egg.

"Hold the fort, old friend." Ronan took two extra pills for the pain. He slipped out the side door. When the sun came up from behind a gable, his pale shadow hobbled ahead of him down the hill. All he could see was a dab of colour in the distance. The only excuse to call it a boat was its proximity to the river. That, and a belief in destiny. The bladder was a problem, unpredictable and impatient. When he reached the hedge, he peed with satisfaction on the safe side of the laurels.

A moment came when the coloured object was unmistakably a boat. That still left unanswered questions. Was she seaworthy? Were there oars? Still, one had to take some risks in life.

"It's a boat alright," he announced at teatime. "You know the routine," he said to Benny when Sara fell asleep. Benny grinned until his face bulged, and saluted in silence.

Back in his room, Ronan phoned again. "I need confession," he said without preamble. The lonely purr of the phone told him the priest had hung up. "Did you hear that?" Ronan said to Malachy. "You'll have to do."

He turned the bedside light low, lay on his back on the bed.

"It's sixty years, more or less, since my last confession." He lit a cigarette, placed the ash tray on his belly, blew slow smoke at the ceiling.

"If it's all right with you we'll skip the preliminaries and go straight to the meat and potatoes." He glanced at Malachy, who raised no objection. "There was a girl – that's the part I want to get at. When I was at the university. We were all young and foolish, what can I say, but in fairness we were also planning to save the world. Debating about Plato and Nietzsche and Moses and the pope, drinking and showing off.

"There was one girl, as I say." How explicit would he need to be? A real priest would probe for the telling details. "When word spread that she was pregnant, Nietzsche proved to be of little help. There were no potential fathers rushing forward to claim their prerogatives. And there was no wronged, high-cheeked girl to point the finger. She had disappeared. It was easy to disappear because none of us looked very far. The summer exams were approaching. We had futures to think about. We hid behind our books until the storm blew over. Not a storm, either: she could have created one, but only a gentle breeze blew through the space she had occupied in our lives. Rumour spread that she was working with nuns in a laundry in the south. No one accused anyone of hardheartedness, much less of fathering the baby. If there ever was a baby. One morning, it was as if none of us had ever met her, or each other. On one ordinary day we became strangers created by this disappeared girl. We walked past each other in silence taking short cuts to the rest of our lives.

"After the exams I would search for her, I vowed. I would rescue her from that laundry. I would cherish her and marry her just as soon as I got my life in order. If there were a child I would be her father, or his father, even if she didn't look a bit like me. Then one thing led to another, and I started teaching, and I never got my life sufficiently in order to go and find her. I was waiting to have a bit of money, a better job. Above all I was waiting for the backbone to claim a daughter or son already two years old and then three, then ten or twenty. Every year the undertaking grew more formidable. I steered clear of marriage, because I would be forced to search first for the other woman.

In the end I felt we were married, wherever she was. An unwritten contract bound us together. I was convinced she had not married either. We were both waiting for the right moment when our lives would finally be in order."

He threw a glance at Malachy and waited. He didn't expect the usual absolution – that came from a higher authority. But this would be a good time for a few words. Malachy, however, held his peace.

"I'll say one Our Father and ten Hail Marys, so," Ronan said. "That should cover it." He prayed them silently, meticulously, the way the cautious Pascal would have done. Beyond the window, half a moon was leaning over. It would be throwing light on the boat. Ronan put on the topcoat and tightened the belt buckle. He put on the woollen cap and scarf. He put his wallet in one pocket and mobile in the other, picked up the flash lamp, and carried the crutch under his arm; that way it would make less noise.

"Thanks for everything, old pal," he tweaked Malachy's toe.

He knocked discreetly on Benny's door. Benny wore a large puffy jacket like a tent, and an orange scarf across his lower face like a bandit.

"It's very mysterious, Ronan," Benny said as they stumbled and slithered down the hill.

"There's a woman lives on the other side." He had to tell Benny something.

"Aren't you the sly devil."

"But keep it quiet, Benny, or Starski will come after us." They stopped to pee behind the laurel hedge, then they pushed on. She might be on the other side – it was a mighty big world over there. If she ever existed. That would have been the year he was twenty-two. But he couldn't remember being twenty-two.

"Do you remember 1942, Benny?"

"Can't say I do."

"Me neither." Ronan felt relieved. That year had never happened. Sometime he'd search for old calendars or newspapers just to make sure.

"Slow down," Benny said, falling behind.

On the other hand, there was, according to some, the golden book. What mattered was whether the recording angel remembered the year in question. Pascal's Wager was more than an intellectual exercise. To be quite frank about it, a man with an immortal soul needed to cover his arse.

He looked back at Benny sitting on a stone.

"Take this, Benny," he handed over the flash lamp. "If you go back now, you'll be in time for the bran flakes."

"Goodbye so, Ronan." Benny's soul had a shorter wing span. They shook hands solemnly.

The moon pointed a finger at the boat. The boat tensed and held together. Ronan unwrapped the chain from around a stone. He shook off old age and infirmity and gave her a push, then a pull, up to his ankles in the dirty water. She moved reluctantly at first, then readily enough, went with him, until it seemed she was pulling him along. There was an oar, and then another, stretched patiently across two seats. Only then did he realize that the boat had been waiting there, year after year, for some codger from the nursing home to grab the bull by the horns and give destiny a last chance. He threw his leg over the side as once he did on summer days. Pushed with the oar in the rushes. Settled himself on the cold seat. Eased the boat out into the dark water where the silver half-moon danced. And headed for the future.

Up in the nursing home, a few lights had refused to go out. He pulled out the mobile.

"Starski? There you are."

"I'll kill you, Ronan," she was affable as ever.

"Benny is safe and sitting on a rock. He'll be home in time for breakfast."

Before she could respond, he threw the mobile in the water.

2. The Mare's Tail

The early sun galloped across fields dodging clouds. Crows prated from telephone wires to others in nearby trees. An old man in a torn topcoat squinted at the day from under a bridge, picked up his stolen radio and hazel stick, and shuffled on into the future. The narrow road dipped and rose until it got lost in the landscape. It still has its moments, he said to himself, the world has, but I'd give a year of it for strong coffee, and two more years for a handful of painkillers.

A tractor came grumbling behind him. He stepped in front and threatened it with the stick until it lurched to a stop.

"That's a grand morning now."

"Out of the way or I'll run you over," the voice was invisible behind a reflecting windscreen.

"You'd be doing me a favour."

The farmer, not wanting to do him any favours, kicked open the cab door. Then began the ordeal of climbing aboard. The farmer, a burly man with a stubble, used several four-letter words and that seemed to help.

"My name is Ronan," the old man said. "I see you have no passenger seat."

"I don't carry passengers. I run them over."

"This is an adventure," Ronan refused to be insulted. "Do you remember that Chinese who defied the tanks in Tiananmen Square?" Silence from the farmer now rattling along at several miles an hour. "The tank tried to squirm this way and that," Ronan illustrated with sinewy movements of the wrist, "but that little Chinese stood his ground, it was a comical sight."

"You're a comical sight yourself," the farmer was not amused.

"They shot him, I heard later."

A thoughtful silence ensued for a mile or two. Because it was spring, leaves were coming to life on trees. Domestic smoke drifted across the road. The tractor stopped without warning.

"Off you go now."

"Just when we were getting to know one another," Ronan said.

"That's my field, the one with the cattle," and he pointed at an empty field.

"I'm told there's a pub."

"You can't miss it."

"That'll be the Mare's Tail, then."

Life was knee-deep in vicissitudes. He should have stayed in the nursing home until the world got on its feet. Starski would have painkillers. He and Benny could observe the river, keep an eye on the boat, life was in no hurry. Ronan bent into the hill, then straightened his big, gaunt frame to descend on the other side.

Eventually a sign signalled a bigger road ahead. A lark and several other birds started to sing. Sometimes, through a crack in reality, optimism stole in. When the pangs of hunger banished all his other pains, he considered this a net gain. A car came along, pristine and friendly, rolling to a stop. The delightful angel agreed the Mare's Tail was in her direction. At first she didn't seem to notice that Ronan smelled like a man who had dirtied his trousers.

"It's beautiful country," he said. "The hills and that."

"You must be a stranger?"

"We're all strangers." He decided she was little more than twenty. Probably a student, with all that this implied, from the humanities to fornication to saving the world. "Is it a woman owns the Mare's Tail?"

"Why do you ask?"

"It's a long story." He longed to open the can of worms. Confession might peel away the regrets and there might be a new man underneath.

"So where did you get the radio?" It sounded like an accusation.

"I stole it," he grinned with a mixture of innocence and defiance. People were unaccustomed to honesty. "I suppose you bought the car?"

"I did." She opened the window to let fresh air in. Silence followed. There was no use blabbering. Real talk took time. "Here we are," she said as the country pub came into view around a bend.

"You could let me off here," he urged before they reached it. "I want to surprise her," he explained lamely. The girl drove away without a goodbye, leaving the impression he had disappointed her.

The countryside was quiet. The sleepy public house was painted yellow, "The Mare's Tail" in smoke-blue letters high above the door. In the gravel parking lot a car and an old tractor waited side by side. He sat on a stone wall. There was a door to the pub and another to the attached dwelling. If she looked out she could see him from any window. It depressed him to think of the sight she would see. For two hours he waited, giving the day time. He went behind a tree and relieved himself, then sat again. If something didn't happen, he would die of hunger or pain – he could no longer distinguish between them. He squared his shoulders, sucked in his stomach, marched forward with as much dignity as he could spare.

In the gloom inside he saw the high counter, tables and chairs, faded pictures on the walls. Dim lights shone on bottles full of false hopes. He placed the radio on a table, took the stick with him to the counter and tapped.

The old woman came through a door. Her face was long and so was her neck that held the head aloft like an inquisitive swan. The hair was grey and wispy. She wore a frilly apron over her long dress. Her inquiring face silently asked what Ronan wanted.

"A pint, please." He had often wondered what this moment, if it was really the moment he thought it was, would be like. Once he had visions of them running to each other with outstretched arms. Twenty years passed and the mighty embrace lost its exuberance. Forty or fifty years and they would surely be strangers. So he went for pity: "A pint for a starving stranger."

"In that case you'd be better off eating."

"I'll start with the pint, if you don't mind."

She gazed a second too long. Sure I'm paranoid, he thought, but I bet she smells me. She stacked the pint with white foam.

"There's only one thing," he said then. "I have no money."

"You could have told me before."

"And what would you have done?"

"The toilet is down there," she pointed at the sign.

"I'm very grateful." He took the porter to a table in the shadows. He fought against swallowing the whole thing at once. After a tentative sip he went to the toilet. As he did his business he worried about the unprotected pint in the bar. There was washing and cleaning to be done, he needed time to dry. He touched walls and furniture, presumably Kate's walls. The unfinished pint waited, sullen in the gloom. The dregs entitled him to sit on.

"I suppose you wouldn't have a couple of pills?"

"What sort of pills?"

"Something for cancer."

She retreated without a word and came back with three white pills. He prayed God for another pint to wash them down, but all God granted was a glass of water.

"Thanks now." She had carried them in her hand, the pills, they had touched her.

A short bandy man darkened the door. He turned out to be a plumber on his way to buy a plastic pipe. He bought Ronan a pint. They agreed about the weather.

"It's a dandy part of the country," Ronan flattered him.

"It is for a fact."

Ronan said the local countryside was the equal of fabled landscapes from Flanders to Greece. The man's pint was disappearing fast. "I find myself in an embarrassing position," Ronan opted for a diversionary tactic. "At my age dementia is never far away. In short, I forget things. In this case my wallet. So I am, for the moment, out of the customary wherewithal."

"No money, is it?"

"Only momentarily. I'm expecting a certain old friend to put things right."

"Don't mention it. We'll have one more round before I get that plastic pipe."

"I'd love to oblige you," Ronan looked contrite again, "but I had another memory lapse and forgot my breakfast. Now my belly thinks my throat is cut, and good porter can ruin an empty stomach."

"You're a terrible man," the plumber was delighted to have someone to rescue.

"If I had one of those sandwiches from that glass case that goes round and round torturing me."

"We'll have one apiece," the plumber was enthusiastic.

"If you insist, make mine the ham."

It took two further pints each to dispose of the sandwiches. The world began to brighten. Kate's pills had performed a miracle.

"That Kate is a remarkable woman."

"Ah now, she's nobody's fool." It seemed like some vague warning.

"Did she marry into the place, or what?"

"No begod, as far as I know she never married. She paid a small fortune for the pub and the farm across the road."

"Are you telling me she owns land?"

"Sure, hasn't she her own bull." The words came floating full of new facts and implications. Ever since the epic Brown Bull of Cooley, a bull of your own was of monumental importance in rural Ireland. "She still drives the tractor." And other information like that. The plumber loved to talk. He forgot entirely about the plastic pipe when a couple of other locals joined in.

A freckled barmaid appeared. The plumber introduced Ronan to every newcomer: "He's a gas man. He forgot his breakfast, but that's nothing: didn't he forget his wallet as well." The neighbours couldn't help liking a man who would forget his own breakfast.

"Did you ever hear of Occam's Razor?" Ronan asked as he helped himself to a farmer's cigarettes. The faces around the table looked suitably blank. He took extra time lighting the cigarette, building suspense. For an interval he was young again in other, grander emporia when great minds waited for him to pronounce on life's secrets. "William of Occam was a philosopher, you see. He espoused the view that entities should not be multiplied unnecessarily. I know, I know, it sounds obtuse until you sort it out. In short, the simple solution should be preferred to the more complex one."

"Sure that's only common sense," a man said.

"Sure, don't I know," Ronan released languid smoke. "People are searching on the moon for answers that are under their noses." The bar was now full and loud. "Do you see what I mean?"

They didn't say they didn't. "Life is hard enough," he said then with surprising compassion, "don't make it harder than you have to." The silence that followed was full of respect. This deference made Ronan ashamed. Occam was an old fart long dead and his razor not worth a damn. Ronan told them about once being a teacher. He mentioned places like Samarkand and Fresno, California, places he had never been. He told them he was working on a codicil to Occam's Razor, codicil was the word he used, while the locals looked at him and each other in awe. The addendum was to the effect that sometimes it was a virtue to complicate the bejasus out of things. He felt their esteem and loved them for it. He had happened upon these good people in his search for the woman who was turning out to be Kate. Planned life was seldom as gratifying as its surprises.

While the barmaid dispensed happiness in glasses of various sizes, the din was interrupted by the strum of a guitar. A big man with a singing mouth, one foot resting on a three-legged stool, broke into song:

'As I went walking down Broadway, not intending to stay very long,
I met with a frolicksome damsel, as she came tripping along.
Her eyes they shone like diamonds, you'd swear she was queen of the land,
With her hair thrown over her shoulder, tied up with a black velvet band.'

The singer's yellow teeth appeared and disappeared within the large cavern of his mouth. There was no link between being handsome and being melodious. Behind the yellow teeth the voice box worked away in obscurity and sent great songs out into the world:

Seven long years' deportation, right down to Van Dieman's Land,
far away from my friends and companions, betrayed by the black velvet band.

Ronan assumed this marked the beginning of a night of singing, but the singer restored the guitar to its battered case.

"Kate never allows more than one song," the plumber explained. "That one was for yourself, I'd say, you being a stranger." This gave Ronan a further warm glow. He nodded off, his head on the table, and no one disturbed him. When he awoke the crowd had thinned. The plumber put a whiskey in front of him. Soon everyone was gone. Kate hovered behind the counter.

"It's closing time."

"I have no place to go."

"One night," she said. She produced a blanket out of nowhere. "I see from your bald head you had chemotherapy."

"I'm better now except for the pain."

"This is not a pharmacy," she said sternly and handed him two more pills. "You can sleep on the bench as long as you make no noise."

"I'm much obliged," he said after her retreating figure.

He stretched out on the floor. There might be no love left, yet he was fascinated, the way people are fascinated by new babies just arrived from the unknown, or mourners mesmerized by a warm body whose soul has already moved on ahead. It was impossible not to be curious about the till. There was no change in it, only a fifty. This was no accident. She had left it for him, no other explanation made sense. Very well, he would humour her. He returned to the blanket and slept like a baby.

Magpies in the field declared a new day. The pills had stopped working. Kate was making small noises next door. In a perfect world he would sweep her off her feet. He would never again be debonair the way he was at twenty, but there was another style of debonair for when you reached eighty. She brought a mug of tea and a scone on a plastic tray.

"You'll have to leave as soon as you finish that."

"Do you know me?"

"Whatever is on your mind, out with it." She was surely his age but he hoped her memory had weathered the years.

"At the university. Were you not there?"

"I was."

"And going to pubs like the rest of us? And, if I may say so, wild? Do you remember that?"

"If it's any consolation, I don't remember you either."

"Still and all, we were there." Now she sat down in the chair opposite him. "If you are who I think you are, we spent nights – I don't know – of bliss, I suppose."

"You're mistaking me for someone else."

"I heard there was a child."

"That's none of your business."

"So whose was it?"

"Mine. No one else's."

"We heard you worked in a laundry."

"I was put to work with a farmer." She went and poured tea in a tall mug. She cupped the mug in frail hands but drank none of it. "The boy was taken away."

"They had no right."

"That was de Valera's Ireland."

"You were not cut out for farming."

"I worked like a man. But at night I was still a woman. I slept in an attic with a pitchfork beside the bed. It went on like that for years. I'd see him watching me, an old bachelor with no one belonging to him. I was a prisoner, no one belonging to me, either. A time came when he started being nice to me. That was worse. One night he slipped a brown envelope under the attic door. Handing over the farm. You might find this hard to believe, but shortly after that he died."

"Good riddance, I'd say."

"He was stuck with a pitchfork."

"You killed him?"

"If I did, do you think I'd admit it?"

"And did they find the killer?"

"They never did."

"And you had the farm?"

"I sold it and bought this place, pub and farm." The morning traffic grew louder outside. "I always knew someone would show up. Eventually I forgot the names, and the faces were growing old anyway, it no longer mattered what they looked like."

"I was busy getting life in order before looking for you. When there would be enough money. The truth is, I lacked the courage."

"Do you remember Camus?" She didn't wait for an answer. "In the daytime, Camus said, birds fly about aimlessly. But in the evening they find a destination. They fly towards something. And the same with people."

"It's you all right." Ideas clung to the world and every so often got spoken. The mind was dragged back to rowdy Dublin long ago where callow youths swaggered and swapped theories about short cuts to happiness. Camus would occasionally be mentioned, along with Nietzsche or Unamuno if someone wanted to show off. "And the child?"

"He's called Scobie."

"It's an odd name."

"We're strangers. He is said to be very successful."

"There's a thing now called DNA," Ronan said. "We could prove it one way or the other."

"Take my advice and go home." She put down the mug of cold tea. "He says he'll kill the father if he ever finds him."

"Don't drive me away."

"I won't. You must go of your own accord." She went and opened the front door. A runty dog walked in from the sunshine, sniffed and left. People had gone to the moon since they were last together, wars were fought, billions of lives lived.

"I hear you have a bull."

"I have."

"That's the biggest surprise. You on a tractor and a bull in the field. Will I not see you again?"

"Not unless you're my son's father."

He arose stiffly from the table. She stood aside to let him pass. His silhouette filled the door on the way out. It did not look back.

3. The DNA Test

A pale, begrudging sun looked down on Dublin. No longer the easygoing city of his youth, Ronan observed; it had filled with people. A high percentage of these seemed demented, especially the motorists. He roamed until hunger insisted, then stole bananas. Behind the glitter he could smell disappointment. He had read about the tiger, frolicsome but festering, giving prosperity a bad name. The luminaries of his youth had been replaced by bandits. History was full of similar lapses and dark ages, but the analogue, yes that was the word, was Dante's Inferno, or somewhere in that region.

A battered medical card saw him through the front door of the nearest hospital. There was no bed, naturally, so he slept on a stretcher. He told anyone he could buttonhole that his cancer was grand except for the pain. He looked large and healthy until one came closer and noticed the gaunt visage and haunted eyes of an eighty-year-old winding down. After a good sleep he discreetly collected the pain pills of those patients who had neglected to take their medicine.

He escaped from the hospital after two early breakfasts, his own and that of a sleeping woman on the next trolley. And came at evening, with the help of information obtained from social workers, to a lavish house in the suburbs. It was painted pink, with touches of black around doors and windows, frightfully dramatic. It was surrounded by trees and exotic grasses that, aesthetics apart, offered Ronan cover to skulk and reconnoitre. He has done well, Ronan told himself, my boy has. That is, if he is my boy. Such an outlandish house makes sense only in the case of a wife. That usually means children. I may be a grandfather over and over.

How to approach the pink fortress was food for thought. A schoolmaster all his life, he had, since escaping the nursing home, acquired the habit of talking to himself. This was more monologue than dialogue: the wise and witty boulevardier of other days advising and admonishing the derelict he had become. In these debates as in real life he had a preference for the big picture: Hannibal crossing the Alps; someone else crossing the Delaware. The pink house, though, called for a more nuanced approach. He could never play the common tramp. He would rather die with dignity than grovel to his own son, if it was his son. But neither could he act as if he owned the place, because reality was still a factor.

Wearing a stained, white suit, he hid his belongings, stored in two plastic bags, behind a honeysuckle bush. He then walked, head high, aiming directly at the front door, scanning each window for spies. The doorbell rang cheerfully as if to greet him. Yet nobody responded. They're out making a difference in the world, he concluded, what else could it be? Then he did what any potential father would be tempted to do: he surveyed the scene. Elegance vied with decadence as he peered through the kitchen window, then the dining room window, then a window near which sat a woman whose surprise and then alarm were followed by a speedy dash through the back door with a poker in her hand.

"Who are you?" Circumstances made the otherwise reasonable question sound like a challenge. She was dressed in black as if she might be a widow, but adorned all over with precious brooches and bangles. She's somewhere between thirty and eighty, Ronan decided. She surely holds some record for facelifts.

"So sorry." The more one needed the *mot juste* in a hurry, the harder it was to find, like hunting for famous last words with time running out.

"Would you prefer to run like the dickens with my dog after you, or wait while I call the gendarmes?" She pronounced *gendarmes* with the proper panache, still holding the poker in the ready position.

"You'll change your mind when I tell you who I am," Ronan held up his chilblained hands in surrender.

"Out of here!"

"I'm your father-in-law. There, you panicked me into saying it."

She produced a mobile phone and pressed several buttons. It was not the best time, Ronan was sure, to discuss whether one had, accidentally or otherwise, offspring, and with whom. In his carefree youth he had wooed a certain Kate. As had others. When rumours of a baby boy spread, Ronan looked the other way. He had, he now conceded, lived a life without backbone. He would die in peace if he could get his backbone back.

So he lurked among the shrubs. He watched a big car come sailing in and a shadow enter the palatial house. Under cover of darkness he visited the scullery and helped himself to cake and a bottle of milk. He tried the garage door and it opened as if he owned it. He slept soundly on the back seat of a vehicle that turned out to be a Bentley.

He was awakened by a man with an iron object he decided was a crowbar.

For most of his life, Ronan, quite unreasonably, had regarded his offspring, if he had any, as a baby. Because of the way things worked out he never got used to the idea of the baby, in this case a boy, gradually growing up and becoming a man. The latter procedure usually took place in the bosom of a family. Ronan knew the mathematics of the thing, but a child one has never seen remains a child unless the imagination takes wing, and this Ronan's imagination had failed to do. His child would be pushing sixty now, about the same age as the man with the crowbar.

"Scobie, is it?"

"No, you go first," the other insisted in a severe tone.

"Ronan," Ronan said. If one could pick a son, his racing mind ran, this would not necessarily be the one. Narrow at the shoulders, it was obvious the orphanage had failed to feed him. A walrus moustache was fine but it required a certain face, not suspicious like this but exuding joviality. Yet there was an elusive whiff of class about him. A gold chain, presumably attached to a gold watch, stretched tellingly across his waistcoat. The newcomer reminded Ronan of some American president of the old school. Presidential timbre was a good foundation to build on. It might even explain the young man's financial success as earlier described, however vaguely, by his mother Kate. "That implement there," Ronan nodded in the direction of the iron bar, "is making me nervous."

"You're trespassing," the other seemed pleased, like a cat with a new mouse.

"And while you're at it, would there be any chance of a glass of water?"

At this precise moment the woman arrived, dressed in yellow and a glossy handbag slung over her shoulder.

"I thought we had seen the last of you," she said in a surprisingly friendly voice.

"Didn't I tell you – I'm the *paterfamilias*."

"Could you get him a glass of water," the man said. "A plastic cup will do," he shouted after her.

"Yes, a plastic cup will be fine." Ronan could discern no shiver of recognition, no paternal quickening of the multiple systems that comprise the human condition. They stared at one another like boxers before a fight. The water arrived in a glass tumbler.

"He's just leaving," the man said, and left.

No such thing, his recovering backbone whispered to Ronan.

"Are you not surprised to see me?" he asked the pair when they returned in the evening. He was sitting on the top step in front of the hall door adjacent to a fountain showering a buxom stone goddess amid lilies.

"You'd better come inside while we sort you out." Ronan was struck by the offspring's insouciance. Civilization had tried since prehistory to make the family a success. Kith and kin made people who they were. Now this generation was acting as if it didn't matter how people got born. "Won't you stay the night?"

"This must cost a sight of money," Ronan suggested after Scobie poured him a large whiskey in the two-storey living room adorned with paintings by le Brocquy and Vallely. "Any harm asking what you're so successful at?"

"Automobiles," Scobie said with pride. "I deal in luxury automobiles. You won't find Fords and Volkswagens in my showrooms. But if you're looking for Jaguars or Bentleys you come to me."

"Luxury, is it?" He was disappointed. He had hoped his son, if any, would make a more distinguished contribution to the human project: a brain surgeon, maybe; or a diplomat making inroads at the United Nations.

Myrtle, for that was her name, thumbed the mobile and soon food arrived steaming from the caterers, soup to cheesecake, and wine to wash it down. Ronan spiced the conversation with yarns about the hunchback of Notre Dame and Kierkegaard the Dane who obsessed over famous last words and wrote his own in advance lest he be taken by surprise. This bored his hosts, Ronan noticed. Their lives were consumed, obviously, by more urgent pursuits such as Rolls Royce gearboxes and questionable tax dodges, with an occasional weekend in Paris to visit the Mona Lisa.

Yet the tall talk, amid brandy and blue smoke, transported Ronan back to early Dublin when spectacled lads and languid maidens debated good and evil and the drawbacks of Purgatory, nights that generally culminated in sins of the flesh. One such night, if the hypothesis held water, gave rise to the young Scobie.

The world was more idealistic then, Ronan was saying, it had a spring in its step.

"What about my mother?" Scobie interrupted.

"Oh that. It was so long ago."

"And you put her, you say, in the family way?"

"It's a long story." On the one hand, one didn't wish to admit one had, long ago, taken liberties with one's son's mother. On the other hand, that was precisely what one needed to have done to lay claim to kinship. "Your mother, Scobie, was a beautiful woman. She still is. I searched the world for her and found her a month ago."

"I'll be off to bed," Myrtle gave Scobie a peck on the cheek. "I keep telling you, dear, not to bring home every derelict you find." She gave Ronan a withering stare. "Scobie is easily taken in by imposters like yourself." She ascended the circular staircase with hauteur like the star of an old film.

"They have a thing now called DNA," Ronan said to Scobie. "I'm told it could be used to resolve this little matter that has arisen."

Scobie added whiskey to his full glass, and a little to Ronan's. If one gave him the benefit of the doubt there was something presidential there. One of the Roosevelts, most likely, the one with a waistcoat. It was disconcerting to hear Myrtle mention other vagabonds when one wanted to be Scobie's only vagabond. The DNA was vital.

"She gave me away."

"She had no option." Ronan told of the old days when the self-righteous gave hell to everyone else. He told of Kate working for a farmer who eventually came to grief at the receiving end of a pitchfork. He waxed lyrical about Scobie's mother protecting her virtue with the same or a similar pitchfork, how she inherited the farmer's farm and bought the Mare's Tail, a pub where, even at her age, she still sat tall on a tractor and was the owner of a bull on account of which she was held in awe by neighbours who remembered the fight Queen Maeve fought for the Brown Bull of Cooley.

"Was she a loose woman or what?"

"Oh no, not loose, I wouldn't say loose."

"Yet, saving your presence, we don't seem to know who my father is. Does that not sound on the loose side?"

"We were to be married," Ronan lied.

"Did my mother know this?"

"Not right away. I was biding my time. Organizing the road ahead. Including provision for yourself if you should come along – though there was no news of you up to that time." The whiskey was great for clearing up loose ends. "Ireland was still a new country. We had plans to make everyone happy, that was a priority. It's just that we ran out of time for the details."

"Because I came along?"

"There were rumours. But Kate had disappeared." Ronan's old mouth puckered. He rubbed his watery red eyes with fat hands. Scobie produced a red handkerchief and Ronan wiped away some salty tears. The fire had burned low. The pain, which moved about his body and never knew where to settle, was calling for help. He pulled out pills wrapped in a serviette. "A drop of water would be a relief. A plastic cup will do."

"It's bedtime," Scobie came back with the water. Ronan didn't know enough about fathers and sons to be sure of proper procedure. He hoped Scobie wouldn't go into a frenzy of hugging and sobbing, not with that funny moustache.

"I ordered one of those DNA kits," Scobie announced next morning over an unbelievable breakfast of flapjacks soaked in Aunt Jemima's maple syrup with rashers and black pudding on the side.

"You're wasting your time," caustic Myrtle said. "Anyone can see he's not your father." Then off the couple went to sell automobiles – to drug dealers, Ronan was convinced, who else could afford such luxury?

"So what did she look like?" Scobie asked in the evening after presenting Ronan with bags full of new suits and leather shoes. Scobie, like nearly everyone else, was eager to know how he came to be who he was. Ronan obliged with nostalgic accounts of how Kate dressed, what she said, with whom she tripped the light fantastic, a mixture of cherished memories and new inventions.

"And when Scobie became a bun in the oven you made yourself scarce," Myrtle interrupted. "You cowardly old thing."

"I kept waiting for the right moment. When I would have a secure job. When I would have enough money. But what I was waiting for all along was backbone."

The DNA kit was delivered by a nurse in a limousine who fussed and bullied while she first jabbed Ronan and then Scobie. The analysis would take time, the nurse, who wore dark blue lipstick, said.

"There's no rush," Scobie was a changed man.

"And while you're at it, a few painkillers," Ronan suggested.

"I warned my mother I'd kill the father if I ever found him," Scobie said later.

"If I turn out to be the father, I'll talk you out of it."

"And if there's anything worse than being the father, it's not being the father."

Next day, as they waited for the DNA results, Scobie took the old man to see his emporium, "Scobie's Automobiles" in lights across the front. Underneath, in smaller lettering, were the shocking words: "Previously Owned." His boy, to put it bluntly, was a second-hand car dealer.

Granted, not everyone could be an astronaut or a poet laureate. The vehicles, besides, looked beautiful and shiny. It was all about the human quest. People had lost all regard for average cars with bald tires. Ronan's pain was back. No boy of his could have reached his full potential selling second-hand cars.

"But wouldn't new cars, if you'll pardon the expression, be better?"

"In the blinking of an eye," Scobie grinned with vindication and satisfaction, "a new car becomes a used car. Used cars last longer."

Day after day, the DNA results failed to materialise. Myrtle and Scobie took Ronan to the Abbey Theatre, to a Temple Bar nightspot, to the zoo. Betweentimes, Ronan would talk about the old days, about Pascal's Wager and other conundrums, a cigar between his teeth.

Along came a day when Scobie bundled Ronan into the Bentley and took him to a clinic. In a pine-panelled office the consultant fingered a blue folder and, after mumbling in circles for a while, told Scobie that, on the basis of their mutual DNA, the subject was not the least bit related to the other subject.

"Would one of those subjects be myself?" Ronan made bold to ask.

The consultant looked at Scobie, who nodded that the DNA had let them down.

That evening, in an atmosphere of gloom, Myrtle ordered Chinese. She lit fat candles and the odour of incense moved effortlessly from room to room.

"Tell us one of your yarns," Scobie said when they got to the brandy and cigars. So Ronan told them about the death of Socrates long ago, accompanied by his sidekick Crito, who wanted Socrates to delay his suicide until sundown and not waste the last day of his life. But Socrates wanted to get it over.

The cigar smoke sailed around the room. "That's how Crito became a historical footnote." There was silence and melancholy, Socrates always did that to people. Scobie wondered was there some message for himself, while Ronan silently hated the nurse with blue lipstick for not doing the decent thing and making him his son's father.

"You'll be going tomorrow?" Scobie said then.

"As you say. It's just that Kate asked me to come over and present my DNA for inspection. At the end of the day a family is what we're all looking for."

"Your DNA is fine," Myrtle said in a kindly tone. "It just doesn't belong here." She had a fat ring on every finger, each one, Ronan was sure, a Rolls Royce among rings.

Early in the morning, his plastic bags full of new sweaters, Ronan walked past Scobie's honeysuckle bushes into the drizzle of Dublin.

"If he looks back, we'll adopt him," Scobie said to Myrtle at the front door. "It takes more than DNA to make fathers and sons."

4. Home Is the Sailor

An incipient moon, just a few inches above the horizon, was, Ronan knew, making waves somewhere. There was a star just above it like the dot over an i. Together they were shooing the old day into the past.

The world was still up to snuff, he decided, despite the bad feet. Sure, there was pain, but what would life be without it? Somewhere deep inside, he insisted, there still resided the debonair fellow once aged twenty-six. What had recently been a new suit was already fit for a scarecrow, but it would be a classy scarecrow. When the road ahead became unyielding, he stumbled from side to side slantwise. He dreamed of a horse, even an ass and cart, because motor vehicles had stopped stopping for him. Yet the cacophony galloping around in his head could only be applause, some mighty endorsement, for an intractable wayfarer carrying his saved soul home on his back.

A sign announced the Riverside Nursing Home. Up and knock on the front door, the intractable part of him prompted the rest of him. But first he sat on a stone and took a half-full bottle from his pocket. "I'll drink to myself," he said to himself, "because I'm all I have left."

There followed a bout of introspection, a habit he had cultivated since he was born. Across from him sat loneliness, taciturn and sulking. He eyed the half-empty bottle. Unaccountably it reminded him of David in the Bible. David and who was it? Not Goliath, that was a different disaster. David and Jonathan was who it was. Your man was parched and Jonathan brought him a carafe of water, it surely was a carafe. Then came the curious denouement. David, touched, would not drink the hard-won water. He emptied that old vessel out on the grass in gratitude. More like a slap in the face, Ronan could not help thinking, it made no sense. Making sense, though, was not the bottom line in the good book. Ronan shifted the bottle from one mottled hand to the other. He concentrated on the contents. He withdrew the cork. Moments stretched into minutes while he decided David was up to something mystical, maybe holy, why else would he be remembered for so long for such nonsensical behaviour? If it worked for David it is good enough for me, he said to nobody in particular as he poured the golden stuff out on the grass, gently, so that it did not even gurgle. And said, as an afterthought: I wonder what was in that bottle anyway.

"I'm back," he said at the front door.

"I'll kill you, Ronan," Starski said before hugging him.

"But I won't be staying long."

Radiators radiated heat down long corridors. Residents smiled befuddled smiles, wondering where they had seen the old man before. Dusk surrendered to dark outside. Inside, Malachy's bed was empty.

"Gave up the ghost, did he?" To which Starski nodded in the affirmative.

An efficient carer upped the heat in the shower and washed away the grime and disappointments. There was hot tea. There were sandwiches. A selection of pills. He slept like a baby until he awoke like a baby. And talked to Malachy the rest of the night.

"All I wanted, old buddy, was to have no regrets."

He heard what could only be Malachy talking back. This made sense. When people moved on, they left behind them all sorts of unfinished business.

In Malachy's case this included the things not said. The words were roaming the world in search of a friendly ear.

Dawn brought light as it had always done. Light in turn revealed a tree. On a top branch sat a crow. Some crows were said to live ten thousand years. This, obviously, was one of them.

"Let me tell you, Malachy, there are a whole lot of people out there in the world. They're strangers mostly, and probably fine people in their way. But it's the other few who really count."

Wishful Thinking

"George W. Bush is a liar!"

"George W. Bush is an empty suit!"

Ballinasloe may seem an odd beginning of the end of a U.S. president. That's why anyone who still clings to the old nostrums will have trouble believing what follows.

Brian drives slowly from the Dublin direction. It is not unusual for a young man who normally speeds like the hammers to slow down when he falls in love. This young man is ordinary except that his otherwise shaved head sports a streak of orange hair down the middle. That and his one arm. In a car designed for one-arm drivers. Brian and Alanna are an item.

"A butterfly?" he queries.

"It needn't be a butterfly. It could be a donkey or a chicken, I guess, but they usually say a butterfly." Alanna is from Pennsylvania. She is only twenty, and already a student at Trinity College. She is pretty as the next one, of sallow complexion, with a ring in her nose, and afflicted with stringy hair she pushes back from her face several times a minute.

The day is bright, with sun in the sky, but cold, so that most people are wearing padded coats and colourful scarves.

A sign says Ballinasloe 12.

"Hurry or we'll be late," Alanna says. This is exactly the sort of remark at which a young man will take umbrage; will slow down and show who's in charge. Especially, one supposes, the type with an orange streak on top and a tattoo on the remaining arm. But Brian just hurries as instructed. This being spring, trees are sucking up life from the earth and making new leaves. It is surprising, he thinks; all the energy it takes just to cover one tree with leaves, not to mention whole forests. And that's not counting cowslips, thistles, fields of grass, and whitethorn hedges in the provinces. Most people don't realise how complicated the world is. Brian has been in college for three years. Normally he would graduate in one more year, but because he's doing art, a subject of infinite scope, his schooling may take longer.

"Park here," she says, and he does. Over there, beyond the traffic jam, is Tesco, doing the usual roaring business on a day when business as usual is a bone of contention.

"They'll sell a million cones today," he says as they pass an ice cream place.

"More than that." She has a more complicated perspective: that thing about the butterfly.

"A million and two, then." He produces Euros for two 99s. "Down it fast," he advises, "or global warming will melt it." Down a hill from the gloomy Protestant church they sit on grass and eat ham sandwiches and bananas from a Grafton Street plastic bag.

Loudspeakers can be heard in the distance, voices amplified and already vibrating over airwaves all over the world, Brian thinks, but not stopping there, the voices sailing off on the breeze, out among the spheres, to be picked up with growing interest by little green persons or whoever has the appropriate technology on local galaxies. Here, closer to home, the huge sound is muffled, punctuated by an occasional electronic screech, and cannot yet be deconstructed into words. It doesn't matter here (Brian thinks), it matters out among the galaxies. Here, people are hurrying along, but there is no rush, it is one of those rare days when time slows down or maybe, if we are lucky, stands still.

"So tell me how that other thing works." He stretches out with his head in her lap and looks at the sun with stainless steel sunglasses, while she fingers his ugly tattoo.

"I already told you."

"Tell it again."

"OK," she says with quiet satisfaction. "This meteorologist named Edward Lorenz was searching for a model that would predict weather conditions, something like that. After experimenting with one set of figures, he decided to replicate the process, just to be sure. Only thing is, he took a short cut and didn't enter the exact same number – he just rounded it out after three decimal points, which anyone would think should be close enough, wouldn't you say?"

"Go on."

"He rounded out the number, as I say, and went off. And guess what: when he came back he found the results were dramatically different. He tried it over and over, just to be sure it wasn't a fluke. So he made up a theory, that the slightest difference in initial conditions, even if it's too small for humans to measure, makes predicting future outcomes practically impossible."

He is an artist and she is a scientist, yet their heads are mutually in orbit around each other as the loudspeakers rumble and the numbers grow, disorganized people cheek by jowl bringing traffic to a standstill.

"This is amazing, this crowd."

"No one could have predicted it," she sighs. "If just one more person attended, or one less, the outcome would be up for grabs."

"Go on." He peels a banana and she bites off half. If this nonsense made sense (he thinks), it could cause trouble. It's a good thing it's nonsense.

"It's called chaos theory. You can see why."

"No."

The flapping of a single butterfly's wings in China, she says, or Tibet, she adds, letting imagination add lustre to the data, produces a miniscule change in the atmosphere. The atmosphere then digresses from what it would have done if the butterfly had kept her wings in the folded position. So, in a month's time, or a year, a tornado that otherwise would have wiped out Fort Lauderdale doesn't happen. Or a drought comes to Africa, initiated by a butterfly nobody knows.

"It's also known as sensitive dependence on initial conditions."

"I'll be damned," he says, observing the citizens of Ballinasloe flapping their indefatigable wings. The words from the loudspeakers are clearer now, and urgent. The name of George Bush breaks through periodically. Always with that W in the middle. Which, Brian says, stands for oil, Bush's middle name. Brian thinks irony is one's best chance of survival in a world of empty suits and rings in the human nose. Irony has kept the world from dropping over the edge.

"Just a tiny hiccup in the initial conditions can change what happens later," Alanna persists (while Brian quietly worries about the risks of someday marrying her). "For instance, take the number two point naught, naught, naught, naught one. Everyone thinks that's practically the same as two. But in the real world it can make a huge difference. And, needless to say, in real life you can never find a nice clean two. There will always be background noise, or someone failed to oil the machine, or there is a moron in the chain of command, a Donald Rumsfeld, say, or a Dick Cheney, and eventually the system goes haywire. I need to pee."

Off she goes to the long line of green latrines where half a mile of strangers are already waiting their turn. A woman emerges from one latrine, hesitates, then returns to the back of the line to wait for another go. She has no clue (he thinks) how one flap of some faraway wing could wreak havoc on local bladders.

The word *war* can be heard floating across Ballinasloe. When the ear is cocked other words float in, such as *hypocrisy* and *arrogance*, not to mention *oil*. Everything now depends on what words connect these key words together. Maybe the speakers believe arrogance is a virtue and George W. Bush needs more of it. And maybe that's what the world needs: more oil and more hypocrisy. If it's true about chaos theory, we will have to take a second look at practically everything. Maybe Bush is right to invade countries against whose leaders he has a grudge. If only Iraq had been a perfect two without that extra point naught, naught, naught, naught one caused by the interfering Rumsfeld and, of course, others, the world might now be a better place.

"George Bush is a liar," the refrain of the fired-up people seems to confirm, in a way Brian cannot understand, Alanna's thesis that every wrinkle in the initial scenario eventually comes home to roost. "George Bush is a horse's arse," the people of Ireland, and a few others sprinkled around the crowd like pepper and salt, say to the world. Sure, citizens sometimes get antsy or even go hysterical, but this Bush is a born-again Christian with two lovely daughters and weapons of mass destruction; this chaos theory has its work cut out.

"Let's join the fun," Alanna suggests cheerfully when she returns from the loo.

"We already did." Losing an arm gives one perspective, Brian tells people when he wishes to gain advantage. A car going the other way once pulled his arm off at the shoulder. The lost arm somehow saved his life, a surgeon in search of a silver lining said, so Brian considers himself lucky. He had no interest in art before the accident. If he had, he would have painted, or sculpted, he believes, with the missing arm, an arm that had already learned a trick or two about coping. Instead he started art from scratch with an untrained but eager extremity full of potential.

"I never realized there were so many people in Ireland," Alanna says. They converge from Church Street and Bridge Street, over the ubiquitous River Suck. They converge from Dunlo Street and Society Street, from Brackernagh and Sli na Habhann. "I'd say a hundred thousand."

"You're crazy. More like a million." They gather in St Michael's Square, spilling out in every direction. There are country farmers wearing wellingtons and dandy lawyers in red ties and priests with Roman collars and youths with streaks in their hair like peacocks. There are couples and strung-out families and rowdy gangs and solitary individuals, islands in this great ocean. Those who are alone mean it, Brian reflects. They didn't come for a lark, like me, or for the company. No, not for the company, for the cause, for the cause *and* the company

– perspective is a curse that goes in circles when life is ambiguous.

Brian and Alanna hold hands, sauntering, not forging fiercely forward like some, nor drunk like a few. A mother carries her sleeping baby in her arms while her angular young husband carries a bigger baby strapped to his back. A dog raises his leg against the wheel of a car that already sports a parking ticket. It is now afternoon and some eat apples or chocolate. Nearly everyone has a bottle of water, an indispensable commodity on this dehydrating planet. A puffy cloud turns threatening. The amplification system finally sends clear, strong words from street to street, "weapons of mass destruction … young soldiers killed … innocent people killed." It's an awful lot of killing for an empty suit.

Alanna and Brian sit on his dusty coat on the dusty street while one speaker rehashes the killing ways of George W. Bush. Another analyses Bush's lies and blunders. Compared with killing, lying seems trivial, until the speaker shows how one thing leads to another. A further speaker blames the unacceptable swagger of this lying warmonger, one thing leading to another. Another says it's because he went to Yale where he invented baseball and became a drunk until he found Jesus who told him you'd better give up boozing or that butterfly will kick your ass. A picture is emerging of a world coming unglued while an allegedly illiterate American rains down discontent on the nations.

"That's Sam Maguire," Alanna says when a new speaker steps forward. He is, it turns out, one of her professors. The speakers are politicians and business leaders, a poet or two, a sports star (the high jump), a mother of eleven, a throw-back to a more innocent time before contraceptives or George W. Bush. This is public Ireland, the community of Celts, and others of course, more wealthy and savvy than ever before (Brian thinks), though not as romantic as the saints and scholars long gone, yet better dressed, and no famine, and no Oliver Cromwell slaughtering insurgents.

Not only the community of people but the community of nations, the butterfly whispers to Brian: not only Ballinasloe but Brisbane and Berlin and Birmingham and so on throughout the alphabet. A day came when people everywhere had a bellyfull of George W. Bush's bellicose swagger. Without realizing what they were doing, they gathered together in spirit and brought chaos theory to bear.

There would be no problem if chaos theory were just that, a theory, but any day now it will move over from theory to fact (Brian thinks), especially if Alanna gets her doctorate and has her way.

It's a mystery to everyone how, on a given day, not so long ago, the world felt a *frisson,* as they say in French, a chill, which overnight, more or less, led to a stiffening of the international backbone. Most people couldn't put a name on it, the malaise and the insight that caused them to say, deep within, fuck it, this Bush is going too far. Great country, America, some said, but this Bush is an out and out disaster. So, when activists started airing ideas, people everywhere were primed and nodded their heads, it's about time, their nodding heads said, and they all got together to do something about it, and the rest would soon be history.

"Did you know the biggest horse fair in Ireland takes place here in Ballinasloe?" Alanna asks.

"No, I didn't know." That would be tens of thousands of horses since time began, maybe millions. All that horse manure – it was imperative to keep the matter in perspective. Farmers' horses with wide hooves ideal for plodding, and sinewy animals sold to Russian czars or besieged Greek governments, a shilling here or there determined in which country and in what battle the brave beast would die.

"The Irish love to talk." Alanna is having an enjoyable outing. And so, it seems, are the Irish. "Does it not remind you of the ancient high kings and their *ollamhs* and *fili* and all that, spouting wisdom and eating wild boar and roast peacock in a glade somewhere – doesn't it remind you?"

"Not a bit." She should stick to science and leave the roast peacock to the Irish. The Yanks may have more scientific know-how but we Irish are better at bullshit.

It is getting late, but no one is leaving. They are waiting for Kathy, the star activist and, it turns out, a combination of the *ollamh* and the *file,* telling the galaxies about the Bush Doctrine that cries to high heaven.

"It's a whole new thing," Kathy says. "If a country gets uppity, George W. Bush whacks it with a preemptive strike. Just as he attacked Iraq for the oil, he may come after Ireland for the potatoes. After telling the United Nations we have potatoes hidden underground. No one wants to be bombed back into the stone age by an empty suit."

"So many people talk daily, but only a few need to be heard," Alanna remarks.

"Something must be done." Kathy speaks with authority: whatever she warns against is more dangerous, and whatever she promises more possible, than if others said so. Brian can't prove this, it's just that a few millennia of knocking about in the world have given humans a feel for the genuine article and likewise for frauds. "A preemptive strike," Kathy meanwhile suggests.

But what do the cheering people do now? How does ungainly earth turn talk into destiny? Bush owns the only remaining superpower. He has Air Force One and the Marines and Wall Street and the Grand Canyon and a British pet poodle.

Everyone goes home. Everyone agrees it was a wonderful day despite a cold nip in the air. The streets and grassy slopes are littered with discarded placards and other souvenirs including dog shite.

By the time you read this, George W. Bush will have made his announcement. You may have seen it on television.

Standing in front of a U.S. flag as big as Delaware, he looks older than when he stole the election from the other fellow. His nervous mouth says the words but as always they are written by others.

"I am a liar," he says. "Worse yet, I am an empty suit. I didn't want anybody to die – honest – but I made up a bunch of garbage about that tyrant over there, you know the one I mean. Over in that place. Didn't want any two-bit foreigner stealing a march on the USA, no sir. And darn it, I won, got him dead or alive, or both, with lice in his hair and weapons of mass destruction in his hip pocket, that's right, weapons of mass destruction, ding-dong, shock and awe, yes siree...."

Tall professional persons in white coats lead Bush away.

This may not be exactly how it played on television, because the world's only superpower needs to save face, but deep down this is the gist.

Somewhere in Tibet an overachieving butterfly is taking a well-earned nap on a flower in a field, Alanna thinks. But Brian believes it's a Ballinasloe butterfly.

He fumbles for the cell phone.

"So how have you been?"

"Oh, you know," Alanna responds from America.

On the journey home from Ballinasloe, while the two were tired and hungry, without willing it, they ceased to be an item. While one butterfly was attending to Bush, another flapped a couple of careless wings closer to home and love slipped out the window on a lonely stretch of road outside Kinnegad.

The Child

Observe the child, seven going on eight. At the door, his mother, in a pink robe and her hair wild, kisses him on the cheek. He wipes the kiss away. The blue bike wobbles up the street because he's puny. Not for nothing his mother shouts after him to be careful.

No one knows what will happen next – not even God if what they say is true, because free will can second-guess even God. No one knows, therefore, that the boy, whose name is Sean, on turning left at the top of the street, will be confronted by several bigger boys, bullies in this case, waiting to mess with him.

"Slow down, kid."

Sean will have no option. He will have two stones in his pockets for protection, but he has been here before, he'll know two stones are not enough. So the little blackguards will shove him around. They will ride his bicycle, yelling childish obscenities. When they are already late for school they will let the air out of his tyres, giving the bike a last kick of contempt, and in a moment they'll have forgotten him as they run ahead in search of an education.

Sean won't cry. He'll imagine the stones in his pockets wounding the enemy causing blood and pain. Yet few would predict he will ever grab life by the unmentionables and kill those bullying little bastards. And the little bastards, if they're not exterminated by bigger bullies, may turn out to be life's gentlemen, with maybe a banker or thoughtful poet among them. But that's just guessing.

It is a mystery how we can get our minds around the past but not the future. This is a trick of time. And a further indication that we have only poorly adapted to life in a cosmos where a billion years in any direction are a mere abstraction.

It gets worse. Once upon a time, when civilization was more stable and therefore more predictable, one could guess how this child would turn out. The law of averages and similar paradigms would kick in, with reliable results. Now, in our vastly expanded and turbulent human condition, the old routines have scattered. Unpredictability is more than ever the norm. It takes nerve, therefore, to go beyond guessing and say what will actually happen.

Sean will, in his turn, bully children younger than himself. He will grow more sturdy than one might have expected. One day soon he will be surprised by puberty. This will confuse the hell out of him but will also stretch his horizons. He will experiment with a little moustache and a honey-blond beard. He will twig to the way cause and effect work, until he notices that most causes have multiple effects. Thus life will get all banged about by ambiguities.

"Eat your vegetables," his mother will say, because nature always and ever insists on vegetables. (No, really: one day she will say it if you give her the benefit of the doubt.)

"The foreigners are coming," his father will have one eye on the television. "There won't be any jobs left." (This, too, is a fact.)

"No shit," Sean will say with the mildly foul mouth he will have cultivated. He will mildly despise his father for missing the boat when life handed out the fiercer virtues.

Just as the past is full of holes, lacunae in people's memories, Sean's future can be forgiven for being more so. As, frankly, is everyone's: buffeted by ambivalence, complicated by assumptions and random circumstances. Yet the future, every nook and cranny of it, is as definite as the past and totally obvious when one stands back far enough. Already psychologists and geniuses and crazies are leaping ahead of clocks and calendars, dishing up what is yet to be.

Thus, for example, Sean will, on an unspecified morning, climb upstairs in a Dublin bus and watch the rain trickle down the glass. The bus will pass the General Post Office. He won't spare a thought for the patriots once handing over the Irish Republic to the bewildered people. Being young, that romantic rebellion will be an empty space in his mind. The rain will ease off at just the right moment, as it all too infrequently does. A classmate will appear ahead of him. Sean will quicken his step, sneak up behind and jostle the classmate. The friends will ignore significant world events in favour of drooling over a nubile girl going in the same direction. "Hold me back," the classmate will say, and Sean will be reassured that sex still holds sway on a wet morning. Life will be that normal.

Sean will meet a girlfriend. Neither of them will know until it happens that the relationship won't last because the girl will find another man dreamier than Sean. (Sometimes, as here, knowing the future could ruin the present, which is a different conundrum entirely.) "Please," Sean will say when he finds out, not knowing what he means.

He will appear again a year later at his graduation. There will be another girl as if the earlier one never happened. His mother will be hugging and waving, in charge of happiness, but it will be his quiet father's eyes that go watery with pride.

Much more detail may be conjured up, but who wants to know? One reason gaps occur in the future as well as in the past is people's short attention spans. Few care that Sean's sandy hair will start thinning early. That the unkempt little beard will turn several shades redder than the thin hair on top. That he will turn from football to golf as soon as he gets a job. There will be several small reasons for this unimportant switch, because the simplest lives are complicated, but one definite reason will be that he will never have been good at football.

His life will be frankly so ordinary that most people won't be interested in the details. His immediate circle will have crises of their own to preoccupy them, and Sean won't be rocking his boat or theirs enough to distract them. He will get a job in the transport sector. He will become engaged, get married for a while, get divorced, grieve awhile. He will follow the county football team for old times' sake. Because he and the whole island will be incomprehensibly prosperous, he will buy a new car every few years, each car a little bigger than the previous one.

Batt Jewel will, in the meantime, be living his own life a county or two away. On a particular Sunday, Batt will enter a sprawling pub called Lenehan's in a country town. He will order a lager and survey the scene. Already the Gaelic football will be in full swing – since it got organized there will scarcely be enough weekends for all the games. Several television sets will be busy with talking heads prior to a match between Sligo and Galway. The pub will fill quickly. This will sometimes be called leisure, something the ancestors never saw coming. The football will have evolved from reckless country skirmishes into show business. The television commercials will still be a perversion we will not yet have managed to abolish.

"Haven't we come a long way," Batt will say to a man sitting on the adjacent three-legged stool. "I remember playing in cow shite in the bad old days."

"Is that right?" The other will look and be satisfied that Batt is old enough to have played in the shite as stated.

"I do for sure."

There will be a pause. Batt will raise a forefinger to order another lager. A commercial will coincidentally be singing the praises of porter. Batt will weigh the advantages of prolonging the conversation.

"Are you for Galway?"

"No, the others," the younger man will answer.

"From Sligo, then?"

"No, to be honest."

"No need to explain. It's only football." The two faces will be turned to the television, but Batt will glance occasionally at the other. "I suppose you play a bit yourself?"

"Not any more," the younger man will answer. "I was never much good at it." A big girl will be singing the national anthem, creating a lull, so the young man will add, "I turned to golf instead."

"Did you now?" Batt will be so affable that the other will look at him. He will see a broad chunky man who will look like a farmer, though in the future farmers and entrepreneurs and everyone else will look interchangeable, all looking like television personalities. Batt will have a seasoned oak face and ears spread wide, far from handsome. He will be wearing a big blue suit with square shoulders and an open shirt. A farmer would be wearing a tie, the other will decide. And since everyone will by then be talking with a TV accent, it will be useless to guess where anyone comes from.

"I'm not much use at the golf, either," he will admit to the stranger.

"Ah now, I'd say you're being modest," Batt will say. "Will you drink another?"

"Why not," he will be warming to Batt, who will raise the index finger again as Galway surge into a four point lead. "Isn't that Duggan like lightning?"

"I don't know Duggan at all. By the time I learn their names, they're replaced by other players." The two will lapse into silence. All around, excited fans will yell and pound the heavy wooden tables when a score occurs.

"You'll have another?" the young man will suggest at half time, because buying rounds will still be the custom.

"You talked me into it." Some will go for a piss while others will go outside to smoke before the game resumes. "My name, by the way, is Batt."

"Mine is Sean." Sligo will stage a modest comeback in the second half.

"My great regret," Batt will say in the middle of the Sligo rally, "is that I never made my mark in football."

"The cow shite, maybe? You'd be a star today on that smooth green pitch."

"I won't lie to you, I'd give up years of my life to be able to catch the high ball like that. Or to have the speed. And then, over the bar, right foot, left foot, and the umpire raising the white flag, or now and again a green one. I would for sure."

"I'd have thought of you as a defender," Sean will be thinking of the mighty shoulders and stocky frame. "A right back, maybe?"

"That's where they used to stick me. In the backs. And I knowing well I had a talent. At home in the evenings, out there by myself when no one was looking, I could score from any angle. I'll tell you, Sean – you don't mind if I call you Sean? – I used to wonder how I could be so accurate."

"I know the feeling," Sean will say ambiguously.

Batt will put his mighty hand on Sean's arm as the drinkers trickle away after the game.

"It's not really Sean, is it?"

"Sure, it is," Sean, a little perplexed, will decide not to be offended.

"Don't worry, I'll find out." The eyes will look grey and teary in the burnished face. He will look, for all his girth, like a man easily hurt, a needy man. "It was a pleasure talking to you anyway."

"Same here."

"A pity about Sligo. But I had money on Galway." He will wink like a conspirator. When they stand up he will be several inches shorter than Sean. He will look stiff on his bandy legs shuffling towards the door, a man who could never score points from any awkward angle.

A week later, after roast beef and trifle in a roadside restaurant, Sean will be back in Lenehan's half an hour early to listen to the talking heads. He will not be surprised when Batt comes waddling through the door, exceptionally pleased with himself.

"I suppose it's not taken?" he will say of the stool beside Sean's.

"I held it for you," Sean will lie.

"Sean, isn't it?"

"It still is." The game will be between Armagh and Laois. "So who are you betting on today?"

"Armagh," Batt will say. "They're resourceful lads."

"They play dirty."

"No. Resourceful," he will insist with grim truculence. "You'll have a whiskey?"

"There must be something wrong with me, I don't like whiskey."

"Go on, it won't kill you." When the spirits arrive, the two will raise the chunky glasses and nod to one another. For a while they will watch the match in silence. The Laois players will appear lanky and destructible. The men from the North will seem more hungry and desperate, lads whose uncles or cousins killed or were killed in that hectic generation that Unionists and Nationalists finally played to a draw.

"I suppose you're married, Sean?" Batt will inquire when a player is injured and the world inside Lenehan's pub pauses.

"Not any more." Sean will hesitate about going down that road with a stranger. "That old divorce thing shouldn't be allowed."

"Ah, is that it?"

"I'm not saying it was anyone's fault," he will try to be fair. "What about yourself?"

"Oh, very married," Batt will be enthusiastic. "And two daughters to show for it." A heavy shower will slant across the field in Clones, while outside the sun will shine on Lenehan's. "Do you go to Croke Park at all?"

"Not a lot."

"Maybe some Sunday, we could give it a try?"

"Well, sure," Sean will be surprised. "I'm afraid I forget your name," he will say apologetically.

"Jewel. Batt Jewel." He will be wearing a fat grey sweater with a blue stripe across the belly. He will be hearty, telling Sean he would divorce his wife if he could muster the courage. "I'm waiting for the girls to leave home." Laois will win.

This routine will become a habit. Batt in his grumpy way will invite Sean to Sunday lunch before some match. "It's not far." Odd, Sean will think, because I never told him where I live.

"His nibs told me about you," the wife will say, and Sean will privately doubt it. The dinner will be delicious. The girls will not appear. The three will talk about surprising topics like the Middle East. Batt will be seen to have a sense of humour. Afterwards, they will move to the untidy living room.

"Leave us alone," Batt will say to the wife. Sean will look at him in surprise. "What?" Batt will say. "You're right," he will add. "I shouldn't have said it like that."

"You shouldn't have said it at all."

The little phone will ring in Batt's trouser pocket. "Not now," he will say tersely and slam the gadget shut. "Feck them."

"Aren't they beauties?" he will say of the two daughters another Sunday. One will be a beauty, the other not so much. "Did you ever hear of McBreen's heifer?"

"Never," Sean will refuse to play his cruel game.

"Ah, feck off," Batt will say affectionately, while the short sister will run crying up the stairs.

They're nothing to me, Sean will tell himself driving home; they're strangers. It's not as if he won't have a social life, including an incipient girlfriend. The following weekend he will decide to stay away. He will sleep late, drive a mile to a greasy restaurant that will serve an Irish breakfast around the clock. He will buy two tabloid newspapers full of poorly clad girls. Breakfast over, though, he will feel uneasy and be vaguely relieved when the mobile rings.

"Where are you?" Batt will sound pained.

"Where did you get my number?"

"Are you not coming over?"

"Can't make it today."

"Ah, feck it, Sean," Batt will be begging. "I held the stool for you. After that fierce breakfast, what else is there to do?"

"How did you know?"

"What?"

"About the breakfast?"

"The same way I knew the phone number. Aren't you like a son to me."

"I'm going to hang up now, Batt." Sean will put the phone in his pocket, then take it out again and, slightly spooked, remove the battery.

A week later, though, he will be back in Lenehan's. He will hold a stool for Batt. He will be determined to be firm about whatever comes up, Batt being no father of his.

"I'm glad to see you," Batt will say. He will insist on a couple of whiskeys. He will offer to bet on one team and then the other, but Sean will have none of it.

"You need to leave me alone, Batt," he will be kind as well as firm.

"I couldn't agree more," Batt will sound pathetic for a huge ape of a capable man. "I got carried away – what can I say?" He will be saturated with men's cologne or another smelly substance, which Sean will consider odd, yet Sean will have encountered most of life's oddities and will take this in his stride. He will have preferences and opinions about everyday life, but there will be few issues he will be prepared to go to war over, polite enough to live and let live, to go with the flow – clichés coined over centuries to describe how most people get by. He will, furthermore, have mixed emotions – if emotions is not too loaded a word – about Batt: a decent skin but eccentric, good company and generous to a fault, but you wouldn't want him for either father or father-in-law. The experts will agree and disagree after Wexford will have beaten Tyrone.

"I'll see you next Sunday?" Batt will say eagerly.

"Fair enough."

Summer will have turned to August. The football will be tougher, the talk more intense. "I have tickets for Croke Park," Batt will say. "We'll go early and make a day of it."

They will meet at the pub. Despite owning a Mercedes, Batt will have two train tickets because the railway station, he will say, is just around the corner. They will reach the city before noon. "I suppose you're hungry?" Batt will wave his short arms and a taxi will take them to a suburban hotel. He will look more elegant than back in the country: a better suit and classy tie. In the hotel, several people will greet him by name – Batt, a reliable name. He will have the roast beef and Sean the turkey and ham, solid country fare, and apple cobbler with ice cream to follow. "I worry about the cholesterol," he will say, but will forge ahead anyway. He will talk about family and regret he never had a son.

He will interrupt dinner several times to take phone calls, send text messages. He will leave the table to do this. He will be apologetic, speaking softly in the city: "Isn't life a curse, Sean?"

"I suppose it could be better."

"One more whiskey to get us through the day?" He will lead Sean to a quiet corner of the lounge. A couple of fat fellows will be talking business, a wrinkled dowager nodding to sleep on a sofa. Sunlight from outside will make life seem happy. The whiskeys will arrive.

"You don't look like a man that gets flustered," Batt will say, eyeing Sean. "You're a cool one."

"Not much to get flustered about," Sean will search in vain for a suitable answer. On television the early game will already have started.

"I suppose you're right." Yet the atmosphere will grow slightly edgy and Batt will seem at a loss. "Would you say we're friends?"

Sean will look around the expansive lounge for a reply, but there will be none handy. "Well, sure," he will say eventually.

"Me, too," Batt will say. He will drain the whiskey from the too-small glass, will knead his chubby hands. He will seem embarrassed. "You'll be amazed at what I'm going to say," he will be looking at the blue carpet, sheepish and self-conscious.

"Is that so?" It will be Sean's turn to down the whiskey.

"I need you to kill a man." Now he will look Sean in the eye. "It's that simple."

"Oh, if that's all it is," Sean, as people sometimes do, will jump to the conclusion that the unpleasant truth is a joke. But he will be thinking frantically in case it's not. From now on the focus will move imperceptibly inside the heads of these two. A short silence will follow, Batt's suggestion sinking in. "We'll be late for the match," Sean will try to change the subject.

"I have a small gun in my pocket, Sean," Batt will say quietly, "and I'd shoot you in a minute to protect myself and my family. Off we go." He will wait for Sean to go ahead of him. The lounge will be the obvious place for Sean to create a scene. But like most people in such circumstances he will hope for the best rather than risk a fuss. Batt will hold the door of the nearest taxi for Sean, lunge in head first beside him. "I can't afford to be friendly for the moment," he will speak tersely, both of them mindful of the taxi driver. "Turn up that music," Batt will then instruct the driver.

I could make a run for it, Sean will be thinking, but it can't be that critical. There might be no gun at all, he will think for a wild moment. No option will seem a solution.

"Why would I do that?" he will ask Batt. "That's if you're serious."

"It's a fair question," Batt will concede. "You'll do it because if you don't do it I'll kill you." This will sound to Sean like a line from a crime novel. He will have read very few crime novels, but he will have read the papers and watched television, his windows on the world, including the world of crime novels. "Don't make me mad at you," Batt will back off a little, "don't make me nervous or hysterical, because I'd like to think when this is over we could still be friends." There will be a sour smell inside the taxi. There will be a woolly bear hanging from the rearview mirror. There will be people getting into or out of cars all around them. It will seem easy to open the door and shout something. Yet people hope for the best, and so will Sean.

"I'm shaking all over, I could never kill anyone,"
Sean's voice will quiver.

"Believe me, I wouldn't ask you if it wasn't necessary."

"Who?"

"He's no good. You'll be doing the country a favour."

"Who's no good?"

"Is it alright if I smoke?"

"For fuck's sake, Batt. It's your taxi. And you have
the gun. Or so you say."

"I'd show it to you?"

"I believe you. Aren't you like a father to me?"

"I said you were like a son to me – it's not the same
thing." He will offer a cigarette to Sean, who will wave
it away. The window will slide quietly down and Batt's
smoke will ease itself out into Dublin.

"Where?"

"He'll be the man in front of you. With rough white
hair like a scrubbing brush. And a brown leather jacket."

"You're out of your mind, Batt."

"I didn't know who else to ask." They will move
slowly through central Dublin. "I'd do it myself if I
could. I'm going to be honest with you now – I wouldn't
sleep nights if I did it."

"Out of your mind," Sean will repeat. "You expect
me to sleep nights?" He will be busy summing up what
life has taught him – about the odds, about the raw,
bloody side of death, about where he went wrong.

"I'll make it as easy as possible for you." Batt will pull
a cap in the Kerry colours from his pocket. He will look

different, jaunty. It will be a good walk after the taxi. For a fleeting second Sean will regret that, whatever happens, he'll miss the football. "Listen carefully now. When the time comes I'll hand you – you know?" He will look at Sean, who will seem to nod. "Along with the raincoat – do you follow?" Latecomers will be elbow to elbow, jostling and excited.

"Shoot a man in the back?" Sean will say loud enough that they will walk a dozen paces in silence until Batt is satisfied no one was listening.

"Ah stop," Batt will say with friendly exasperation. "Better him than you." Sean will not answer, unable to believe what will seem to be happening, gobsmacked and confused. "What you do is, you wait for a goal. Then, in the middle of the cheering and pandemonium, you go for it. "

"Would a point not do? They might not score a goal."

"Kerry always scores a goal. And the crowd always shouts louder after a goal." They will walk another dozen steps in silence. "But go ahead," Batt will relent, "a point will do, if that's how you feel." Sean will, against all the odds, feel relieved.

"Then what happens?" he will ask.

"How, happens?"

"After?"

"Don't you want to know how to use the what-you-call-it – the instrument?"

"I want to know what will happen."

"You'll be grand." Batt's tone will be conciliatory. "This happens all the time, and no one is the worse for it. Except maybe for the other party."

"It does not."

"What?"

"Happen all the time."

"Don't you watch the news at all? Do you live on Mars or what?"

It will take pushing and shoving to get to their seats. Sean will notice that a man in a leather jacket is directly in front of him. With stiff dirty-white hair as predicted. Sean will resent the stupid bastard for not staying home; for doing whatever he did to bring today upon himself. He will be of indefinite age. Sean will consider shooting himself if and when Batt gives him the gun. "But why should I?" his conscience will argue back.

Before they are properly settled in their seats, Kerry will score a goal. Before anyone is ready for it.

"Just do it as planned," Batt will say loudly enough for all Croke Park to hear. Croke Park, though, will be caught up in the game. So much will have gone into getting the players ready for these seventy minutes. Sean will steal glances at the man in front. He will appear mild and not a bit guilty, stupid bloody bastard when he could have stayed home and watched on television.

Instead of shooting himself, Sean will consider shooting Batt. First thing when he gets the gun. Batt meanwhile will be shouting down at the players, giving them hell. Enjoying himself. What is everyone to do once the shot is fired? Or should it be several shots? The scenario will be clear as a nightmare. Including the option to cut and run. Once he has the gun.

"If there is pressure on the small of your back," Batt will say about this time, "that will be a gun. There is a friend of mine sitting behind you. To be sure, don't you know?" Batt will slap Sean on the back like two friends having a good time. "I can read your mind, son, I can for sure."

Half time will come and nothing accomplished. Batt will take two bananas from under the raincoat and offer one to Sean. "Or would you prefer chocolate?"

"Fuck you," Sean will be expecting the gun instead.

The man in front will be laughing, telling a joke to his neighbour.

"There's only a point in it," Batt will say, "so there will be huge excitement after the next score." Once the game restarts, Batt will hand over the raincoat to Sean. Their hands will touch and then Sean will feel the gun, grip it, warm and sweaty, and no one will notice, everyone waiting for the next score. Sean will be wondering whether the gun is real, and how exactly to use it.

When the score comes it will be a beautiful curling ball from far out.

Observe the child, four going on five, trotting alongside his father by the sea. No one knows that a bully who will later harass him will indeed grow up to be a banker and then be murdered beside a country canal. No one at this point cares that the child will one day point a gun at a man in Croke Park, with consequences one can only imagine.

No one knows the facts because there are no facts yet. Consequently there is neither comedy nor tragedy nor insight. Time taunts the race that never learned to look ahead and make itself at home in the future. Wars will take place. Tsunamis and other bad news, the predictable generalizations. New personalities wait to be famous. Thugs wait to kill. Their victims wait. Everyone waiting. This seems a waste, but of what?

"You're a right boyo," Batt will say to Sean on the train. He will wave a bottle of whiskey and laugh like a hyena, only more cheerful, the wooden face flushed the colour of mahogany. Kerry will have lost the game and Kerry fans will be muttering in four-letter words. Sean will be laughing after several swigs from the bottle. On the plastic table between them ham sandwiches will be half-eaten and disgusting.

"No flies on you, Batt," Sean will reply. Behind the jollity Batt will be a volcano. Fields will fly by, sheep grazing as if football did not exist. All in the future: the sheep have not yet been born.

"A flea and a fly in a flue," Batt will intone, because nonsense will have survived.

Around this time Sean will take a small stone from his pocket, an inch across going on two, incorporating, on closer inspection, a fossil from previous aeons, a fossilized frog or other critter, spreadeagled all those years, yet faintly comical and even happy. "I found it in a field."

Batt will allow a trickle of whiskey into his square mouth to steady his imagination.

"That stone contains all the secrets – earth, air, fire and water." Sean will not explain further. The future offers no clue about whatever point he is making. Logic fails to throw further light. The brain may have leaped ahead of itself but abstractions will still pose problems. From another pocket Sean will take another stone of similar size. Embedded in this second stone will be what seems a snail's shell, petrified now. "I found it beside Lake Derravaragh. If you don't keep them apart, they might copulate and wreck everything."

"You're making it up."

"I'm a collector." Sean will massage the small stones with his pale hands, then place them in the same pocket where they will knock against each other with a slightly stony sound. "I collected stones since I was a child." The train journey will stretch interminably because the elements will be playing tricks with life and scarcely anyone will know the time except by their watches. Much the same as now. Batt will fall asleep while the whiskey whispers thoughts. Sean will regard the older man with affection. He will ease the bottle out of Batt's hand.

(The future refuses to reveal who will have the gun. Though the future has not forgotten the gun.)

"I was interfered with as a child," Sean will say at a certain stage. "Years afterwards I met one of the perpetrators, who had in the meantime become a banker. I had often wondered, if the occasion should ever arise, would I ignore him entirely or reprimand him or kill him. In some cases reprimanding isn't worth a damn, it goes blowin' in the wind. I have to agree with you, there's nothing like killing." Sean will hand the bottle to Batt, who will hold it by the neck and think sluggishly about life.

"You're like a son to me," Batt will say. "I hoped you'd marry one of my daughters."

"The nice one would never have me and the other one is ugly." This will be the whiskey talking but also the cruel truth.

"And their father a criminal," Batt will help the conversation along.

"I drive as far as Paris," Sean will explain for no reason. "I drive down the leg of Italy. I belong to that great army that keeps the multinationals in business. I know every bend in every road. But I always come back for the football." They will now be on the railway platform.

"The stones?" Batt will inquire. "Did either of them lay an egg?"

Sean will remove the two stones from his pocket. They will look the same as before. "Anyone can see they're not the same. They're older now. And they're in a different place. But the key difference is the molecules.

Do you seriously think they looked like this when time began? Just like yourself is not the same man who used to kick a football over the bar in that field."

As autumn blows the leaves into winter, Sean will decide to give football a rest. Batt will phone begging and threatening, he will promise the pretty daughter in marriage. So Sean will go back to Lenehan's.

The nations will be in turmoil. After the construction bubble bursts, and no more buildings to build, people will have lost their purpose. The media will begin discussing, among other things, the end of the world.

Yet an institution as complicated as the human race will not fold overnight. Among the durable relics will be Gaelic football and public houses in a symbiotic relationship. In the spring, Lenehan's will install high-definition TV. Years will pass, years that, thrown together, people will refer to vaguely as life.

(These are, needless to say, only the bare facts. And furthermore, all this may make more sense in the future than it seems to make now. Not that it doesn't make sense now.)

Batt Jewel will have abandoned his stool in favour of a round table in a corner. A pint and a whiskey will await his attention. He will complain when Sean arrives late.

"It's her fault." The reference will be to Batt's daughter, the stumpy one, now Sean's wife, who will order a white wine after giving daddy a kiss on his leathery cheek. Kildare will be playing Cork.

The more the end of the world will seem near, the more the future will be spotty and uncertain.

"You took a fierce chance."

"There was no gun in my back."

"That bastard let me down," Bat will be amused. "A second cousin, and I paid him two hundred quid."

"And the fella?"

"He's living in Tipperary. We're the best of friends."

Further months will pass. The wife will be pregnant despite the upcoming end of the world.

"I'll give you two to one on Leitrim."

"I'd have killed you that day in Croke Park."

"Sure, don't I know."

Observe the child. When he dies, an old man, the two stones in his pockets will be buried with him, next door to his deceased wife. In a few million years the stones will resume their interrupted evolution. They will go wild becoming something else, because that's life and the future wouldn't have it any other way.

Death Shall Have No Dominion

There is a fly on the wall. Not the proverbial fly but an inquisitive insect that presently approaches the portrait of a dead ancestor. Owen Bui has forgotten who the ancestor is. On his back in the sweaty bed, Owen's stare is vacant and his breathing shallow. Sometimes cracks come into focus in the ceiling above. These then shimmer and transmogrify into roads and rivers. Inspired by his medicine, he can identify neighbours' houses or young lads kicking a football or a tractor lurching along faster and louder until the cracks in the ceiling return and leave him confused.

Agatha comes in all business, pulling aside drapes and agitating dust. She opens the window so that sounds enter: crows complaining and a cow in need of the bull, but beyond that an indiscriminate rumble of life, the creaky noise of earth on its axis.

"So how are we today?" She seldom looks at him anymore.

"Couldn't be better." They were about the same height when they married, but eventually she grew smaller after two children took their toll. Lately she dresses desperately flashy for her age. There seems to be a red dress and a green item over her shoulders. He suspects there's lipstick, here in the middle of nowhere. He thinks she still loves him, though it's far from the same as once. Love was always shifty, like a weather vane veering about to please the wind.

"Reilly is coming up the road. If he dawdles start falling asleep."

"Hurry with the tea, it might shift him."

The bedroom is austere: a big press for her clothes, a small one for his. Reilly sidles in apologetically as if going to confession.

"Is it yourself, Reilly?" Owen does not look in the other's direction.

"Good man, Owen." Reilly is a leathery entity under a peaked cap. "I'll smoke if you don't mind."

"And why wouldn't you?" Sunshine plays with the blue smoke up near the ceiling. When Reilly blows out the match he looks around for what to do with it.

"Agatha?" Owen raises his hoarse voice. "Is there an ash tray at all?"

She hands a tin tray to Reilly, who places it on the threadbare carpet and, if he remembers, aims the ashes at it from a distance.

"And is it serious?" Reilly scans the other for symptoms.

"Nothing to write home about." Country people don't condone lies, so they decorate the truth until it means something else.

Agatha arrives with tea and a slice of loaf. Reilly looks at the cigarette in his hand, decides there's too much of it left to throw away, places it on the ash tray on the floor, takes the tea and bread and looks apologetically at Agatha. "Many a field Owen and me ploughed," he explains. "Many a rabbit we caught."

"He told me," Agatha says drily.

"And we're not finished yet."

"And we're not finished yet," Owen Bui repeats with less conviction.

They talk about the usual imponderables, from the townland to the wide world. Since both mumble, and neither can hear very well, they talk past one another, answering questions never asked and lapsing into silence when a reply is called for. Owen closes his eyes and pretends to sleep until the other exits. The difference between asleep and awake is not as pronounced as it used to be.

"Do you see that fly, Agatha?" he asks her when he awakens. "No need to kill him. Just shush him out the window."

"When I shush him out the window, he always comes back."

"No, this is a different fly."

But Agatha chases the intruder with a plastic swatter until the latter goes to ground. Owen sleeps to escape the pandemonium. In his sleep he hears his cousin Susan arrive in her Hyundai. He hears Susan and Agatha hugging at the door. Agatha whispers and Susan pipes

273

down. He can see her without waking, fat and dressed in jeans, hair an artificial red and her arms bare to the elbows. He hears them breathlessly enter the sick room. There is a great silence, the room full of old shadows and suspicions. Even in his sleep, Owen knows Susan knows the identity of the ancestor in the picture. Sometime he'll ask her, and that will start a long story about how the ancestor, named Tom – that was it, his grandfather's brother Tom, who went to Pennsylvania and never returned but sent the portrait when he was elected mayor of some small town run by the Irish between the wars.

Owen Bui is of two minds about people. Entertaining them can be a nuisance. On the other hand stands loneliness. Were it not for Agatha, he might as well die. The boy, a teacher in Barcelona, and the girl, a hairdresser, have lives of their own. They will come home soon and clinch his hunch that he's history. Sure, he loves them. He would, if the occasion arose, die for them. But such occasions never arise, so he goes on being, in the final analysis, irrelevant.

"What's the name of that footballer in Barcelona?"

"What are you talking about?"

"Never mind – it's just that I need something to talk about when the boy comes home."

"The boy is a man now." She closes the door, leaving loose ends.

"Get up, you old rogue." Margaret Greene, an old rogue herself, owns the petrol station and the Centra beside it. Owen, even in his present condition, wonders was she flirting sixty years ago or would it have come to anything or was it only his imagination. It's too late to bring all that up now. More and more, he thinks, the issue is not so much what was done or said as what was not done or said. A body could go mad regretting. Margaret sits on the side of the bed, squeezes his sick hand, leaving Owen to wonder was the life he lived the one for which he was cut out or a different life entirely. After Margaret has left, a silly old woman now making odd noises with her dentures, thoughts still go crazy inside Owen's head.

"Ah, Owen!"

"Well, Owen!"

Mostly the lads arrive in the evening, sometimes in twos or threes, so that extra chairs need to be introduced along the wall. In a rainy country like this, no conversation gets started until the weather is dealt with. Then there is football and war. Eventually it is safe to move into the past.

"Do you remember the time you won the high jump – was it in Cavan?"

"Do you remember the year we won the championship?"

Agatha arrives with a tray. There is a mug for everyone except Owen. Crumbs fall on the carpet amid the ashes.

"Do you remember Roscommon races?"

"That wasn't Roscommon."

Owen, looking up at the ceiling, does not remember. He has no recollection of a racehorse. He was never on the football team. No matter – they are arguing among themselves and have forgotten him. He glances sideways with curious eyes. They have known each other a lifetime. Yet Owen Bui sees strangers. The last time he looked they were fresh-faced and gangly, kicking a football and hoping for women and some trying to grow beards. Somewhere, a while ago, they rounded a corner and found they had gone droopy and baldy but no one said a word. The way they are laughing now, they can't see the reaper coming up the road.

Owen always thought he would be afraid, but fear keeps getting pushed up ahead. There is no knowing what to worry about, he with neither pain nor ache. He is admittedly tired. But, to be honest, he has been tired all his life. Couldn't kick a football now, but he never could. There's less to regret than people think.

"That man never sinned in his life – isn't that right, Agatha?"

"Not that I noticed."

The boyos have deserted him, thinking he is asleep. By the sound of things there is another mug of tea. Owen gazes at a future without bread and jam. No bother. The gut has said goodbye to all that.

"Isn't it great there's no hell anymore."

"Oh, I wouldn't rule out hell."

The debate fades to a murmur in the kitchen. Owen contemplates the future. No longer mighty and hairy, God is easy-going, sitting on a log and mad at no one. Could everyone have it so wrong for so long? God sitting on a log and fishing, God sunburned by his own sun who before was pure spirit like a white sheet against a white sky. Unless it's not a he at all but a she? If he could get this sorted out, especially at this critical juncture, Owen would call in the others. He would ask Agatha to uncork bottles of porter. He would tell them what no one ever told or was told, so forget Manchester United and Bin Laden. Not that he wants to be a prophet. That is the great boon of death's door: you reach a stage where you don't care. You're tired from a lifetime of living, but apart from having to urinate, you are content. Soon the urinating, too, will be a thing of the past, another threshold crossed.

In case of a revelation on the other side, he decides to take the mobile into the coffin. There may be facilities yonder for that kind of thing – everything ever dreamed of is supposed to be waiting there. He is surprised no one thought of this before.

"That fly is at it again," he says in the morning.

"The doctor will be coming." The poor doctor made a bags of the chemo. Owen is surprised that he no longer minds. It took him the second half of his life to let go of what he tried so hard to have in the first half. He'd try singing this minute, but it might scare Agatha. Before he goes he will thank her for everything.

Beyond the ceiling he sees his own funeral. Agatha steps out of a limousine. Without Agatha, life, if it will still be life, will never be the same.

"Good man, Owen." Reilly is back.

"How is it out there?"

"The river is high." Pause. "Margaret Greene was asking for you."

When Reilly is gone, the Margaret for whom Owen waits is sixty years younger than the Margaret who fails to show up.

The lads arrive and smoke and murmur. Owen learns tons about himself. When they think well of him, it's because of how little they know.

"Ah now, he was harmless."

He dies. Or so it seems – no one knows exactly when death occurs or what it actually is, it may be all in the mind. What follows is commonplace: the undertaker, the coffin, the whiskey and tea and condolences, the kind words and fond memories. Owen sees them, hears them, nods in agreement. He is at Agatha's elbow helping out, cheering her on.

At the funeral, he can't resist counting the cars.

He wakes up in the coffin and knows instinctively he is under the ground. Out of habit he looks up. The lid is only a few inches from his nose. He never got round to saying thanks to Agatha. He forgot to take the mobile. This is typical, he realizes, no one is ever a hundred per cent ready to go. He notices his mind working. He took it with him then; it's not that easy to get rid of a mind.

No sign of God. Who may be gone fishing. Owen regrets the time spent on football and war. He finds himself compiling a bucket list in case there are options.

The distance is so short between here and before, yet he can't see anyone, can't hear bird or tractor. It is useless to fret about Manchester United or even Agatha, who may, for all he knows, have moved into the grave next door – time is a different turkey down here. He thinks of banging on his own coffin. She might bang back.

A buzzing begins. There is a fly in the coffin.

There is, after all, life after death.

All That Delirium

A Rolls Royce crawls along a stony road in the Dublin Mountains. It belongs to Rodney Reilly, the magnate. He is accompanied by Jo Golden, a writer.

"Whoa, Lar!" and the chauffeur pulls over amid boulders. There is a sublime stillness in the morning. Rodney, who fancies himself a typical Irishman and therefore a poet, asks Jo if she remembers Wordsworth emoting about London Bridge. "A sight so touching in its majesty. Do you remember that?"

"No." Even in real life some women are beautiful. Jo is one of them. Circumstances hint she is also intelligent, ambitious, born to the silver spoon. She is a senior correspondent for *Forbes*, the megamagazine of the materially successful.

"Are you sure you have the name right? Reilly without the O?"

"I know."

"If it wasn't Wordsworth, it might be Gerard Manley Hopkins."

"Wordsworth will do."

"I can see we're going to get along famously." He knows Jo is most at home with real estate and money, life's bread and butter respectively. But he wants her, before the day is over, to see him not only as the fabulously wealthy renaissance man he is, but as the quintessential Irishman that the Irish have been trying to produce for thousands of years, but have only recently perfected as this once-distressful country emerged from misery to become the envy of the global economy.

"Why are we here?"

"You just finished asking one of the great questions, girl." His big fist knocks on the glass partition that in discreet Rolls Royces separates the hired help from those who hire them. "Lar!"

Lar holds the door for Jo. They drink in the brisk morning. Sheep are busy with breakfast. White clouds in the distance have silver linings. Because this is a great day, birds fly in spectacular formations. They're crows, but Rodney Reilly sees swans and snow geese and a scattering of eagles up from Kerry.

Once the firmament above is in order, attention returns to earth below. Little is happening: a few wars, commerce thriving, consumers consuming, good people loving and a few haters hating. The main event today is the launching of Rodneyville in, yes, Ireland. It falls into the category of consumers consuming, only more so. Some complain that the name does not do this extravagance justice. To which Rodney, in his rollicking way, responds: "I built the fucker, do you think I'm going to name it after my grandmother?" A reputation for irreverence is money in the bank. Not that money in the bank is everything, but everything wouldn't be the same without money and the bank and his good friends the bankers. At his best, the talking heads on television say that Rodney combines the wit of the late Oscar Wilde and the vision of the legendary Eamonn de Valera, or, some suggest, the more recent Bertie Ahern.

What is this great thing called Rodneyville?

As the world evolves, people can't keep up with names for its diversity and especially its superabundance. Rodneyville is a case in point. It isn't wild Vegas or civilized Paris or enigmatic Constantinople or mythical Atlantis. It is all of the above. Beyond the bricks and mortar in which ordinary property developers specialise, Rodneyville is a symbol, a harbinger. It is only a small stretch to advise Jo it is a shining city on a hill.

This new hill is in Dublin 4, though this in itself is a bone of contention. Dublin 4, traditional neighbourhood of the privileged, had to be re-zoned when an endless stream of Reilly lorries failed to stop transporting the other counties into the city. Every hillock and small mountain from Cavan to Waterford has been flattened to provide for this monumental endeavour. Thus, while craters dot the provinces, Dublin 4 has been growing higher and wider. This, the whole world agrees, from Wall Street to peasant cottage, is a time of thunderous progress: a time of unfettered ambition, of bonhomie and good cheer. Greed has at last lost its stigma. Best of all, everyone agrees this zest will last forever. Nearly everything that used to be said of heaven in the old days is now attributed to this new paradigm. Not that there was anything wrong with heaven, which still has a few followers.

(If this hype sounds overheated, it is worth remembering that there is nothing more natural than exaggeration. Consider the shamans and seanchaí of old. They didn't become legendary by understating the obvious.)

"I'll tell you why we're here," Rodney is saying, though Jo's immense poise, enigmatic as Sheela na Gig, is making him nervous. He knows this superwoman is more than her extreme good looks. For no reason at all, Plato's cave comes to mind. That's the kind of mind he has, impressionistic: insights flying in from faraway places at just the right moment. Jo, he now intuits, has a role in that cave somewhere. She is the writing on the wall or the shadow cast by the sun – he can't quite remember how the Plato story went but he knows she fits. "Have you ever wondered what God thought on the eighth day, when he looked down on creation, he surely couldn't resist feeling satisfied? Have you ever thought about it?"

"It was the seventh day."

"Was it the seventh? Anyway, don't you think he felt good? God? I'd say he felt like I'm feeling."

"Maybe better."

"No. He couldn't possibly feel better."

"But why me?"

"Because your publication represents all that I hold dear." He wills Jo to admire every aspect of the great achievement below. "You name it, it probably happened down there," he waves his arm in a heroic arc. "Brian Boru and the Battle of Clontarf. This was always a great city waiting to happen. Never recklessly progressive, I'll grant you. Now, if I may say so, we are changing that. It's no longer enough to write poetry down there in the moonlight. Or show off in the Abbey. We have taken commerce by the scruff of the neck." He tells her about the apartment buildings, the malls and fun palaces and parks. He tells about the Reilly Tower Hotel in the most understated manner he can imagine: "Only my good friends in Dubai have a taller tower."

Jo listens with a smile at the corners of her lips, lips that would only be spoiled by lipstick. Lar takes constant messages on several electronic devices, but Rodney waves them aside. Today the whole world wants to see and hear him and in short, spread the message that Rodney Reilly has fulfilled his promise. Well, hell, let the whole world wait.

"Some say the human race should never have moved indoors." He wants her to admire Rodneyville, but most of all he wills her to notice Rodney Reilly the visionary, such as comes along scarcely once in a lifetime. "This hesitancy to put a roof over our heads has left us at a loss. Oh, we've had our moments. Some early ziggurats, perhaps. A few good tries in ancient Egypt, and a thing or two in Greece. You could throw in a Gothic cathedral, I suppose, but spare me those flying buttresses. Closer to home we have Le Corbusier and Frank Lloyd Wright and that crowd, but I don't think they'll stand the test of time. The world has been waiting for the next quantum leap, and isn't it ironic that it should appear in a poor little country like Ireland?"

As he makes this speech, prepared by his public relations people, Rodney fights bravely not to sound bombastic.

Yet, about this time, when his cup should normally be running over, an infinitesimal wrinkle appears in reality. Rodney is forced to concede that Jo is possessed of a begrudging attitude that fails to display a hint of awe.

There is no sight more inspiring than a pink Rolls, driven by his wife Cissie, followed by the blue Rolls crawling into the great city. "Remember," Rodney says to Jo, "God had all the advantages. There were no strikes, no Hitachis breaking down, no bankers to wine and dine. God, if you want to know, had it easy."

It is mid-morning. The media helicopters form a procession above the Rolls Royce procession below. The day, in short, is going according to plan. The circus converges on Dublin's Parnell Square.

"Did I mention why I took you with me this morning?"

"Why did you take me?"

"I was hoping I could persuade you to write my definitive biography."

"Me?"

"It would make you famous."

Guests pour into the nearby art gallery, most recently called the Dublin City Gallery the Hugh Lane, a ridiculous title that lends itself neither to nickname nor acronym. This is why Rodney Reilly has made a donation to the gallery. Rumours range from a million to a billion. In return he has been allowed to rename it the Dublin City Gallery the Hugh Lane the Rodney Reilly.

Not only that, Rodney is donating a small masterpiece from his private collection, a little-known item by the late Pablo Picasso. It is called "The Bald Guitar."

"It is a masterpiece because I say it is," Rodney elbows an overweight trustee over a lunch of Mayo salmon, Offaly potatoes and the works.

"I'll grant you I was unaware of it," the trustee loves salmon and the works. "I can't imagine why he called it 'The Bald Guitar.'"

"I can help you there." Rodney hates salmon but is prepared to do whatever greatness takes. "The maestro was tired of those funny noses and there was no mistress needing to be painted. So he took to doodling on the guitar picture, over by the woman's ear – little doodles that look like tadpoles. So he called it 'The Bald Guitar.'"

"But why?"

"Oh now, he was an odd one, Picasso."

All day there is eating and drinking, loud laughter and extravagance. Every politician in the country has been invited. All banks have been closed.

"Glad you could make it," Rodney says to everyone who comes forward with outstretched hand. The excitement moves from one venue to another, one magnificent array of victuals to the next. Fine speeches are delivered by those who specialise in the spoken word. When Rodney is called, audiences are secretly glad to find him short and sweet. Such a man does not need verbosity, his achievements speak for themselves. So he tells them he is glad they could make it.

In the private lounge of one of his hotels, Rodney sits with a few cronies after the crowds have gone home. There won't be many more days like this one, he is thinking, I hope nothing has been left out. Cronies have a sixth sense and know when to go home, so they go when Jo arrives.

"This is a surprise," he says.

"I know."

Jo, Rodney notices, never crosses her legs. The knees never drift apart. If they drifted even two inches, his day would be complete. She sips champagne and grows more beautiful. Rodney vows again to be faithful to Cissie unto death. It's the least I can do, he ruminates: it's my only chance to suffer the pain that all humans are doomed sooner or later to suffer.

He fears Jo sees through him. He detects no affection, no wonder, nothing at all in the lust neighbourhood. The more it is not there, the more he needs it, without knowing what it is. So he continues to trawl because everything short of heaven is only one surprise away, one gift away.

"What do you think of Picasso, really?"

She gazes at him.

"The only date I ever remember, for some reason, is 1881, Pablo Picasso's birthday. Did you know that?"

"No."

"No matter what event you mention, wars or scandals or whatever you have going, it means nothing until I measure it against 1881. If 1853 comes up, I have first to do the addition or subtraction. I think: Picasso would not be with us for a further twenty-eight years. Or twenty-seven or twenty-nine, because of the untidy way birthdays sometimes work. Everything else is a blank. Well, except Jesus maybe, whose date has always been 1. And now I hear they're disputing that. But I can tell you for sure it wasn't 1881." Pause. "I wish I knew how to bring the day to a good end."

Drizzle never fails to get under Rodney Reilly's skin. Still, because the gremlins are making inroads, he decides to drive the scenic route – down O'Connell Street. First he circles Parnell Square for nostalgia's sake. Past the art gallery that now bears his name. Francis Bacon is in there kicking and screaming. Rodney admires the ruthlessness with which Bacon turned his friends' faces into pork chops or banana skins, then drove over them, if only metaphorically, with a JCB. He has two Bacons in the dining room at home, one an anonymous pork chop and the other a howling pope in a glass cage, one of the deceased Innocents.

South of the river, the traffic is dense and chaotic. The city is dysfunctional, the country is. People especially are creaking to a halt. Not their BMWs and little toy cars with spoilers, not their dishwashers and high-definition things – consumerism remains healthy, thank you – nor their boozing and fornicating: all that goes without saying. It's something more abstract, maybe metaphysical is the word. Their heads are missing the point. Rodneyville was a great success, to take an obvious example. But after all the right things have been said, he still can't break the celebrity barrier like pop singers do. And *Forbes*? Are you joking? Jo's article didn't even make the cover.

On, then, to Dublin 4. He passes several of his own landmark creations – buildings any civilization would be proud of. The Rolls turns left of its own accord into an oasis in the middle of which sits the Huffington Hotel. It belongs to his early, practically reckless period, when he was more interested in making his mark than making money.

He has reserved an alcove where the sun shines even on cloudy days. The maître d'hôte (it is that kind of establishment) murmurs that the usual beverages will be delivered at once. In the dozen years he has been dropping in, no one has ever asked him to pay. He does not understand how this works, or what remote edict was issued to the effect that he is, and will always be, so to speak, on the house.

Although Rodney is punctual to a fault, he knows that Deputy Garda Commissioner Barney Eccles will be there ahead of him. At school they played rugby together and like all rugby players they bonded. Barney exudes substance and singularity. Framed by the window, he makes Rodney feel short and lumpy.

"I hope I'm not taking you away from anything, Barney." They shake hands, neither is the type to indulge in embarrassing hugging.

"Devil a thing. How the hell are you?" The demeanour is down-to-earth and humble.

"Grand. I'm grand."

"You don't sound grand."

"Why don't we break the rules, Barney, if there are any, and drink that bottle of whiskey?" But Eccles waves the idea away. Rodney has only to look at the waiter, who is honoured to read his mind and pour fresh coffee instead. Rodney often imagines that in his own iconic hotels he wields the kind of mysterious influence that God must wield in heaven, just rattling around getting obeyed and no need to express his wishes or even think them because they have been anticipated.

"It was a great day anyway."

"I couldn't have done it without you."

"All I did was keep the rabble under control."

"You were always too modest, Barney."

"I know. I'm the best second fiddle I know." Barney leans forward, confidential. "I often thought, Rodney, watching your career, that a time would come when all the buildings were built, when you got tired of making money – I thought you'd run for office. And there's only one office to run for."

"There isn't a politician in the country who doesn't owe me, I'll grant you that. They'd have trouble running against me."

"Whatever I can do to help, just say the word."

"I'm going to surprise you now," Rodney says. "All I ask is that you don't overreact or make a scene." He looks intently at Eccles, who looks surprised, maybe startled. He nods his head the way Rodney thinks he would nod to a suspect to start confessing. "This is embarrassing." He tries to suck a last drop from the empty coffee cup. "I never thought I'd be saying this to anyone."

"Out with it."

"I need you to put me in jail."

"Stop the joking, Rodney. You were never funny."

"I wish you weren't so straight-laced, Barney. I wish you were a gas character who'd pull out the handcuffs and ask questions later. There must be many a time you wanted to nail me, I don't know, for making more money than you, or maybe for not being the good friend you deserved. Many a time I'd have loved to nail you, especially over women. Over your moral superiority, I suppose. You would make a good Taoiseach yourself. And if you run I'll make a contribution."

"What is it, Rodney?"

"Jail may not be the answer. But it would be a start."

"Sure, Rodney."

Pregnant pause. Further chat would be superfluous. Rodney rises and Barney rises. They shake hands solemnly, wondering how everything can be fixed. "There's a hell of a lot of sadness in the world, Barney. People talk about nearly everything, in the pubs or on television or at home in the kitchen, but they seldom talk about sadness. No one seems to have a handle on it. After you get me locked away, and justice done for starters, you might, after you become Taoiseach, look into sadness."